The
Nidderdale
Murders

ALSO BY J. R. ELLIS

The Body in the Dales
The Quartet Murders
The Murder at Redmire Hall
The Royal Baths Murder

The Nidderdale Murders

A YORKSHIRE MURDER MYSTERY

J.R. ELLIS

THOMAS & MERCER

Text copyright © 2020 by J. R. Ellis
All rights reserved.

Published by Thomas & Mercer, Seattle

www.apub.com

Amazon, the Amazon logo, and Thomas & Mercer are trademarks of Amazon.com, Inc., or its affiliates.

ISBN-13: 9781542017435
ISBN-10: 1542017432

Cover design by @blacksheep-uk.com

Printed in the United States of America

To the Otley Writers

Prologue

Crutching Close Laithe
Yarnthwaite Barn
Hawkswick Clowder
Pikesdaw Barn

It was a crisp, clear Friday morning in mid-September on the high moorland fells above Nidderdale, one of the Yorkshire dales. Early mist had cleared and the sky was blue. The lush fields were dotted with sheep and cows. The trees in the scattered areas of woodland were still in full leaf, but the bright green of summer was slowly fading to yellows and browns.

The quiet peace of early autumn which pervaded the scene was suddenly disrupted by a series of loud explosions and the sound of birds whirring into the air. Puffs of smoke could be seen above small walls within the heather. The strange, mechanical cry of the red grouse, which seemed to call a panicky *go back, go back, go back, go back, go back, go back* as if in warning, could be heard among the heather. Birds flew up quickly and tried to wheel away, but many shuddered, flapped pathetically and fell to the ground as the bangs continued.

At one of the butts, four shooters were steadily blasting away at the birds that had been driven up by men who could be seen beating in the heather. Some distance away on each side were two more butts, from which yet more shotguns were being fired and birds cut down. The fellside resembled a battlefield.

The four men were all dressed in expensive weatherproof jackets, brown corduroy trousers, green wellies and flat caps. One of the group, Alexander Fraser – 'Sandy' to his friends – broke his shotgun to reload. He was a retired judge, a tall, powerfully built man with a shock of wavy hair which had once been blond and was now grey. He lived just outside the nearby village of Niddersgill in a seventeenth-century manor house and owned the shooting rights on the adjacent fells. He employed a gamekeeper and a team of people to maintain the grouse moor, and recouped money in the season from organised shooting parties such as this, for which he could charge a hefty fee. He looked forward every year to the Glorious Twelfth of August, which marked the beginning of the season, and he was a stickler for everything running smoothly.

Fraser peered into the smoke and frowned.

'I must say, those bloody beaters are a bit on the slow side. I'm going to have to have a word with Davis. It's just not good enough,' he said to the man standing next to him in the butt – a tall, thin individual with a balding head, who was a minor aristocrat called James Symons. He lived in a small, medieval fortified manor house in Wensleydale.

'Not to worry,' said Symons. 'We're bagging plenty. I think your gamekeeper's done a good job. It's a splendid morning's shoot, don't you think, Rawnsley?'

The third man in the row, short and stocky, fired both barrels of his shotgun before replying. Gideon Rawnsley ran an elite-car showroom near Ripon and supplied many of those present with their Jaguars, Bentleys and Range Rovers.

'Fine,' he replied laconically. Rawnsley was somewhat socially beneath the others and said little. He always accepted these invitations, whatever the cost, as he regarded them as being good for business. He got on pretty well with the others although he had some issues with Fraser.

The fourth man was taking a little break and a swig of whisky from a leather-covered hip flask. Henry Saunders wore rimless glasses and seemed to have a perpetual supercilious grin on his smooth face. He was a wealthy banker from London who had known Sandy for many years during the latter's time in the capital. They'd been at school together.

'It's all good, Sandy,' Saunders said. 'I'm thoroughly enjoying myself. It's so relaxing to be up here, and so invigorating to have a gun in your hand.' He looked around. 'It's what these moors are for, isn't it? There wouldn't be much point coming up here otherwise, would there? It's a bit of a wasteland.' He laughed.

'Wait a minute,' said Fraser. 'What the hell's going on over there?' He pointed to where the beaters were slowly progressing through the heather. There appeared to be some kind of scuffle and voices were being raised. 'I hope it's not one of those bloody saboteurs again. Do you know, one of these days I'm going to blast them with both barrels. I'm absolutely sick of—'

'Steady on, old boy.' Symons put his hand on Fraser's arm; the latter had been instinctively raising his gun. 'I think the beaters have it under control.'

'Yes, I think you're right,' replied Fraser as he peered down the slope. 'I can see Davis escorting someone across to the track and one of the beaters has got another. He's got the bugger's arm firmly up his back. Good for him! Now perhaps we'll be left in peace.'

Fraser's hope was fulfilled, and the shooting continued uninterrupted until twelve thirty, when a couple of Land Rovers could be seen bumping and rolling up the track from the direction of the village. They stopped at a bothy, a small, stone-built refuge some way behind the grouse butts.

'Ah, that's lunch, everyone!' announced Fraser and, as shoot captain, he blew on a horn to indicate the end of the morning's session. They all made their way to the bothy where the provisions were being unloaded. As they discussed their successes or otherwise they were served glasses of champagne and fed hot asparagus soup, followed by a range of luxury canapés, sandwiches, pies and desserts. The food had all been prepared by staff at the Dog and Gun in Niddersgill, the local inn and restaurant where the shooters were staying. A sumptuous dinner would be served there in the evening.

After he had eaten, Fraser came out of the bothy to speak to his gamekeeper, Ian Davis. Davis and the beaters were sitting on a wall eating the sandwiches they had brought with them and drinking from flasks of tea.

'What was all that row about then, Davis?' Fraser said.

Davis was the son of a local farmer. He was in his late thirties with a young family and had lived in the dale all his life. He hastily swallowed his mouthful of corned-beef sandwich. 'Nowt to worry about, Mr Fraser, it was just a couple o' them sabs. We got rid of 'em.'

'Yes, I saw you,' Fraser said irascibly. 'But how did they manage to get there in the first place? Don't you patrol the area to make sure there's no one around? One of these days one of them will get shot and no doubt that will be regarded as being our fault. Not that it would bother me in the slightest; they deserve everything they get.'

'We did have a look round, Mr Fraser, but it's such a wide area, like, and they're crafty, they hide in the heather until the shoot starts and then they stand up with those placard things and get in the way and—'

'I know what they do, but I'm expecting you to do a better job of preventing it. And also, those beaters were a bit lackadaisical this morning. You need to get them to show a bit more energy and enthusiasm.'

Davis glared sullenly at his boss. 'Yes, Mr Fraser. It was because those sabs came that we—'

'No excuses, Davis. Now see to it.' Fraser turned round and went back into the bothy, leaving his gamekeeper seething with the injustice of this rebuke. Davis kicked a stone against the wall in frustration. The beaters were looking on with a combination of amusement and sympathy. Sandy Fraser was generally known for his arrogance, especially in the way he treated his employees.

'Right, come on then, you heard him,' said Davis. 'Let's get into position, they'll be out soon. If you see any more of those sabs, strangle them with the bloody heather.' This produced some laughter and they all trooped off back to the moor. Privately, Davis was wondering how long he could stand working for that bastard, but as his wife didn't have a job at the moment and they had two small children, he had no choice but to grin and bear it. But sometimes, he thought as he screwed up his fists, he could just . . .

He shook his head to dispel the violent images that came into his mind.

The afternoon shoot went well and the satisfied party rode back to the village in Range Rovers, followed by an old jeep stuffed with their trophies.

∾

In the village of Niddersgill, local postman David Eastwood made a late delivery of post to the Dog and Gun Inn. He toured the dale in his red postal van and it was always late afternoon when he reached his final locations. He popped into reception, where Rob Owen, who was joint owner with his wife Sheila, was behind the desk looking at the computer screen and rattling away at the keyboard. Rob was tall with black curly hair and a moustache.

'Afternoon, Rob.' Eastwood handed over a wodge of letters and the usual junk mail.

'Afternoon, David,' replied Rob, not looking up from the screen.

'Have you got that shooting party in tonight?'

'We have indeed.'

'I thought so. You can hear the guns going off from well up the dale. I don't envy you. They're not a pleasant crew, are they?'

'Maybe not, but they bring in good money.'

'Yep. I'm sure they do, and business is business.'

'It sure is.' Owen still didn't look up from the screen, and Eastwood, realising that he wasn't going to get a long chat, went off to do a quick round of the village before driving away in the red van in the direction of Pateley Bridge.

Inside the inn, the atmosphere was frenetic. In the kitchen, Sheila Owen was run off her feet. It was the busiest time of year, when shooting parties made large group bookings, ordered food to be taken up on to the moors, and dined together in the evenings, often occupying the large table in the main dining room. They were lucrative business but also very demanding, none more so than those organised by Sandy Fraser. Fraser scrutinised menus and wine lists and nitpicked about everything. His guests were little better, always exclusively men and usually of the worst type: rich, arrogant and misogynistic. She'd had to deal with a number of complaints from waitresses and chambermaids about unwanted attention and physical contact. It was made worse by the fact that Fraser lived locally and he brought in too much money to turn away his business.

It was 5 p.m. Sheila looked around the noisy kitchen at her team, who were working hard preparing the evening's meal. She sighed and pushed a lock of auburn hair back under her cap.

'Harry, get a move on with those onions and carrots; the onions very finely diced please, carrots finely sliced too.'

'OK, Chef,' replied the young commis chef.

An added pressure was that tonight the members of the shooting party were not choosing from the normal menu but would be eating some of the grouse they'd shot. This meant that a Land Rover had had to rush back from the moors to the inn with some of the dead birds, which then had to be hastily prepared for roasting. Removing all the shot from the carcasses was more difficult than it looked. Sheila was taking responsibility for this meal, while her sous chef, Greg Cooper, attended to the regular menu – which, unfortunately, would have fewer specials tonight due to the extra demands on the kitchen.

'How are you doing, Greg? Ask Harry to give you a hand when he's finished preparing for me. He's quite capable of doing some of those dishes; he must have seen you do them so many times.'

'I'm OK. I'd rather be doing this than cooking for that shooting party and Fraser.'

'Yes, it's a challenge, but you could manage it.' She was looking down at her preparation surface when she said this and didn't notice the look of hatred on Cooper's face when he mentioned Fraser.

Sheila contemplated the dish she was cooking for the twelve people in the shooting party: roast grouse with sauce Albert, puréed sweet potato, and braised savoy cabbage with bacon. The key was a good sauce: smooth and creamy, with the mustard and horseradish flavours not as strong as they might be for beef. The cabbage and sweet potato were being prepared by another commis chef. *Blast!* She remembered that they were also serving sautéed potatoes. Who was in charge of those?

Then someone called out to her: 'How's it going?'

Rob stood by the open kitchen door, hardly daring to come in. He ran the bar and accommodation side of the business, and normally steered well clear of anything to do with food. He knew his wife was under pressure this evening.

'It's fine. Just go away,' replied Sheila, light-heartedly pointing a knife at him.

Rob held up his hands. 'Wow! OK, I get the picture.' Laughing, he made a swift retreat from the kitchen and went to the dining area, which was split into a number of separate rooms, the largest to be occupied by the shooting party. They would be sitting down to eat at seven thirty, after their gin and tonics in the bar.

Everything seemed in order. The table was set and included two jeroboams of a red *grand cru* Burgundy on silver trays. These had been specially ordered in by Sandy Fraser at considerable expense. Rob shared his wife's ambivalence about Fraser's shooting parties. They were not the easiest people to deal with, but they were a source of revenue that the Owens didn't want to lose, especially at this time of year when the high-summer tourist season was over and the main restaurant was not as busy as Rob would have liked. He went round the table, tweaking the cutlery and glasses. It was difficult not to share his wife's nervousness before an evening like this.

~

Sandy Fraser returned to his manor house when the party arrived back in the village. He walked up the stone-flagged path, which was flanked with cottage-garden plants, to the solid wooden door, overhung with a now rather tired-looking late climbing rose. His wife Miriam called out from the sitting room, which overlooked a substantial garden to the rear: 'How was it, darling?'

Fraser went to join his wife, who was sitting in an armchair facing the garden and reading a book. 'Fine, apart from those bloody saboteur people. They had another go at disrupting things; damn nuisance, they never give up.'

'Can't the police do anything?'

'Too lily-livered; they're afraid of being taken to court if they use any strong-arm tactics.'

'Well, don't *you* do anything. You know what happened last time.'

'That wasn't my fault. The chap had a weak heart; he shouldn't have been up there.'

'I know but . . . Anyway, would you like a cup of tea?'

'Thanks, but I haven't really got time. I need a shower and then I must get back to the inn for a drink or two before dinner.'

With that, he went upstairs, leaving his wife to contemplate another evening alone as the late-afternoon sun slanted in through the window.

~

At six thirty the shooting party were starting to gather in the bar, where there was a tab for their drinks. They occupied a number of bar tables, and one of the staff brought their drinks over. Fraser insisted on black-tie dress for these dinners, while he himself always appeared in a kilt of the Fraser tartan. This was an affectation, as his family had had no connection with Scotland for hundreds of years, although he had been to boarding school there.

At the bar itself, a number of the locals were gathered, drinking pints of beer and lager. Alan Green, sitting on a bar stool, wiped beer from his brown moustache. His red face reflected his outdoor life – he was a gardener and odd-job man. Next to him on stools were Peter Gorton, a burly character who ran the local shop and newsagent, and Wilf Bramley, a farmer in his sixties wearing a battered tweed jacket and grubby corduroy trousers. He was the sole farming tenant of Sandy Fraser, who owned the land on which Wilf's farm stood.

They were joined by Ian Davis, the gamekeeper, who came in looking exhausted.

'Evening, Ian,' said Gorton. 'You look well and truly buggered.'

'So would you if you'd been out wi' that lot,' replied Davis, glancing over to the shooting party and frowning. 'I'd forgotten they'd be in here. I've had enough o' them for one day.'

'Not to worry,' continued Gorton. 'Ignore them, they'll be going in for their posh meal soon. What're you having to drink?'

'Oh, cheers. Pint of bitter, please.'

Gorton turned to the bar and attracted the attention of a young woman with long blonde hair, tied back.

'Kirsty, pint of bitter for Ian, please. Do you fancy another, Alan? Wilf?'

'Aye. Cheers, Peter.'

'Aye, go on then, ta,' said Bramley, as he and Green finished their pints. Green's accent was north-eastern and he sometimes got teased and called 'the Geordie lad'.

'Coming up!' Kirsty grinned at the group as she pulled the pints.

Davis took a drink from his glass and glared again at the shooters, who were involved in increasingly loud banter with each other and oblivious to the people at the bar.

He turned back. 'One of these days I'm going to take a swing at that Fraser. He's been at me all day.'

Kirsty laughed. 'Steady on, Ian, that won't get you anywhere. Just ignore them; don't take them too seriously.'

'That's easy for you to say.'

'But it isn't – we get a lot of shit from those shooting-party people. They're always making remarks and brushing up against you, touching you up and stuff.'

'You don't surprise me.'

'Yesterday Jeanette was cleaning the rooms, and when she knocked on one of the doors a voice shouted "Come in", so she did, and there was this oldish bloke stark naked on the bed with his legs spread apart – big hairy belly, one thing sticking up and the rest dangling down. She turned round and went out, said she'd never seen anything so disgusting in her life.'

This provoked some laughter, but the prevailing mood remained hostile to the difficult visitors.

'The mucky bugger!' declared Bramley, shaking his head.

'Bloody perverts!' said Green. 'Think they can do as they like because they've got money. I've done a few jobs for Fraser, always tries to screw you down to the lowest price, as if he wasn't rolling in it.'

'We all know Fraser's a tight git. You should see t'rent he charges me and ah've only a small farm. He put it up ag'ean last year an' ah'm really struggling.'

'Why do Rob and Sheila put up with him and all these posh shooters?' asked Gorton.

'Why do you think?' replied Kirsty. 'They bring in a lot of money. The Owens don't like it either, but they just have to grit their teeth like the rest of us.'

'Oh, bloody hell!' said Davis. 'Look who's here. What's he playing at?' He put his hand over his mouth to suppress a laugh.

Sandy Fraser had appeared at the bar in his Fraser kilt, complete with sporran, long white socks with black brogue shoes, black jacket, white dress shirt and black bow tie. He even had a knife tucked into his sock. There was applause from the party and someone called out: 'Well done, Sandy, every inch the clan chieftain!'

Fraser grinned and accepted the accolade while the people at the bar giggled into their beers.

Just before half past seven, the shooting party moved on to their private dining area, many of them already well lubricated. In the kitchen a huge operation went into action serving three courses of high-quality food to the party, the centrepiece being the roast grouse. Wine was decanted from the jeroboams and consumed in large quantities. After the meal they went into the residents' lounge for coffee and port, one or two stepping outside briefly to take the evening air and to smoke a cigar.

~

Back in the kitchen, Sheila was exhausted, but satisfied that everything had gone well during the evening service. She sat near the door with a glass of wine. The kitchen was clean and quiet; all the staff had gone home. The peace was shattered by Sandy Fraser, who came through the door red-faced from drinking wine.

'I thought I would find you here,' he said. 'I just wanted to say a good meal on the whole, but I'm not sure about that sauce Albert you did with the grouse.'

'Oh,' said Sheila, surprised.

'No, I thought it was rather too strong. All right for beef, but don't you think you should have toned the flavours down a little for grouse?' He chuckled. 'I mean, we spent all day bagging them and then when we came to eat them, it was difficult to tell what kind of meat it was. A pity really. Well, not to worry, I'm sure you'll do better next time. Actually, there's a superb little place in London, been going there for years, excellent for game. I can get the chef to give you a few tips if you like. Anyway, good night.' Without waiting for a reply, he went out of the door and joined the others in the lounge.

A few minutes later Rob came in and found her crying. She explained what had happened.

'What a bastard!' he said.

'How could he say that?' she said, drying her eyes. 'I know that sauce is perfect for grouse and you adjust the mustard and horseradish so that it's milder than for beef. He comes in pontificating, and he's not even a chef, offering to get me help! It was so humiliating. I know I shouldn't take it to heart but it's been such a long day and I've just had enough.'

'I know, love.' Rob put his arm around her shoulders.

'It's a good job he left quickly or I might have said something I shouldn't.'

'Well, don't. It's only a few times a year and we make a lot out of them.'

'They may not come back after this if my food is so awful.'

'Rubbish! There's nowhere else round here with a kitchen anywhere near as good as yours and he knows it. He's just one of those arrogant know-alls who thinks he's an expert on everything. Come on, it's late, let's get to bed.'

She smiled at him, took off her apron and hat, and they left the kitchen.

∼

When Fraser joined the others in the lounge, the party was starting to fragment. Following all they'd eaten and drunk after a day on the hills, some were dozing in armchairs and a few had called it a day and gone to bed. Fraser joined a group of hardened drinkers who were still knocking back the port, as well as some whisky which had appeared from somewhere. This group included the men with whom he'd shared the grouse butt: Symons, Rawnsley and Saunders. Partly due to the influence of alcohol, Rawnsley's mood had changed. He'd become rather raucous. He welcomed Fraser by raising his glass.

'Here he comes, His Lordship! Is that how you address a clan chieftain?'

There was a ripple of laughter, but some embarrassment at this rather abrupt and coarse greeting.

'Well, no. If I was the clan chief, you'd address me as Fraser,' replied Fraser, humouring Rawnsley.

'What if he doesn't pay his bills, and gets into debt?'

There was a shocked silence. Symons froze in the act of raising his glass to his lips; Saunders looked away. Fraser looked at Rawnsley with contempt.

'You've had too much to drink. I'd go straight off to bed if I were you.'

Rawnsley laughed. 'Only a joke, calm down. I'm sure you're going to pay me soon. Not before time though, is it?'

'Steady on, old boy,' said Symons. 'This is not the time or place, surely you can see that?'

Rawnsley had raised his voice and the remaining people in the room looked over. 'What is the right time then? He owes me a lot of money for—' Saunders stood up and gripped Rawnsley's arm. 'Hey, get off me!' Rawnsley protested, but he could not escape Saunders's strong grip.

'Come on,' said Saunders in a low, controlled voice. 'Sandy's right. It's time you went off to bed before you make a complete fool of yourself. You'll feel different in the morning.' He steered Rawnsley out of the room and shut the door.

'What a vulgar little man,' remarked Symons. 'What was all that about?'

Fraser sat down in an armchair. 'Oh, take no notice,' he said with a dismissive wave of the hand. 'I owe him some money for the new Bentley sports. I've had quite a lot of outgoings recently so I've delayed payment.'

'No excuse for bringing the subject up now,' observed Saunders.

'No indeed,' continued Symons. 'The man's just not . . . Well, you know what I mean.'

Fraser and Saunders understood: Rawnsley was not a gentleman, but his crass talk and his departure had spoiled the atmosphere. It was also after midnight and they were now the last people in the lounge.

Saunders yawned and stretched. 'I suppose we ought to call it a day. Want to be sharp tomorrow, see if I can beat you all in the shoot.'

'Not a chance,' laughed Symons, 'but you're right.' The three men got up and left the lounge.

~

The loft space of the Dog and Gun had been converted into small apartments which housed the live-in staff. In one of these rooms overlooking the front of the inn, there were two people squashed into the single bed. Kirsty Hemingway, the bartender and chambermaid, and Harry Newton, the young commis chef, were in a relationship but they kept it a secret. Harry's brother had got into trouble while conducting an affair with someone in his office and had warned him off mixing romance and work.

Harry was already snoring, but Kirsty was still awake. She found it hard to sleep when Harry was with her. The bed wasn't big enough. She often kicked him out and back to his own room if he kept her awake for too long.

It was quiet outside. She lay listening to some owls calling in the distance and then the sound of someone closing the door of the inn and walking away. Then she heard voices being raised, disturbing the peace of the night. She got out of bed and went to the window, which was open as it was a warm night. She had a good view of the front of the inn. The external lights were still on. There was a man standing with his back to her wearing a kilt, so that must be Sandy Fraser – she'd seen him dressed in this manner earlier in the evening. He was facing another man and blocking her view of him. They were arguing loudly.

Then the other man moved into view and raised a shotgun. Kirsty saw Fraser put his arms up and cry 'No', but the other man fired the gun at close range. She saw Fraser drop to the floor, blood pouring from his chest, and she let out a piercing scream. The assailant looked up towards her and she saw his face clearly. Then he ran off with the gun into the darkness.

Kirsty rushed over to the bed. 'Harry! Harry! Wake up!'

Harry jerked awake. 'Bloody hell! What's happening?'

Kirsty was shaking him and crying. 'Get up. It was horrible!'

'What was? Have you been dreaming?'

'No! I was looking outside.' She pointed to the window. 'I've just seen Alan Green shoot Mr Fraser. I think he's dead.'

One

Numberstones End
Lumb Gill Wham
Seavey Crook Bank
Lower Wham

Detective Chief Inspector Oldroyd had reached the point in the Saturday-morning Harrogate parkrun when he thought he was going to die. Halfway through the flat three-lap course around part of the Stray he was gasping, and his legs felt as if they were turning to jelly. However, he'd learned that stopping was counterproductive, so he struggled on at a slow jogging pace as the ten-year-olds and runners with buggies sped past him.

Oldroyd's partner, Deborah, was out of sight and far ahead of him. She was the one who had persuaded him to take up running. While she usually finished the five-kilometre run in twenty-six or twenty-seven minutes, he was still trying to beat thirty-six minutes. Despite this, he didn't feel as embarrassed as he had done in his schooldays. The whooping and clapping from the volunteer marshals made him feel triumphant. When he reached the funnel which led to the finish line, Deborah was there urging him on.

'Well done, Jim! Keep going. You've done it!'

With a tiny sprint at the end, Oldroyd got to the line and collected his finish token. Gasping for breath, he waited in the queue to have the token and his barcode scanned. Later on he would look at the results and see if there was any improvement in his performance. He had just reached double figures in the number of parkruns he'd completed. Deborah wore her 'hundred' shirt with pride and was well towards two hundred. She was waiting for him in her running tights, looking slim and toned.

'Great stuff, Jim!' Deborah high-fived him.

Oldroyd nodded. He was bending over trying to get his breath back, and contemplating a reward for his Herculean effort. His first words when he was able to speak again, were 'I think we deserve some breakfast after that. Let's go to Walton's.'

They put on their thin running jackets and wandered across the Stray towards West Park Street and Walton's, a luxury-food shop with an excellent cafe. This was the blissful part of a Saturday morning when he was off duty and did the run. He had to admit that he felt good when the exertions were over and he could enjoy a nice breakfast without feeling guilty. For the rest of the day he would feel a little tired, but much better in terms of his mood. He was experiencing the 'runner's high' that he'd always derided. They ran twice a week and he was gradually losing weight and felt much less sluggish. He'd also cut down on alcohol.

'OK,' said Deborah. 'Now don't go spoiling it all by ordering some kind of meaty fry-up.'

Oldroyd looked at the menu, at last feeling capable of conversation again. 'No, you're right, I'll go for the smoked salmon with scrambled eggs on sourdough. And coffee.'

'Good choice. Me too.'

After they'd eaten their breakfast they were just savouring a relaxed moment and had ordered a second coffee, when Oldroyd's phone rang. He took it out of his pocket.

'Blast, it's Tom Walker. I wonder what he wants.'

Detective Chief Superintendent Walker was Oldroyd's boss. They'd worked together for many years and had a good relationship, both being diehard Yorkshiremen. They were on first-name terms in private.

'Morning, Tom.'

'Jim, I'm sorry about this. I know you're off duty, but something big's come up.'

Oldroyd's heart sank. 'Oh? What's that?'

'There's been a murder up in Nidderdale, village called Niddersgill.'

'Yes, I know the place. But can't they deal with it at the Pateley Bridge station?'

'The problem is, the victim's a bit of a bigwig: Alexander Fraser – local landowner, former judge. Watkins is already on my back asking me who's on the case. He never shows any bloody concern if it's some ordinary person who's been bumped off, but if it's someone like this he starts jumping up and down.'

Matthew Watkins was the trendy chief constable of West Riding Police, despised by Walker for his management jargon and his obsession with image.

'So, could you go up there? I'm sorry to ruin your weekend, but I need someone like you to take care of it. You can take your team with you.' Oldroyd's team normally consisted of Stephanie Johnson and Andy Carter, two young detective sergeants who were also in a relationship.

'Fine, Tom. I'm out at the moment and I'll have to go home to get changed. I'll be there as quick as I can.'

'Good man.'

Oldroyd ended the call and sighed. 'Duty calls, I'm afraid. I told you what it would be like when you're with a detective. I've got to go to a murder scene in Nidderdale.'

'Not to worry; at least it's a nice place for it. I've got plenty to be getting on with. I'll do some reading for that conference I'm going to.' Deborah was a clinical psychologist who worked in her own practice. Oldroyd was pleased that she seemed to cope well with the disruptions to their private life caused by his job.

'Good. We'd better get back and then I'll go and find out what's been happening.'

~

'It's absolutely gorgeous up here today. Look at that view!'

It was another fine autumn day as Oldroyd drove his old Saab up the road that wound its way through Nidderdale towards Pateley Bridge. A broad sweeping landscape of farms, drystone walls and fields was spread out before them, soaring up the hillsides with higher fells in the distance. Steph was sitting next to him and Andy was in the back. Luckily they'd both been on duty at the Harrogate station when Oldroyd had arrived. Steph and Andy tried to arrange the roster so that they worked together on their weekend shifts and could then spend time together on their weekends off.

'Fabulous, sir,' said Andy, smiling to himself. A Londoner, Andy had grown to love the Yorkshire landscapes since he'd moved to the north, but he still found Oldroyd's rapturous enthusiasm quite amusing.

'Is this village beyond Pateley Bridge then, sir?' asked Steph.

'Yes, through Pateley Bridge, turn right and drive up towards Gouthwaite Reservoir. It's a lovely little spot.'

'And someone's been murdered outside the pub?'

'The Dog and Gun in Niddersgill is more than an ordinary pub; it's what you'd call a country inn. People stay there and the food has a good reputation, but yes, according to Superintendent Walker, someone was killed with a shotgun. There'll definitely be lots of shotguns around here at the moment. The shooting season is in full swing up on the moors.'

'So that's where they go up and blast away at birds?' asked Andy.

'Yes: it's usually red grouse around here, and it's big business these days. People pay a lot of money to take part and they come from all over the world. This man who was shot, Alexander Fraser, he owned one of these grouse moors – wealthy man, retired judge, and prominent local with political connections. That's why Walker's sending us out to make sure everything's dealt with properly and swiftly. Matthew Watkins doesn't want any bad publicity.'

'I see,' said Steph. 'The local people won't like us muscling in, will they, sir?'

'Maybe not, but there's a good inspector at the Pateley station, Bill Gibbs, who's probably up there now. I've known him a long time, he used to work at Harrogate, and I think he'll appreciate our help if things prove difficult.'

The car turned a sharp corner to the left, headed down the long, straight, picturesque main street of Pateley Bridge, and over the bridge spanning the River Nidd.

Oldroyd turned right at a signpost listing destinations in the upper part of Nidderdale, including Niddersgill, How Stean Gorge, and the remote settlements of Middlesmoor and Lofthouse high up at the top of the dale. They soon reached the village, which had a picture-postcard prettiness. Stone-built cottages clustered around a pond and a village green with a permanent maypole. There was a small primary school, a small church and Peter Gorton's shop, but the centrepiece was undoubtedly the Dog and Gun Inn which overlooked the pond. It was a long, low, seventeenth-century stone building clothed in Virginia creeper that was starting to turn red. Tasteful extensions at the side and back had increased the residential capacity and created a large dining area.

Oldroyd pulled into the car park in front of the inn, in which a small number of cars were parked at right angles to the building. The detectives got out and walked over to an area cordoned off by incident tape, where they found a number of people apparently waiting for them, including Inspector Gibbs. He was a balding man in his forties, with a dogged expression which broke into a wide smile when he saw Oldroyd.

'Ah!' said Oldroyd. 'I'm glad it's you, Bill. This is DS Carter and DS Johnson – Inspector Bill Gibbs.' The introductions were acknowledged.

'Welcome to Nidderdale, sir,' Gibbs said. 'I'm pleased to have your help. We don't have a big staff up here in Pateley. My DS is out on another investigation and I'm here with a DC.' He indicated a young officer, Ian Potts, who nodded to Oldroyd and said, 'Sir.'

Oldroyd looked at Steph and smiled reassuringly. Territorial feelings were not going to be an issue here. A tall man came over – Tim Groves, a forensic pathologist with whom Oldroyd had worked for many years.

'Morning, Jim,' said Groves. 'Inspector Gibbs said you were on your way, so I thought I'd wait and give you a briefing. The body is on its way back to Harrogate. He was shot at close range by a shotgun. I'll be able to tell what bore it was after the post-mortem. He was probably hit in the heart and died pretty much instantly; time of death was about midnight. Officers from Pateley have been here all night, but I couldn't get here until this morning. Anyway, I'll be off now. I wish you luck in capturing the killer and I hope it turns out to be fairly straightforward.'

'That's very rarely the case where I'm concerned, Tim,' laughed Oldroyd.

'I know. At least you've got a lovely setting for your work. OK, I'll be in contact.' He strode off to his car, carrying his bag of instruments.

After a brief examination of the murder scene, the detectives went inside. Gibbs had already set up an incident room in the residents' lounge, the scene of Sandy Fraser's last conversation before the angry words he'd exchanged with his killer. They all sat down in the comfortable chairs and Gibbs went through the details.

'We were called at twelve thirty a.m. by a Mr Rob Owen. He and his wife, Sheila, own the inn. The victim, Alexander "Sandy" Fraser, was dead when we arrived. Shot, as Tim said. He'd had dinner here with a shooting party, after which he'd sat here with members of that party until midnight, when he left to walk home. He lives in an old manor house just out of the village. It was late and there was no one around apart from the assailant. The good news is that we do have a witness.'

'I thought you said there was no one around?' said Oldroyd.

'There wasn't outside, but a woman called' – Gibbs consulted his notes – 'Kirsty Hemingway saw what happened from her bedroom window, which overlooks the front of the building. All the exterior lights were still on and it was a clear night.'

Oldroyd smiled at this. Gibbs had always had a reputation for thoroughness. 'She saw two men arguing, one of whom she recognised as Fraser even though his back was turned to her,' Gibbs continued. 'This was because he was wearing a kilt.'

Oldroyd raised his eyebrows.

'Apparently he always wears a kilt to these dinners with his shooting parties. It's a kind of tradition.'

'I see, go on.'

'She then saw the other man lift up a shotgun and shoot Fraser in the chest. When he did this, he moved to a position where she had a clear view of his face. She says she's sure that it was a man called Alan Green. He's a gardener and odd-job man, lives somewhere in Pateley Bridge. He'd been in the bar earlier in the evening so he knew Fraser was here. Looks like he waited until his target left and then confronted and shot him.'

'Is there any sign of him?'

'No. No one I've spoken to knows an address for him. I've been on to my people at the station and there's no criminal record for such a person. We've got officers out in Pateley searching for him.'

'Right. Well, first off I think we need to talk to this girl – Kirsty – again, as our star witness. How far have you got with taking statements?'

'Not very. The residential part of the inn was pretty full last night with members of the shooting party. I've given the instruction that everyone is to stay here and I've had a quick word with the Owens. I've been round to inform the victim's wife, Miriam Fraser. Unfortunately I didn't have a female officer who could have stayed with her. I think that's everything.'

'OK . . . so I want you,' Oldroyd addressed Potts, 'to start organising statements. See if anyone else saw anything suspicious. Who else knew this Alan Green, and what can they tell us about him? Was anyone aware that Fraser had enemies? You know the sort of stuff.'

'Yes, sir,' said Potts.

'Also find out if guns were kept on these premises and whether any have gone missing. Steph, can you go round to check on Mrs Fraser?'

'Sir.'

'It's an old manor house just out of the village, turn right when you get to the main road. You can't miss it,' said Gibbs.

The three of them left, and Gibbs went into the kitchen where Kirsty was sitting with Sheila Owen, drinking coffee. Sheila had an arm around the younger woman's shoulders. They both looked tired and shaken.

Gibbs brought Kirsty in to see Oldroyd, who introduced himself, sat her down and smiled encouragingly. 'You've told Inspector Gibbs what you saw from your bedroom window. That must have been a terrible shock.'

'It was.'

'I won't ask you to go through it all again, but you're sure that the man you saw with the gun who shot Mr Fraser was this Alan Green?'

'Yes. I had a good look at him and I'd been talking to him in the bar only a few hours earlier. The inn lights were shining straight on to him. I recognised his face and he had the same clothes on: green jumper and brown cord trousers. He comes into the bar fairly regularly. I'm sure it was him.' She looked at Oldroyd. 'What I'm worried about, as I told the inspector here, is that he looked up and saw me watching. He knows I'm a witness so what if he comes for me?' For a moment she looked panic-stricken.

'Don't worry, we'll protect you. What else can you tell me about him?'

'Not much. He does gardening and stuff for people. He lives in Pateley and cycles or walks up when he's got a job, and he likes coming into the bar here. It's not far. He has a north-east accent so he must have come from up there originally. He was in the bar earlier,' she repeated, and looked as if she could scarcely believe it.

'Did he say anything? Did you notice anything unusual about him?'

'No.'

'How well did you know Mr Fraser?' asked Gibbs.

'Not at all, really. He only comes in the bar with his party when the shoots are on. I've seen him and his wife dining here a few times.'

'You must hear a lot of local gossip, working in the bar.'

'Yes, I suppose so.'

'Did Mr Fraser have any other enemies? Did anyone ever express animosity towards him?'

Kirsty looked very uncomfortable. 'I don't like to say.'

There was a flash of the steely side of Oldroyd. 'Well, I'm afraid you'll have to; this is a murder enquiry and you can't withhold information.'

She bit her lip, twirled her hair with a finger and seemed to be frantically thinking of what to say.

'A lot of us don't like him and his shooting parties,' she began. 'They don't behave . . . well when they're here.' She told the detectives about the groping and harassment. 'Mr Fraser was big-headed and he didn't treat people well. He . . .'

'Yes?'

'Look, I'll tell you but don't tell anyone I said it. Ian Davis is Mr Fraser's gamekeeper. Mr Fraser was always on his back and Ian often got angry. But I . . .'

'Was he angry last night?'

'Yes, as it happens. Fraser had pulled him up over something on the shoot. But look, Ian would never harm anyone, and anyway I saw Alan Green, so it definitely wasn't Ian or anybody else.'

'OK, well, thank you,' said Oldroyd kindly, trying to calm her down. 'Now, stay in the inn and don't go out anywhere unaccompanied. There will be officers around for some time. OK? And I'm just coming up to your room now so you can show me the window from where you saw Mr Fraser being shot.' She nodded and they left together.

~

Gibbs and Andy chatted for a few minutes until Oldroyd returned.

'So, sir,' said Andy, 'if the killer knows he was seen, he'll make himself scarce.'

'Yes, we're going to get a message out to the locals to be aware that he could be hiding in a barn or outhouse and he could be dangerous, as we assume he's still got the shotgun.'

'Did you work with DCI Oldroyd, then, sir?' asked Andy, curious to find out about his boss's previous colleagues.

'Yes, in Harrogate. It's a few years ago now but I'll never forget it. I learned most of what I know from him. You're lucky to be part of his team. There aren't many like him.'

'I know, sir. I came up from the Met. He had a bit of a reputation even down there. He teaches you to think, doesn't he?'

'That's right. And never to assume you know all the answers without investigating properly and considering all the possibilities. He once told me that he was very affected by all those cases in the seventies when people were wrongly convicted. He said it was lazy, arrogant policing and we had to do better. The thing is, he has such a fine brain and—'

At that moment, Oldroyd returned. 'Fine brain, eh? You must be talking about me.'

Andy and Gibbs laughed.

'Well,' said Oldroyd, 'I've seen the view she had from her bedroom and it's some distance from that window to the murder scene, and it was night-time. I put that to her but she remains adamant that she saw Green, and the light from the hotel shone on his face and so on. I still think she could be mistaken or that she could be covering for someone else. There are no other witnesses.'

'True,' said Gibbs.

'It's not conclusive enough for us not to consider other possibilities. She seemed very alarmed when we questioned her about Ian . . . what's his name?'

'Davis, Ian Davis the gamekeeper,' replied Gibbs.

'Yes. I think he's high up on our list.'

Gibbs consulted his list again. 'There's also Wilf Bramley, a farmer, and Peter Gorton, who owns a local shop. They were in the bar earlier in the evening with Green and Davis. They might have noticed something.'

'Excellent work. I think it would be a good idea if you went back to Pateley and supervised the search for Alan Green, and left us to question people here.'

'Yes, sir, that's fine. We need to catch him as soon as we can. The problem is we've got no photograph or anything. We need to ask around and find out who knew him.'

'OK, off you go and I'll keep you up to date. If anyone here can tell us where he lived in Pateley I'll let you know.'

Gibbs left for Pateley and Andy went to help Potts, who was continuing to take statements. Oldroyd took a break to take in his surroundings. The lounge at the Dog and Gun was very luxurious, with a thick carpet, an array of comfortable sofas and a range of sporting prints on the walls. There was an open fire which would be very cosy in winter. There was a pleasant view across the village pond with a glimpse of the fells beyond. He settled into an arm-chair and spent a while thinking about the case as he gazed out of the window. It was good to get a few minutes of calm. He was just wondering about whether to bring Deborah here for a nice week-end away when Andy returned with Potts.

'I think we've got it sorted, sir,' said Andy. 'We have statements from everyone, and we've gathered some useful information. Before he left last night, Fraser was in here with three of his shooting friends: James Symons, Gideon Rawnsley and Henry Saunders. They were the last people to see him alive apart from the witness to the murder and, of course, the murderer. Apparently, there was an argument between Rawnsley and Fraser, and Saunders had to get Rawnsley out of the room and off to bed.'

'Was there, indeed? So we need to talk to those three.'

'In terms of the staff, sir,' said Andy, 'the owners Rob and Sheila Owen have had quite a lot to do with Fraser over the years and know the village well, so they'll be worth talking to.'

Oldroyd slapped his legs. 'OK, excellent! Let's get moving. We'll start with the Owens as they're close at hand. Inspector Gibbs has gone back to Pateley to pursue our chief suspect, so we need to see what we can find out here.'

~

Sheila and Rob Owen sat in front of the detectives looking rather dazed. After their gruelling day they had been up most of the night, and it had been chaos with the police, the ambulance, and disturbed guests wandering around asking what was happening.

'I know you're very busy, so I'll try to be quick. Before I ask you any questions, I have to tell you that it will be necessary to close the inn for a while. Unfortunately, it's a crime scene. None of the guests should be allowed to check out until I give the word. We'll try to keep it to the minimum time possible,' began Oldroyd.

Andy sat, ready to make notes.

The Owens took in this information passively, as if they'd been expecting it.

'So, what happened last night?' continued Oldroyd.

Sheila glanced at Rob, who started to speak. 'We were in bed asleep; it had been an exhausting day. We were woken by Kirsty banging on the door, screaming that someone had been shot outside. She was nearly hysterical. I told her to stay with Sheila and I went down. Mr Saunders and Mr Symons were just coming up to their rooms so I asked them to come with me and see what was going on. The three of us found Mr Fraser on the ground just past the inn buildings. He'd obviously been on his way home. There was blood on the ground and a big wound in his chest. I felt for a pulse but couldn't find one. We went back in and I called the police and ambulance. I think you know the rest.'

'So who locks up at night?'

'All the doors except the front are always locked and operated by a code. The front door is locked at eleven o'clock, but residents have a key and Mr Fraser had one on this occasion as the leader of the party. There's a rota for staff to stay up until the last guest goes to bed and then go round to check everything and turn out the lights, et cetera.'

'Who was on duty last night?'

'It was Greg Cooper, Sheila's sous chef. We all do a shift on that rota so that no one has to do it too often. We can't afford to employ any security staff. Greg came out to see what was happening, but like the rest of us there was nothing he could do. He went back inside and spoke to the residents, who were asking what had happened.'

'Did you see anyone else outside?'

'No.'

'OK. Now, you say that you met Saunders and Symons on the stairs. Would it have been possible for one of them to have fired the shot and come back into the inn?'

'Well, yes, I suppose so. Going by what Kirsty said, quite a bit of time must have elapsed as she ran to our door. But she was insistent that she saw Alan Green.'

'Yes, she's told us. So what do you know about Sandy Fraser and what was your relationship with him?'

Rob looked very tired with the effort of talking, so Sheila took over.

'He came to the village about six years ago when he retired. I think he was a judge. He bought the manor house which is just down the road, towards Gouthwaite Reservoir, and a grouse moor. He runs shooting parties right through the season, and we have a contract with him to supply accommodation and food at midday up on the moors when the shooters take a break.'

'So, does this arrangement work well?' asked Oldroyd.

Sheila glanced at Rob. 'It does on a business level. He's a good customer and pays his bills, though not always promptly, but we've never found him an easy person to deal with. He's very demanding and pernickety about things – always complaining about something.'

'But he's never gone elsewhere?'

'No, it's too convenient for him here, close to the grouse moor, and I think he knows we provide a good service. It's all about him showing off the fact that he's in charge, and knows about everything. Last night we prepared a special meal for them consisting of the grouse they'd shot, served roasted with a sauce and vegetables. We put a lot of effort in. Every party gets that on their final evening here. They usually stay two or three nights. So he comes in afterwards, very lukewarm about it all and complaining about the sauce I prepared for the grouse. I could have stuck a kitchen knife in his back.' She put a hand to her mouth. 'Oh, I'm sorry, that was a tasteless remark. Of course I wouldn't really have harmed him, I—'

'I can see that would be very annoying. Never mind, just carry on.'

'Well, he was like that, always picking you up on some detail, never satisfied. Ian Davis, his gamekeeper, found him a difficult person to work for.'

'Where does Davis live?'

'In a cottage on the back road. He's got a wife and two children and I think they struggle a bit, so I don't suppose he can afford to lose his job.'

'OK. Did Mr Fraser have any other enemies that you know of?'

Rob replied this time: 'I can't say anyone liked him, but someone who'd want to kill him is another matter. I know Wilf Bramley

31

had no time for him. He was in the bar last night as well. He's an old tenant farmer of Fraser's. He complained a lot that Fraser charged him too much rent.

'There are also two people who've made his life difficult with the shooting. Liz Smith campaigns against blood sports and she's conducted shoot sabotages with the group she's part of. And there's a bloke called Tony Dexter. He lives in a tiny converted barn high up on the fellside across the dale. He's a bit of a loner, a writer and environmentalist. He's opposed to grouse moors because he says they damage the habitat and the environment. So Fraser had some run-ins with those two.'

'And where does this Liz Smith live?' asked Andy.

'In a caravan in a field just out of the village – pays a bit of rent to a farmer who doesn't seem bothered about her beliefs, probably just welcomes the cash. It's a bit of a dump and it's plastered all over with posters about cruelty to animals and stuff.' Rob smiled. 'I always thought it was quite amusing that Fraser had to pass her caravan every time he came in and out of the village. She works with another woman in a local pottery. You'll have passed it on the way into the village – very artistic stuff but bloody expensive.'

'I see. And is that all?' asked Oldroyd.

The Owens exchanged looks again.

'I don't know of anyone else who you could call an enemy of his, Chief Inspector,' continued Rob. 'But, as I say, he wasn't popular. Of course, we don't know anything about his life before he came to Niddersgill.'

'Did you know any of the people in the shooting party? I'm thinking particularly about the three who were with him in this lounge before he was shot,' asked Oldroyd.

'None of them apart from Mr Saunders and Mr Symons, who were friends of Mr Fraser and they've stayed here before. I've heard of Gideon Rawnsley. He runs an upmarket car business in

Harrogate. I didn't know any of the others, did you?' Rob looked at Sheila, who shook her head.

'OK, thank you. You'll need to make statements, but by all means go back to work. We'll release all your staff when we've talked to them.' Oldroyd got up to leave. 'By the way, any chance of some coffee and a bit of lunch?'

'I'll order some sandwiches and drinks for you,' replied Sheila. 'Thanks.'

'Before we go, Chief Inspector,' said Rob, 'there was one thing I saw which I ought to tell you about. But I don't want to get anyone into trouble.'

'Go on.' Oldroyd had suspected that there might be more.

'When I went out to tend to Mr Fraser, I caught sight of the back of a black van parked behind that terrace opposite. When I went back out with the ambulance people, it had gone.'

'Do you know whose van it was?'

Rob seemed reluctant to continue. 'No, not for sure, but it looked like David Eastwood's. He's the local postman, delivers all the post to the villages round here. He comes in the daytime in his red post van, but if he comes here at night he uses his own van.'

'Does he live in Niddersgill?'

'No, he lives in Pateley Bridge. He wasn't in the bar here so it was odd that his van was here at that time of night, except . . .' Rob looked sheepish.

'What Rob's trying to say is that Dave has a bit of a reputation as a womaniser. He could well have been visiting someone in the village.'

'For . . . romantic reasons?' It never ceased to amaze Oldroyd what went on behind closed doors in the little dales villages.

'Exactly,' Sheila said.

'I can see why you don't like reporting that, but you're right to mention it. We'll have to follow it up and hopefully eliminate him from the enquiry without causing too much upset to those involved,' said Oldroyd discreetly.

The Owens nodded and left.

'Well,' said Oldroyd, settling back in his chair and reflecting on what they'd been told. 'What do you make of things so far?'

'I take it you're considering whether one of his three friends could have bumped him off?' said Andy.

'At least two of them seemed to have had the opportunity but we don't know any motive yet. We might know more when we've interviewed them.'

'Real motives are a bit thin on the ground so far, aren't they, sir?' said Andy, looking at his notes. 'I mean, the Owens obviously didn't like him but you'd hardly murder someone who brought you a load of money in, even if they didn't like your sauce.'

'I wouldn't have thought so. It's going to be interesting to speak to those animal rights and environment people. Emotions can run high with those issues.'

'Yes, sir, but this might all prove unnecessary if we can find Alan Green,' said Andy.

'True, but I'm already thinking that this may not be as open and shut as it seems,' continued Oldroyd. 'For a start, as you said, motives are not clear: what was Green's? No one has yet given us a reason why he would want to kill Fraser. The second point, as we discussed, is that we can't rely totally on this witness. She may be mistaken and there's no one to corroborate her story.'

'You still think Kirsty might be covering for someone else?'

'It's possible. A neat little plan. She has a nice vantage point from which to say she saw the murderer, and she did, but was it who she said it was? Was it actually Symons or Saunders, as they were well placed to follow Fraser out and shoot him? Or maybe Rawnsley didn't go to bed but nipped out and lay in wait for him.'

'That's all possible, sir. Also, we'll have to follow up with this postman. It's suspicious that his van was there just at the right time and then it disappeared.'

'Yes.'

The coffee and sandwiches arrived.

'The questions are building up and we've got a lot of people to speak to, and unless I'm wrong, and Alan Green is found quickly and confesses, my instinct is that it's going to be a hard slog.' Oldroyd looked at the food. 'So we'd better get stuck into this first. But leave some for Steph.'

~

Steph walked the short distance out of the village to the Frasers' seventeenth-century manor house. It was small but beautiful, with attractive mullioned windows. There was a garden full of roses and nepetas which were still in bloom, if a little ragged now at the end of the season.

She walked up the path and knocked on the door. It was answered by a woman with glasses and short greying hair, dressed in a tweed skirt and a cardigan. Her eyes were red.

Steph introduced herself, and Miriam Fraser invited her in.

Steph followed the woman into a sitting room full of chintzy sofas. A large grandfather clock stood in a corner and a cat lay asleep on one of the sofas, on top of a sheepskin throw.

Mrs Fraser sat down in an armchair, while Steph sank into the sofa next to the cat, which looked round, yawned and went back to sleep.

Fraser's widow looked clearly agitated. 'I would offer you some tea, but I'm too . . .' Her hand went to her mouth.

'No. That's fine, don't worry about it. You've had a terrible shock. Could I make you some?'

The woman shook her head, closed her eyes and seemed unable to reply.

'I know this is very difficult, Mrs Fraser,' Steph said, 'but we want to catch whoever is responsible and you can help us. Is it OK if I ask you a few questions?'

Mrs Fraser sighed, grimaced and seemed about to refuse, but then nodded.

'I presume the last time you saw your husband was yesterday evening?'

'Yes. He came back from the shoot and changed for the dinner at the Dog and Gun.' It was clearly a big effort for her to speak.

'Did he seem OK?'

'Yes. He was his normal self. He told me not to wait up for him, as he would be late back as he usually is when he goes to the shoot dinners. Then he gave me a kiss and . . .' She started to cry, dabbing her face with a handkerchief.

Steph waited until she appeared to have composed herself. 'And what did you do when he'd gone?'

'I watched television until about eleven o'clock and then I . . . went to bed.' She struggled to finish the sentence.

'I'm sorry. I know this is difficult but it's really important. Has your husband been his normal self recently? Has he been worried about anything? Anything to do with money perhaps, or the grouse moor.'

'Not that I know of. I left all the financial stuff to Sandy. He was very good with that side of things and I never had anything to do with the grouse moor. To be honest, I don't like it: grown men firing their shotguns at defenceless birds.'

'I understand. Did your husband have any enemies, Mrs Fraser? And I don't mean just around here, but maybe someone in the past. Just try to think back.'

'No,' she said after a pause. 'Sandy could be quite abrasive and domineering. I think he was a judge the barristers feared, so he was never popular, but I'm not aware of anyone who was a real enemy – someone who would want to harm him.'

'And you were married a long time?'

'Thirty-nine years. We were coming up to our ruby wedding.' She had another little weep.

'Do you have any family, Mrs Fraser?'

'Thomas, our son, is a barrister in London – father's footsteps and all that. Henrietta studied environmental science and she works for the National Trust in Wiltshire. She and her father had some fierce rows about grouse shooting and blood sports, I can tell you.' She smiled for the first time at this family memory.

Steph continued. 'The main suspect at the moment is a man called Alan Green. Did you know him?'

Mrs Fraser looked puzzled. 'Green? Oh, you surely don't mean the odd-job man? Sandy got him to clean out the gutters and trim the hedges, stuff like that. What could he possibly have against Sandy?'

'They didn't have a row about anything?'

'No. I think Sandy got him to lower his estimate for the work, but it was all amicable.'

'Now, this is a hard question, Mrs Fraser, but I have to ask it. How was your relationship with your husband?'

The woman gave a cynical little laugh. 'I think you can tell what I thought about Sandy unless I'm a wonderful actress. We had a marvellous marriage. Sandy could be difficult with other people, but he treated me like a queen. I couldn't have asked for more.'

Steph smiled. 'I see. Is there going to be someone coming to stay with you, Mrs Fraser? Your son or daughter perhaps?'

'Yes, my daughter's coming on Tuesday. I'll be all right until then.' She turned to Steph. 'I think . . . before you go, there is something else I've remembered.'

'Yes?'

'It was about two years ago. Those hunt-saboteur people were causing trouble up on the moor. Sandy couldn't bear them spoiling his shoots, said they could lose him a lot of money. One day some of them appeared and Sandy chased one of them with a stick. He lost his temper quite easily. He ran after this man, who fell. Sandy tried to pull him to his feet and he found that the man was dead. They called the ambulance and there was a post-mortem and everything. It turned out he had a rare heart condition and could have died at any time. It wasn't really Sandy's fault, but I wonder if some of those people hold Sandy responsible for the death of one of their group. I suppose if they did, it could be a motive to kill him.'

∾

Inspector Gibbs arrived back at Pateley Bridge station, eager to pursue Alan Green, but he soon discovered that there was very little to go on. No adverts for his services seemed to have appeared in any local publication. Brief enquiries earlier had yielded nothing. It was time to be more thorough, so he and his officers would have to go out and patiently ask people in shops and pubs whether they had heard of the suspect. A photograph would have been very helpful because sometimes people went under different names, but all they had was a basic physical description, and the north-eastern accent.

The police station was a modern building at the top of the beautiful, long main street in Pateley Bridge. Gibbs organised a small team of officers to cover all the shops, cafes and pubs on both sides and he set out with them. It was not an easy task. It was Saturday afternoon and the street was bustling with people. Everywhere he went, Gibbs felt that he ruined the relaxed atmosphere by bring-ing a message of horror and fear: a local man murdered and the murderer on the loose, probably still in the neighbourhood. Smiles dropped from people's faces and bright conversations stopped abruptly.

Two hours later, Gibbs met up with his team at the bottom of the street. The results of their enquiries were poor. One or two people said they thought they might have seen someone answering Alan Green's description in a pub, but no one recognised the name as someone who was a regular, or who had done work for them or for anyone they knew.

The officers walked back up to the station with nothing to show for their efforts. But they were professionals and not about to give up. Gibbs knew that people like Green, who lived somewhat itinerant lives, could be difficult to locate, often because they had left a trail of petty crime behind them and didn't want to be found. Green may have lied to people about where he lived, but it had to be somewhere not too far from Niddersgill as he appeared not to have a car; maybe he lived in one of the many villages or hamlets nearby. The task of finding Alan Green had only just begun, but what also concerned Gibbs, as it did Oldroyd, was that they still had no idea why he'd killed Fraser; both man and motive were elusive.

~

Gideon Rawnsley sat opposite Oldroyd and Andy. Potts had gone to check on the statement-taking. Rawnsley appeared chastened and downcast, and was clearly suffering from a hangover.

'Well, Mr Rawnsley,' began Oldroyd, 'a number of people have testified that they saw you having an argument with Mr Fraser not long before he was murdered. So, shall we start with that? Can you tell us what it was about?'

Rawnsley looked very sheepish. 'It was my fault. I was drunk and I shouldn't have raised the issue. Sandy hasn't paid me for his latest car and it was starting to annoy me. We work on very small margins with luxury cars, and we get a lot of customers like Sandy: wealthy and posh but very lax when it comes to paying their bills. I don't suppose money matters to them. But it does to people like me, who have a business to run.'

'Did you threaten him?'

Rawnsley shook his head. 'No. As I said, I was drunk – it was all swagger. I tend to get like that when I've been drinking. It would all have blown over; Sandy and I got on well, really. He enjoyed talking to me about cars, vintage ones and stuff like that. I do a bit of business in vintage stuff and if I ever got anything unusual in, Sandy would come down to have a look. He wouldn't have invited me to this shoot if we didn't get on, would he?'

'Maybe not. Have you known him for long?'

'Ever since he came to the area.'

'Did he have any enemies?'

'Not that I'm aware of. But I only knew him after he'd retired from his job.'

Rawnsley had made the same point as Rob Owen about Fraser's previous life. That needed to be researched as soon as possible and might yield someone with a motive more compelling than what they were finding so far in Niddersgill.

'Did you know a man called Alan Green, who works as an odd-job man in the area?'

'No, never heard of him.'

'What did you do after you were ejected from this lounge?'

'I just went straight to bed. I was already feeling bad about the way I'd behaved, and I was going to apologise to Sandy and the others at breakfast. But I never got the chance.' He seemed genuinely sad and regretful.

'Is your bedroom at the front? Did you hear anything?' asked Andy.

'No, it's at the back. I went straight off to sleep until Henry Saunders woke me up this morning. He told me there was a hell of a mess going on, the police were here and Sandy had been shot.' He shook his head. 'I'm very sorry about it all. It's shocking, but I had nothing to do with it.'

Henry Saunders sat down casually, with his long legs crossed, and looked straight at Oldroyd through his rimless glasses.

'How long have you known Mr Fraser?' began Oldroyd.

'For more years than I care to remember, Chief Inspector. We were at school together in the early seventies. We've always got on well although there have been periods when I didn't see that much of him.'

'When was that?'

'Well, Sandy was in chambers in London and then became a judge, but he moved up to the north a while ago. That's when he discovered these grouse moors out here in the wilderness.'

Oldroyd frowned as He suspected a slur against his beloved county. It might well be wild on the fells but it was also beautiful. In fact, the wildness was part of the beauty.

'Now that Sandy's retired, I come up to see him quite regularly, especially at this time of year. My wife and I came up for Christmas a few years ago. Quite delightful to get away from it all. You really are miles from anywhere up here.'

Oldroyd wasn't sure whether that meant in Nidderdale or the north generally, but he didn't pursue this particular question.

'I take it you were on good terms with him?'

'Good Lord, yes. Sandy was a sound type, solid through and through. Man of the old school, like me.'

Again, Oldroyd refrained from exploring what Saunders actually meant by that.

'Were you aware of any enemies? Anyone who wished him harm?'

'No.' Saunders shook his head.

'What happened last night in here?'

'Oh, that idiot, Rawnsley, had too much to drink and started to harangue Sandy about some money problem. I ask you – there's a time and place, isn't there? So I steered him out of here before he made a damned fool of himself and told him to go off to bed, and he did.'

'And you roused him in the morning?'

'Yes, well, I thought he would have a hangover and had probably slept through all the commotion.'

'And he was in his room?'

'Well, he answered me and he came down here pretty quickly.'

'Do you think he would have been capable of attacking Mr Fraser?' asked Andy.

Saunders laughed. 'I don't think so, Sergeant. There was nothing dangerous about him; he was just, how shall I put it, a little out of his social depth. I'm not sure why Sandy invited him unless he was buttering him up and hoped to get a good deal on a car.'

'I understand the row was about payment for one of those cars. Did Mr Fraser have any money problems as far as you were aware?'

'Sandy? I shouldn't think so. He's always been well heeled – family money, judge's salary and all that. Maybe he didn't pay his bills as quickly as some people would have liked, but nothing serious. I don't think he'd run up any significant debts. Not that he would tell me.'

'But he might, as you work in the financial world, don't you?'

'True, but I think a proud and private man like Sandy would have to be very desperate to seek help from someone about a matter like that, even from a friend. It would be an admission of failure.'

'You referred to the commotion. What did you hear at the time of the murder?'

'James – that's James Symons – and I went out of this room with Sandy at about a quarter past twelve, and he left the inn by the front door. James and I were talking and going slowly up the stairs to our rooms. We'd nearly got to the top when I heard a muffled bang. It sounded like a shot outside. I asked James if he'd heard it, and he said no. We were about to continue up the stairs thinking I'd been mistaken when we saw that young woman run past us screaming and then start banging on a door. It must have been the Owens she was rousing, because the door opened, she went in and then the husband came running out and said someone had been shot. We went back down with him and then outside to where we found Sandy on the ground.' He paused and looked very grim but still controlled. 'It was a terrible shock, especially when we realised he was dead.'

'Did you see anyone?'

'No. Whoever did it had already disappeared. I hope you find them, Chief Inspector. It was an absolutely vile thing to do. You will always have my full help and cooperation.'

'Thank you,' replied Oldroyd with a faint touch of sarcasm. It always amused him when people of wealth and influence seemed to imply that they had a choice about whether or not to cooperate with the authorities. At some level they appeared to think they were somehow above all that. 'And what happened then?'

'Basically, James and I left them to it. There was nothing we could do. We came back inside and had another drink. There was no point going to bed, it was pandemonium with the ambulance and police cars arriving, people waking up and wandering about asking what was going on. We were pretty shook up, as you can imagine. We got a few hours' sleep at about four a.m. I phoned my wife this morning and she can't believe it. I trust you've been round to see poor Miriam. The police said we had to remain here.'

'Yes, she's been informed. Detective Sergeant Stephanie Johnson is with her now. She'll be looked after, don't worry, but we have to follow the procedures correctly.'

'Absolutely.'

'Did you know this man, Alan Green, who we'd like to question?'

'No, but I understand he's some sort of local odd-job man. Sounds a funny business, can't see why someone like that would want to kill Sandy.'

'All right, so that's all for now,' concluded Oldroyd. 'We'll need to speak to Mr Symons next. I assume he's around.'

'Yes, he's in the bar. There's nowhere else to sit apart from our rooms now that we can't come in here. I'll tell him to come along.'

'Thank you.'

~

James Symons, the last of the three men who had sat in the lounge with Fraser before he was murdered, relaxed on the sofa with a smile on his face.

Oldroyd asked him to describe what had happened the previous evening and he gave the same account as Henry Saunders. Of course, Oldroyd was aware that there had been ample opportunity for them to agree on a story if they were trying to cover up something.

'How well did you know Mr Fraser?' he asked.

'Not tremendously well. I got to know him when he moved into the area. We share a passion for shooting and we met on the circuit, you know. He came over to my patch in Wensleydale and invited me back, and it went on from there. We also meet at various social functions.'

'I see. So were you aware of any enemies he might have had?'

'I knew little about his life outside shooting, but I think it's worth mentioning these confounded saboteurs, forever causing trouble and sticking their noses in. I've had problems with them over in Wensleydale and I've seen Sandy get very angry with them. I think there was an incident with them a few years ago, but I can't remember what it was about; I wasn't there. One of them died of a heart attack, I think. In fact, the afternoon before he was killed, there was a group up there causing a nuisance.'

'I see. We'll find out exactly what happened. To your knowledge, was he ever personally threatened by them?'

'No, and I realise it's a long shot, but you never know with these people – they're fanatics and some of them will stop at nothing. They may have wanted revenge.'

'I take it you didn't know Alan Green, who a witness has identified as the killer?'

'No, I didn't. Why are you asking me about all these people if you've got a clear suspect?'

'We can't be certain at this stage as to the precise nature of what happened. We have to examine other possibilities. Did you think Mr Rawnsley was a threat after his row with Mr Fraser?'

Symons smiled again. 'I couldn't see him as being capable of murder, Chief Inspector. He was just a silly little man who lost control of himself – very embarrassing but not killer material, if you see what I mean.'

'Another person has been mentioned to me as an opponent of grouse shooting: Tony Dexter. I understand he's an environmentalist?'

Symons laughed. 'Oh, him! Yes, he's an environmentalist, and a poet, and an artist and goodness knows what else. He turns up to council meetings sometimes, and writes to the local paper arguing that grouse moors damage the habitat and tosh like that. Again, I can't see him as a murderer, he's just an amusing eccentric – no one takes him seriously. He lives up on the fells somewhere near here I think.'

'Yes, we'll track him down. And what's your business, Mr Symons?'

'Oh, I suppose I'm what you'd call part of the local gentry, Chief Inspector. I have a large estate to run in Wensleydale – Uredale Manor, I'm sure you've heard of it – and I've been High Sheriff of North Yorkshire and all that kind of stuff.'

'Indeed.' Oldroyd didn't add that he was not an admirer of the remnants of feudalism, either in his own county or in any other part of England. 'So did Mr Fraser fit into this social circle, would you say?'

'Oh yes. He wasn't a significant landowner, but he's come from the right background, same school as Henry, so I'm told. It always helps a lot if—'

Oldroyd didn't want to hear any more of this kind of thing, so he brought the interview to an end in a curt fashion. 'Yes, well, that will be all for now. Thank you very much, Mr Symons.'

~

Steph returned just as Oldroyd and Andy were about to go over what they'd learned so far. She ate her share of the sandwiches during the discussion that followed.

'So, what did you make of Mrs Fraser?' asked Oldroyd, drinking his second cup of coffee but ignoring the biscuits that filled a plate.

Andy was showing restraint. He, too, was trying to lose weight.

'She's devastated, as you'd expect, sir, but I felt it was genuine,' Steph said. 'There's nothing to suggest she had anything against her husband, no womanising or violence or anything like that, unless she was keeping something from me.'

'Did she identify any enemies?'

'Well, she admitted Fraser could be difficult: "abrasive and domineering" were the words she used.' Steph consulted her notes. 'But she didn't know of anyone who'd want to harm him. I asked her about Alan Green and she remembered him as the odd-job man and gardener who'd done jobs for them, but again she couldn't see any reason why he'd want to harm her husband. Just as I was about to go, she told me about an incident with the saboteurs.' Steph outlined the details.

'Good. We've already heard a bit about that from Symons, and you've told us more. We need to research who was involved and who might have had a connection with the dead man and so on. Andy and I have interviewed the three companions who were with Fraser just before he was killed, so we'll bring you up to date. What did you make of them, Andy?'

Andy looked at his notes before replying. 'Well, sir, I was interested in the accounts of hearing the shot, and I like your suggestion that Symons and Saunders could be in it together, and that one is giving the alibi for the other. There was easily time for one of them to go outside, shoot Fraser and nip back in before the alarm was raised. They were both a bit too controlled and smooth with their answers for my liking.'

'That would mean that Kirsty Hemingway was in on it, too, and is falsely identifying Alan Green as the killer.'

'Yes, unless she got confused and mistook one of them for Green. It was dark after all. I know the lights were on but she can't have seen the face for very long. She seems very sure it was Green on the basis of a brief glimpse.'

'That would be very convenient for the murderer, wouldn't it? To have someone else identified as the suspect. But I'm not sure I can believe that.'

'I take it we've still no idea about a motive for Symons or Saunders?' asked Steph.

'No, but something might emerge when we've done some more digging into Fraser's past. What did you think of Rawnsley, Andy?'

Andy frowned. 'Seemed a bit of a wimp to me. Can't see him shooting anyone, and why one of his regular customers? Even if he did delay paying?'

'I agree. Of course, he could have faked the drunkenness and then doubled back and gone outside to lie in wait for Fraser, but that's all fanciful.' Oldroyd sat back in the armchair. 'OK, no point speculating any more at the moment. Next on the list is this game-keeper who appears to have had a difficult time with Fraser. He lives in the village so I'll pop over there with Steph. You stay here, Andy, and make sure everything's in order. Check the statements; I want to know if anyone saw or heard anything unusual last night. Speak to that young woman again and see if she's remembered anything else. Then we'd better go down to Pateley and see how Inspector Gibbs is getting on with the search for Alan Green. I haven't heard anything from him. He should also remember the case when the saboteur died.'

'OK, sir.'

～

Harry Newton was at work in the kitchen. The service was very much reduced and most of the staff who lived out had been told not to come into work that day. The remaining staff were preparing a limited menu for the residents and inn staff. Oldroyd was going to allow the bar to open as it was the only one for miles around, but the rest of the inn was sealed off from the public. Sheila Owen had been present to give the staff instructions, but had then gone off to lie down for a while, having been up for most of the night.

After Kirsty had woken him up and gone out to raise the alarm, Harry had nipped back to his room across the corridor. He'd hated having to do this but he felt it was more important that they remained discreet after his brother's experience.

He was peeling vegetables when he heard a tap at the open back door of the kitchen just behind where he was working. Kirsty put her head round the door. He put down his knife and joined her outside.

'How are you feeling?' Harry asked.

Rob Owen had given her the day off due to the trauma she'd been through. Her face was very pale. 'Not great. I wished you'd stayed last night. I needed a cuddle when I finally got back to bed.'

'I know. I'm sorry; I just thought it was too risky.'

'Maybe. I wonder if anyone's really bothered.' She lit a cigarette and leaned against the wall. He'd never seen her smoke before.

'I didn't know you—'

'I'd given up,' she said. 'I need something to calm me down.'

'It'll all settle down when the police have finished combing through the place and they leave.'

'Do you think so? I don't know if I'll ever feel good about being here again, apart from you of course.' She smiled for the first time and he found it reassuring.

'You will, it's a good place to work; but if not, we'll leave and go somewhere else.'

She didn't reply to this, seeming distracted. 'I keep remembering Fraser being shot. It was like watching a scene from a crime film, except it was real.' She took another drag on the cigarette. 'The worst thing was recognising Alan Green. I couldn't believe it.'

'No, I'll bet.'

She was gazing up into the sky as she recalled the scene. 'There was one thing I didn't tell the police.'

Harry looked at her. 'Why not?'

'It sounds stupid and I'm not sure about it. It was probably nothing, but when the gun went off I screamed and he looked up towards me. That was when I got a good look at his face. But . . .' She shook her head, took a final drag on the cigarette and threw the butt on to the ground. 'I swear he didn't seem bothered about me seeing him, and I'm sure he almost smiled at me before he turned and ran off.'

'So?'

'Don't you think that's weird? Why would he not care about being seen? It makes me think he's not bothered because he knows where I am. Harry, I'm scared. I nearly didn't tell the police who I saw, because I'm afraid he'll come back to get me.'

She started to cry and put her arms out towards him. He embraced her. 'Look, you're letting your imagination run away with you. I can't really see Alan Green as some kind of ruthless killer. If you're right and it was him . . .'

'It was, Harry.'

'OK, well it must have been some argument that got out of hand. I'm sure the police will find him soon and that'll be the end of it. Anyway, he knows you'll have told the police you saw him, so he can't silence you, can he?'

'Harry! That's an awful thought. I suppose you're right, but he might want to get revenge on me.'

'I doubt that. Now give me a kiss and then I'll have to get back to work. I'll see you later. Go back to your bedroom and lie down.'

They kissed and she walked off silently towards a nearby back entrance, which led to the residential section of the inn. She was looking cautiously around her and he had the impression that she was far from reassured.

~

The detectives' call at the Pateley Bridge station proved fruitless in terms of information about the whereabouts of the increasingly mysterious Green. The four detectives were sitting in Gibbs's somewhat spartan office. It reminded Oldroyd of DCS Walker's office at Harrogate HQ: that of a man who disliked bureaucracy and paperwork and who preferred to be out doing police work in the field.

'There's no sign of him so far here in Pateley,' said Gibbs. 'Which is where people in Niddersgill seem to think he lived. I'm casting the net wider now, into the surrounding area and all the little hamlets. We need to move quickly; having a murderer on the loose is going to cause a lot of fear around here.'

'So we've no documents, no bank account or anything, sir?' asked Steph.

'No.'

'Is there any indication that anyone had phone contact with him, sir?' asked Andy.

'No again. It's extraordinary that in the modern world someone could keep such a low profile, isn't it?'

'The problem,' observed Oldroyd, shaking his head, 'is that even if you find his hideout, wherever it is, he's unlikely to be there, though it might yield some useful documents and information. He's probably far away by now, following a planned escape route, though that's no consolation to the frightened populace. Keep at it, but we can't ignore other possibilities until we find him. Even then we may find that other people are involved. There's something very odd about the whole thing. There's usually an obvious motive in a case like this: robbery, revenge, jealousy. This man shot another local for no apparent reason and it was out of character. He had no history of violence or aggression. Then he disappears.'

Gibbs agreed. On a more positive note, he had further information to offer on the death of the saboteur in which Fraser had been involved.

'I remember that case, Jim, though I hadn't made the connection until you mentioned it. It was a few years back and it was ruled as accidental death, if I remember rightly, but the saboteurs made a huge stink about it; they said this bloke would never have died if Fraser hadn't chased him and threatened violence. I'll get all the details for you.'

'Thanks, Bill,' Oldroyd said. 'Of all the motives I mentioned earlier, I've thought from the beginning that revenge might well be the one in this case, and this incident may be the thing we're looking for.'

∽

Oldroyd and his partner Deborah still retained their separate apartments, his overlooking the Harrogate Stray and hers in nearby Knaresborough. When Oldroyd arrived back at his, there were two recorded messages on his landline. One was from his daughter Louise.

'Hi Dad, how're you doing? I'm sure you'll be busy as usual, but is it OK if I come up for a few days before term starts? I've got to collect some stuff from yours, books and clothes and things. Also, I've managed to get in for the degree ceremony on Thursday. There was a cancellation. Auntie Alison's coming. Can you give her a lift? Robert and Andrea can't make it but Mum will be there. I'll come back up with you after, if it's OK? So call me back soon. Bye.'

Louise was going back to Oxford in October to do an MSt in Modern History. She retained bases at both Oldroyd's flat and with her mother, Oldroyd's estranged wife Julia, in Leeds. Oldroyd smiled. He enjoyed the company of his feisty daughter, who had been the one to persuade him that he had to move on after several years of forlornly hoping that Julia would ask him to come back to her. He was glad, too, because it meant he had met Deborah.

Oldroyd, and no doubt also her mother, had been urging Louise for some time to organise her degree ceremony. She'd spent a year off after having graduated, working in London at a women's refuge and then taking a couple of months to backpack in the Far East, so it had not been a priority. Nor was she enthusiastic about the more arcane aspects and rituals of academic life. This last-minute arrangement was typical of her. He would have to make time to go down to Oxford, but it would be difficult now that he was involved in this case. And it was never easy meeting Julia. He shook his head.

The other message was from his sister Alison, an Anglican vicar in the village of Kirkby Underside between Harrogate and Leeds. Alison was inviting him and Deborah to dinner on Friday at the vicarage, a large, rambling building which Oldroyd loved for its quirkiness and many reminders of a different, peaceful and comfortable age. At least for the pampered clergy who'd lived there. He called it the Jane Austen Vicarage.

He rang back for a brief chat with Alison, and to accept her invitation. Although it would have to be postponed, as Alison would also be coming to the hastily arranged degree ceremony.

Finally, he sat down with a cup of tea. Not long ago, before Deborah had taken his diet and his general health in hand, it would have been a glass or two of red wine after work.

Deborah was going to an early film showing with some friends this evening and she would be coming over later. Oldroyd settled down on the sofa after putting on a CD of Schubert's *Impromptus*. He liked to relax when he got home in the evening and collect his thoughts about the case he was working on. There was often insufficient time and opportunity during the frequently hectic activities of the day to reflect on what was happening. These piano pieces always calmed him down and prompted him to think deeply.

The murder of Sandy Fraser seemed to be reasonably straightforward. Although Oldroyd had speculated about the young barmaid being involved in a plot and deliberately misidentifying the killer, he didn't really think it was likely. The disappearance of Alan Green seemed to imply his guilt. It was not the action of an innocent man. Nevertheless, Oldroyd's instincts were telling him that something was not right.

Was it the lack of motive so far identified? Why would an odd-job man and gardener kill a man like Fraser? If he had, there must be some history between them. Murders did take place in villages and not just in Agatha Christie novels, but had Fraser lived there for long enough to make real enemies? Had something from his past pursued him to Niddersgill and exacted a bloody reckoning?

Oldroyd closed his eyes to listen to a particularly exquisite passage of the Schubert.

～

When Deborah arrived at the apartment, it was dark. She found Oldroyd asleep on the sofa. The CD player was switched on but the CD had long since played to the end.

She nudged him. 'Wakey, wakey! I can see you're ready to paint the town red on this Saturday night. Maybe I should have chosen a younger man.'

Oldroyd stirred and yawned. 'It's your fault for exhausting me with all this running. Plus, I've actually been working all day.'

'Poor you. And I suppose you'll be going in tomorrow as well?'

'Yes, sorry. It's always like this when a serious case blows up.'

'Not to worry, I can arrange to meet Dawn in Leeds.'

'Good. Look, I can't be bothered to cook. Let's go for a drink and then a pizza.'

'Good idea.'

'How was the film?' said Oldroyd, getting up from the sofa.

'Excellent, you would have liked it – set in small-town America. You thought you knew the characters, but when the film moved on to the backstories you realised the early bit was only scratching the surface of their lives.'

Oldroyd was putting on his jacket as Deborah opened the front door.

'Interesting – that's exactly how I'm feeling about this murder in Nidderdale.'

'Honestly! You relate everything back to work.'

'I know, it's bad, but I'll forget about it when I've got some wine and some food inside me.'

'Right. I don't want work mentioned one more time this evening!'

Oldroyd was happy to agree but he couldn't guarantee that. Unbeknown to Deborah, his thoughts might stray back occasionally.

Two

Tatham Wife Moss
Quaking Pot
Black Edge Shake Hole
Jingling Pot

On Monday morning, David Eastwood arrived in his red van to deliver the post. It was another bright day with clouds drifting overhead, and all seemed peaceful and tranquil in the beautiful village. The only physical indication that something violent had happened was the blue-and-white incident tape draped around an area near the entrance to the Dog and Gun. But the place seemed unnaturally quiet and there were fewer people about as he worked his way around the houses and cottages surrounding the green.

People seemed to regard him as a reassuring presence, as a number of them came to the door to collect their post from him directly. Some of them confessed they'd not been out of their houses since the murder of Sandy Fraser, and Eastwood was the first person they'd spoken to. He saw in the worried faces of the older villagers, who'd mostly retired to Niddersgill from the towns and cities, a certain perplexity, a sense that things were just not right: they'd come here for peace and tranquillity, not for murder and mayhem.

He'd nearly finished his deliveries, and was about to call in at Gorton's shop for a can of Coke and a brief chat, when he saw an old Saab enter the village, drive up to the inn and park near to his van. A man got out and walked quickly over to him. He held up a warrant card.

'Are you the postman David Eastwood?' asked the man.

'Yes.'

'Chief Inspector Oldroyd. I'm leading the investigation into the murder of Sandy Fraser. Is that your van?' He indicated the red post van.

'Yes.'

'Do you also possess a black van in which you visit this village when you're not working?'

'Yes.'

'Can you come over to the inn please? We need to ask you some questions.' The tone was friendly but firm, and Eastwood felt he couldn't refuse.

~

In the hotel, the postman was shown into the residents' lounge, where he and Oldroyd were joined by Andy and Steph. He still had his postbag, which he laid on the floor.

'I assume you've heard about what happened here on Friday night?'

'Yes. I heard about it on television. He was shot outside here, wasn't he?' replied a nervous-looking Eastwood.

'He was. Now, we have a witness who claims to have seen your van parked just across from here behind some houses. Were you in this village on Friday evening?'

Eastwood was clearly shocked, and hesitated. He seemed about to deny it but then uttered a quiet 'Yes'.

'And why were you here?'

Eastwood sighed and hesitated again. 'You see, it's private, and . . . and secret, if you know what I mean.'

'Were you visiting a female friend?' asked Oldroyd bluntly.

Eastwood squirmed a little with embarrassment. He looked away from Oldroyd only to encounter a cold stare from Steph.

'Yes, I was, but please can you not make it public? My wife . . . doesn't know. She thinks I'd come to Niddersgill to meet some friends at the Dog.'

'I see. Well, you've done the right thing by telling us. Too many people in these situations take fright, lie to the police and get themselves into all kinds of difficulties when the lies are revealed. We'll need the name and address of the person concerned and we'll have to interview her to check your story, but other than that – how shall I put it? – your secret is safe with us.'

Eastwood looked relieved. 'Her name is Theresa Rawlings. It's number one in that row of cottages: Gouthwaite Terrace. At the end of the row. I was parked at the back. It's true that you could have spotted the end of the van from the inn. I would have parked further down the lane, but there was no space.'

'Did you hear or see anything unusual that evening?'

'I . . . er, *we* heard a bang which sounded like a shotgun, but round here you think nothing of hearing that, even at night and especially at this time of the year. There are shotguns going off all the time. Just after that I left and drove back to Pateley. I noticed some people outside the Dog, but I thought nothing of it.'

'OK,' said Oldroyd. 'That seems to tie in with what our witness said, so we'll leave it there for now.'

A sheepish Eastwood picked up his bag and left to continue his round.

Andy was grinning. 'Caught having his bit on the side, sir! The look on his face! He was starting to go as red as a beetroot when you forced him to confess.'

'Serves him right, the little rat,' said Steph, not looking in the least bit amused. 'I can't stand men like that. He has the poor little woman at home, no doubt looking after his kids and cooking his dinner, and he comes out here cheating on her. He probably does it all over the place. Very convenient, isn't it? To have two vans, and drive around the dale amusing himself.' She would have liked to have expressed this in more colourful language, but felt her boss might not approve.

'No, not a pleasant individual,' agreed Oldroyd, who got up from his chair. 'Anyway, send a DC round to interview that woman and see what she has to say. We'll have to get moving now; we've a lot of people to interview today. Steph, I want you to go round to talk to Liz Smith, while Andy and I go in search of this chap Dexter, who lives up on the fells in a barn.'

~

Oldroyd and Andy headed up a steep and winding bridleway out of Niddersgill on to the fells above the village. They walked between drystone walls with sheep and cows grazing in the fields at either side, as they headed towards the higher moorland. Rob Owen had explained how to get to Tony Dexter's small converted barn. The bridleway was just about passable for a four-by-four, but not for Oldroyd's car, so they had to walk.

As they ascended the path, the heavy stone embankment of the dam of Gouthwaite Reservoir with its Victorian castellated stone-work came into view, and then the beautiful long stretch of water behind. Oldroyd thought it was the most picturesque reservoir he knew.

'What do we know about this bloke then, sir?' asked Andy. He was enjoying the walk. He'd come to love these sweeping Yorkshire landscapes and the wonderful bracing air that filled your lungs as you got up on to the tops.

'Not much. Apparently he styles himself as a poet and environmentalist and had a few run-ins with Fraser about grouse shooting. I wouldn't say he was a prime suspect, but he's worth talking to.'

Rounding a corner on the rocky, uneven track, they saw a low barn which at first looked empty, but as they got closer, they could make out a rudimentary vegetable patch in front of the door, together with compost heaps and birdfeeders. The blades of a small wind turbine were spinning round and a bicycle was leaning against a wall.

'This looks like the place all right,' said Oldroyd. He walked past the leeks and onions and knocked on the door. After a pause, it was opened by a tall, thin, wiry man with wild hair and a bushy beard; he was dressed in dirty jeans and jumper.

'Hello,' he said cheerfully. 'What can I do for you?'

'We're police officers,' replied Oldroyd as he introduced them and they showed their warrant cards. 'We'd like to ask you some questions.'

The smile immediately left Dexter's face. 'Oh, what on earth for?'

'Have you heard that Sandy Fraser has been murdered?'

'What? No. It takes a while for news to get to me. I haven't been down to the village since Thursday. When was this?'

'Friday night. Can we come in please?'

'Yes, of course.' Dexter led them into a large kitchen and dining area which must have covered the whole of the ground floor. There was a mezzanine floor above with a door that likely led to a bedroom. A large window gave a panoramic view over the dale. In one corner there was a desk with a computer and a large bookcase behind it against the wall. Oldroyd saw that the shelves were full of books on nature and the environment: landscape, ornithology, global warming, ecosystems and so on. There was also a substantial poetry section, mostly poets who wrote about nature in different ways: Wordsworth, Hardy, Edward Thomas, Ted Hughes. There were a number of old sofas and chairs around the room, all covered in colourful drapes. On the floor were faded, dusty rugs.

'Please, take a seat.' Dexter looked down at his dirty clothes. 'I'm sorry I'm in such a grubby state, I've been gardening all morning. I still have a lot to do here. I've been here three years and my next project is to create a big vegetable patch at the side of the house to add to what you saw at the front. It'll keep me in food for much of the year. Can I get you a drink? Tea? I don't drink coffee I'm afraid.'

'Yes, tea will be fine,' said Oldroyd, glancing at Andy for confirmation. They were thirsty after their walk. Dexter went over to the hob and put the kettle on. Oldroyd and Andy continued looking around the room. The walls contained some prints but also posters from environmental campaigns. Dexter brought the tea over in large mugs emblazoned with campaign slogans: 'Frack Off: Say No to Fracking', 'No to Nuclear Power', 'Save Our Bees'.

Dexter sat down on an armchair and put his hands on the arms. 'I take it if Sandy Fraser's been murdered, you must be looking for suspects, and you've heard that he and I didn't get on.'

'That's not far from the mark,' replied Oldroyd. 'So tell us more.'

'Well, let me say first that I didn't kill him.'

'Do you have an alibi? Where were you on Friday evening?'

Dexter shrugged his shoulders. 'No, I don't have an alibi. I'm a bit of a loner. I don't go down to the village much and I live here by myself. I was here on Friday night, but I can't prove it.'

'Do you possess a shotgun?'

'No.'

'OK. Well, tell us what you thought about Fraser.'

'I didn't like the man, but it was what he did and represented that I objected to the most. Grouse shooting is very damaging to the environment, Chief Inspector. Wildlife such as mammal predators and birds of prey are killed because they threaten the grouse, and the burning of the heather releases carbon dioxide into the atmosphere. These people – they're all wealthy – they think the countryside is there for their amusement. They create an artificial environment which benefits the grouse but at great cost. They also dig drainage channels which leads to a very fast run-off of water. That's why the towns in the valleys below many of these moors have been flooded.' Dexter was starting to get angry. 'Anyway, that's just the beginning. I could talk to you all day about how destructive it is.'

'But of course Sandy Fraser disagreed with you?'

Dexter laughed. 'He certainly did, but it was his manner that I found so offensive. I'm no coward: I went round to his house and confronted him on his doorstep. I told him what I thought without being aggressive. He invited me in but he wouldn't engage with the issues. He thought it was an outrage that anyone should even question what he did with his own land, that kind of attitude – said it was none of my business.'

'Have you ever done anything to disrupt the grouse shooting?'

'No, Liz is your person for that. Liz Smith. She's an animal-rights campaigner and very much into direct action. I respect her and her group, but I don't really see the point. The shooters get so annoyed that they become more determined to carry on. You have to defeat these people with argument and persuade politicians to change the law.' He took a drink of his tea and looked at Oldroyd. 'I suppose that's why I'd say to you that it wouldn't make sense to me to get rid of Fraser. Someone else would just come and take his place.'

'Unless he got to you on a personal level.'

Dexter laughed. 'Yes, but I can assure you he didn't. No one does.'

Oldroyd looked around at the landscape prints. 'These hills and dales mean a lot to you, don't they?'

'Absolutely, Chief Inspector. It may not be a completely natural landscape; it's been affected by human activity for thousands of years and there's lots we could do to improve it, but there's a wild beauty which really gets into your soul if you spend a lot of time here.'

Oldroyd nodded and smiled. He couldn't have agreed more. 'Who did those paintings?'

'A local chap, John Gray. He has a studio attached to his house in the village. He's more of a recluse than me. You don't see much of him. I wandered into his place one day and he would hardly talk to me – said he had a cold and his voice was bad. He just carried on painting, facing the canvas away from me. Very rude and anti-social. That's what some artists and writers get like. They spend so much time by themselves, they forget how to relate to people. I understand it when you're in this landscape. You feel you could merge with it and become one with the trees, heather and streams. Anyway, I liked his work so much that I bought those prints and had them framed in Pateley Bridge. By the way, Gray must have known Fraser too. When I went to his house that time I saw some of Gray's paintings on the wall, and they looked like originals.'

'So how come you ended up here, sir?' asked Andy, thinking that Dexter was a bit of an oddball, and not as interesting as Oldroyd seemed to find him.

Dexter took a deep breath and appeared to think about the answer for a moment. 'Like many people, I've had problems in my life: divorce, job issues, you know. I just decided to pack in the rat race and come up here. I got this place fairly cheap; it was in a bad state and I've slowly done it up. I make enough money with my writing to survive and I've never regretted it for a moment. My life has purpose now: I'm involved in crucial campaigns to save the world from destruction.'

'What sort of writing do you do?' asked Oldroyd.

'I do articles for various online sites and print journals. And I write poetry. Mostly about the landscape and its natural life.'

'I thought so, judging by your poetry collection,' replied Oldroyd, nodding towards the bookshelves.

'Oh, you're obviously a literary man yourself, Chief Inspector.' Dexter's eyes brightened with enthusiasm. 'I'm especially inspired by the natural structures in the landscape around here – you know, Brimham Rocks, and Jenny Twigg and her daughter Tib.'

'Who are they?' asked Andy, bewildered. Being from Croydon he still struggled, not only with the Yorkshire dialect but with a number of the rural traditions and beliefs that locals took for granted.

Dexter laughed. 'They're two outcrops of millstone grit up on the moors not far from here.'

'Like the ones we saw that time at Brimham Rocks,' said Oldroyd, referring to a previous case where he and Carter had nearly been murdered at that strange Yorkshire beauty spot.

'Right, sir. Don't remind me.' Andy shivered at the memory.

'The difference is that those two stones are standing together in a sea of bare moorland,' said Dexter. 'You can see them for miles, except if you go up there in mist or fog, and then it can be quite a shock when they suddenly loom up at you. Actually, if you get to them you're probably completely lost as they're off the main track.' Dexter seemed to enjoy the eeriness of it all, but Andy didn't welcome a reminder of his Brimham Rocks experience. It had been freaky and misty that day too, but this had probably saved them as it had concealed their position from their attackers and enabled them to escape.

Oldroyd brought things back to the questioning. 'Did you know Alan Green? He's an odd-job man.'

'I've heard the name. Does he do gardening as well? I think I've seen him around the village.'

'Yes. Did he ever do any jobs for you?'

'No, Chief Inspector. I do everything myself. It's important to become more and more self-sufficient in preparation for the world to come. If the human race is to survive, we'll have to grow more of our own food and live sustainably.'

'Quite,' said Oldroyd, while Andy looked sceptical. 'Were you aware of anyone else who might have wished to harm Mr Fraser?'

'No, Chief Inspector, I can't help you there. I've not lived here that long, though I don't think Fraser was here much before me.'

Oldroyd would have liked to stay longer and talk to Dexter about the Yorkshire landscape, but time was limited and there were other people to interview. Dexter came outside with them and pointed to the moors. 'Jenny Twigg and her daughter Tib are just up there on the moor. There's a story that the names are based on two women who ran an inn and murdered someone, so it ties in well with your investigation. A bit uncanny, though, isn't it?' he said, laughing.

'Quite,' repeated Oldroyd.

~

Steph walked down the narrow road out of Niddersgill, between the drystone walls. She was looking for the field where Liz Smith had her caravan. She needn't have worried about missing it: posters with screaming slogans about cruelty to animals adorned the side of the small, shabby caravan which was parked near to the wall overlooking the road. Entering the field through a nearby gate, Steph wondered what the villagers thought.

As she approached the caravan she heard music, presumably coming from a radio, and saw that there was a window open. She was in luck. She went up the metal steps and knocked on the door. It was opened by a woman in her thirties with longish dark hair tied back. She was wearing jeans and a chunky, brightly patterned cardigan which looked home-knitted.

'Yes, who are you?' she asked suspiciously.

'Detective Sergeant Johnson,' replied Steph, showing her identification.

Liz Smith frowned. 'Police? What do you want?'

'We're investigating the murder of Sandy Fraser. I presume you've heard about it?'

'Yes, good riddance as far as I'm concerned, but I don't know anything about it, sorry.' She was starting to close the caravan door.

'I'm afraid I need to ask you some questions,' insisted Steph. 'Can I come in please?'

Liz sighed and pushed the door open again. Steph followed her.

Inside, there was a basic kitchen at one end and a table and seating at the other, which presumably converted into a bed. It was a cramped space, made more so by the mountains of magazines and posters, piles of clothes, rows of boots and shoes, and the cardboard boxes containing vegetables and knitting wool. On the table was an old laptop with a cracked screen.

Liz pushed things aside to create a space for Steph to sit down at the table, while she sat by her laptop on the other side. 'As I said, you're wasting your time, but go ahead.'

'I understand that you and Mr Fraser did not get on.'

Liz made a sound that indicated contempt. 'That's an under-statement. He was an arrogant bastard who thought he had the right to butcher wildlife. Not only that, he organised parties of people, mostly men let's be honest, to come and do it.'

'So you and some other people tried to sabotage them?'

66

'We did. We're part of an animal-rights group, all above board, nothing secretive. We don't do violence, not like the shooters. I mean, people are animals too, aren't they? So it would be a bit hypocritical to harm them.'

'You were there on Friday, weren't you?'

Liz looked at Steph with defiance. 'Yes, we were. If they have a right to shoot, then we have a right to try to defend the birds.'

'Isn't that dangerous, given that shotguns are going off all the time?'

Liz shrugged. 'I suppose it could be, but we're committed to helping the innocent birds.'

'And doesn't it cause conflict? Did you have a confrontation with Mr Fraser on Friday?'

'No, the beaters chased us off. They're the ones who are violent. They'll beat you up if they get the chance. But I think we saved a few birds, sent them up out of the heather before the shooters were ready to aim at them. That's all we can do. These people are powerful and dangerous.'

'Have you ever been treated violently yourself?'

Liz paused. 'Yes. But not since I came here. It was down in the Calderdale area. We were set upon by a group of beaters with their sticks. The police, of course, weren't interested; we were trespassing, causing a nuisance, blah-blah. They always side with the Establishment.' She looked challengingly at Steph.

'Well, I hope not,' Steph said. 'The police are here to protect everyone's rights.'

Liz grunted cynically. 'If only that were true.'

Steph pressed on, ignoring this comment. She didn't have time to enter into a discussion about the role of the police. 'There was a much more serious incident concerning Mr Fraser a few years ago, wasn't there?'

'Was there?' Liz's tone remained sullen and insolent.

'I think you know what I mean.'

'Yes, the murder of Sam Cooper,' Liz blurted out angrily.

'So I take it that you blame Mr Fraser for this man's death, despite the fact that it was ruled as accidental?'

'Me and many others. I was there. Fraser chased him with a stick shouting at the top of his voice. Sam must have been terrified. He dropped down unconscious and died. It was horrible. The authorities just covered it up like they always do.'

'Did you and others in your group want to get revenge on Mr Fraser?'

Liz laughed derisively. 'Of course, but not by killing him. We make sure that we're there to disrupt every shoot he's involved in.'

'Where were you on Friday evening, just after midnight?'

'Here asleep at that time. I'm an early riser.'

'Can anyone confirm that?'

'I'm afraid not. There isn't anyone I'm shagging at the moment, male or female, and I don't get many visitors staying in this little shack.'

Steph ignored the provocation. 'Do you possess a shotgun?'

Liz burst out laughing. 'What would I do with one of those? They're instruments of death for wildlife in the countryside: rabbits, crows, pigeons, as well as game birds.'

'OK.' Steph looked at her thoughtfully. 'You don't appear to like living in the countryside very much, so why do you live out here?'

'Isn't that obvious? It's to be near my work, as it were. We have a duty to try to protect animals from what goes on out here. We want to make sure farmers are looking after their animals properly and we do our best to prevent any random killing for sport.'

'Who's "we"?'

'Me and the others in the group. I'm not going to tell you who they are. We've had enough harassment from the police in the past. We don't do anything that's against the law.'

Steph also ignored this for the moment, though the time might come when they would need to know who else, beyond the people of Nidderdale, might have had a motive for killing Fraser.

'I take it these people don't live in the village?'

'No, they travel in when we've got a protest on.'

'So why don't you? Wouldn't you be happier in the town, away from all this abuse of animals as you see it?'

Liz smiled. 'No, I'm an awkward bugger. I like to be here and a thorn in their flesh. They know I'm here watching them.'

'You must get abuse from people.'

'Yeah, from some. I'm actually more sympathetic to farmers than you might think, as long as they look after their animals properly. It's their jobs and livelihood. I think it's wrong to kill animals for food, but I don't blame the farmers. Actually, you'd be surprised at how many local people tell me they support our cause, especially against the grouse shooters. Killing animals for pleasure is obscene. I don't care how many of those poor birds they eat or sell to restaurants, their main motivation is the shoot. I'm not popular with those people, I can tell you. It's a wonder I wasn't the one you found shot dead.' She laughed again.

'Do you know a man called Alan Green?'

'Never heard of him. If he's local, I don't mix much, so there's a lot of people I don't know.'

'Did you know anyone else who might want to cause harm to Mr Fraser?'

'Any animal-rights campaigner who knew about him,' Liz answered flippantly, and then became more serious. 'But no, I never heard about anyone else who threatened him or anything, though I don't think he was popular with the people who worked for him.'

69

'OK. Thank you,' said Steph, getting up to go. 'That wasn't too hard, was it?'

Liz gave her a half smile. 'No. I wonder what will happen now with the shoots. Who will take over that moor? I can't imagine his wife or family wanting to run a grouse shoot.'

'It could be sold.'

'Probably. Anyway, we'll be ready for whoever comes next. The fight will go on.'

~

In the bar at the Dog and Gun, some of the local regulars were having a lunchtime drink. Kirsty was not behind the bar. The atmosphere was subdued and the murder was the main topic of conversation. It was rare for something so dramatic to happen in a small rural village.

Peter Gorton was taking a break from the shop and having a drink with Ian Davis and a man called Vic Moore, a freelance copy-editor who lodged with the artist John Gray. Vic was chunkily built with black hair, and he always wore dark glasses due to an eye complaint. He came from the Midlands originally and still had a Birmingham accent.

'The village is like a flipping graveyard,' he said. 'There's nobody about. I have to admit, I looked around me when I walked over here to check there was nobody around with a gun. It's no fun having a murderer on the loose, is it?'

'A few people have phoned me saying they're not leaving their house and could I deliver things to them,' said Gorton. 'What the hell do you think's going on? I hear Kirsty's saying she saw Alan Green shoot him. Can you believe that? Alan? What the bloody hell for? He was in here only a few hours before. He said Fraser was a bit of a bugger, but he wouldn't kill the poor sod because of that, would he?'

Davis took up his pint glass and drained half of it in one draught. 'Naw. Kirsty must have made a mistake. Mind you, it's funny 'ow he's buggered off, isn't it? I hear t'police can't find him. They were looking all over Pateley yesterday afternoon according to my mate Barry.'

'He always seemed a decent chap to me, though I haven't known him all that long,' said Moore, who was sipping from a whisky and soda. 'But you never know with people, do you?'

That set people around the pub shaking their heads and muttering at the puzzle of it all.

'Have the police been to talk to you yet?' said Gorton to Davis.

'No, but I'm expecting 'em. I know it'll get out that him and me didn't get on that well, but let 'em come, I've got nothing to fear. I hope that woman sergeant comes – she can interview me any time.' He sniggered.

'That's enough of that, Ian, or I'll dob you in to Jenny,' said Jeanette, who was covering for Kirsty behind the bar.

'Get away with yer, and pull me another pint,' said Davis, who had now drained his glass.

'From what I hear, they've spent their time interviewing his shooting cronies, and that inspector and his sergeant were seen walking up towards Dexter's place,' said Gorton.

'And the woman went to see Liz Smith,' said Moore.

'Yeah, I wonder what she made of her: madwoman in a caravan,' laughed Davis. 'Actually, do you think she might have done it? She hated Fraser, didn't she? Especially after that do a few years ago. Mind you, didn't we all?'

'I assume they're still after Alan. Do you know where he lived in Pateley, Vic?'

'Me? No. I thought he lived somewhere round here.'

'No. He's not a villager. He came a few years ago, just before you. He started doing jobs for people; he always said he lived down in Pateley, but nobody seems to know where,' said Gorton, taking a drink of his beer.

'He did some gardening for John a while back, he just took cash in hand. I suppose he's one of those private sorts – doesn't like people knowing too much about him,' observed Gorton.

'Maybe he had a mysterious past,' said Davis.

'Alan?' asked Moore.

'Yeah – well, they say still waters run deep.' Davis glanced out of the window and saw Oldroyd and Andy coming into the inn. 'Ey up, t'coppers are back. Careful what you say.'

'They've got you lined up if they can't find Alan,' said Gorton with a teasing smile. 'They already suspect you, the disgruntled employee who's handy with a shotgun.'

'Bugger off!' laughed Davis, and drained half of his second pint.

~

Steph had got back earlier and was already in the lounge when Andy and Oldroyd came in. The inn staff were going to supply some lunch again and Oldroyd, a bit peckish after his walk, was looking forward to it. But first there was work to be done in reviewing what they'd found out. Steph reported first.

'Well, she's a character all right, sir, very outspoken and not at all defensive. She admitted straight away that she hated Fraser due to the animal-rights stuff and, as we expected, there's a lot of anger about that incident where the sab bloke died. She and the sabs blame Fraser; she called it a murder. She has no support for her alibi that she was in bed in her caravan at the time of the murder. She only had a few hundred yards to walk to here so she could easily have done it. I was wondering if she or someone else could have disguised themselves, so Kirsty Hemingway thought she saw Alan Green, but it doesn't really make sense because how would the murderer know that Kirsty would be looking out of the window at that moment, or that anyone else would see them at that time of night, in the dark? Also, why would Alan Green disappear like this if he's innocent?'

'You're right,' said Oldroyd. 'I suppose the murderer could have wanted to disguise themselves just in case anyone did see them, but in that case why not just put a mask on your face? No, I think we have to conclude that Kirsty saw, or thought she saw, Alan Green. Unless she's lying, but we've no evidence yet of anything like that. So, what did you think of Dexter, Andy?'

'I thought he was a bit of an oddball too, sir, and he's another one who had no time for Fraser. It's quite feasible that he walked down to the village that night and did him in. Like Liz Smith he can't prove his alibi, and, by the way, it strikes me they've got a lot in common: they were both enemies of Fraser and both live alone without much contact with the villagers. I wonder if there could have been any collusion between them. They both wanted the grouse shooting stopped, for different reasons.'

Oldroyd frowned. 'Maybe, but it's not a very convincing plan as neither had a good alibi and, in the end, what would they gain? Just because Fraser's gone it doesn't mean the grouse shooting won't continue. Someone will buy that moor with the shooting rights, and on it will go.'

Andy shrugged. 'I think you're right, sir. We could just be wasting our time developing unlikely theories when it'll probably all be resolved as soon as Alan Green is found. I'm sure a motive will emerge. Maybe they knew each other somewhere else before they came to the village.'

Oldroyd looked at Andy and smiled. He was very pleased with the progress that his two young detective sergeants had made over recent years in their analysis of evidence. He remembered that when Andy had first arrived, he'd been eager to slap the handcuffs on the first likely suspect who emerged in a case. Now he was much more thoughtful, and recognised that things were often far more complex than they appeared.

'That's a good point, Andy. We don't seem to have uncovered a very convincing motive so far in any of the people we've interviewed, so we're going to have to dig deeper; and the answer, as you imply, might well lie in the past. We need someone back at HQ to investigate Fraser's financial situation. That might reveal something interesting. We'll also look at Bill's report on that incident on the moor.'

'I agree that Alan Green still seems the likeliest suspect,' said Steph with a sigh, 'but somehow things don't seem right.'

This gave Oldroyd further satisfaction, because he'd also taught them to pay attention to their instincts and feelings about a case, as well as to their reasoning. Doing this prompted you to continue to examine the evidence and to look for things you might have missed.

'I agree, so we can't just sit back and wait for Alan Green to be found, the work has to go on. Next on the list is this gamekeeper, Ian Davis. There was clearly a lot of tension between him and his employer. We'll also have to talk to this farmer, Wilf Bramley, who was Fraser's tenant, and the shopkeeper, as they were both in the bar. But we're not doing anything before this . . .' His eyes lit up as the sandwiches and coffee were brought in.

～

Jenny Davis stood in the cramped kitchen of the small cottage down a back lane in Niddersgill which she and her husband Ian rented. Their two young children were playing in the living room. She had to go in periodically to deal with squabbles, but right now she had a rare moment of peace.

She washed and dried her hands, pushed a lock of hair behind her ear and poured herself a glass of wine. If Ian could go to the pub, she could have a drink at home. On days when he wasn't out on the moors he came home for his lunch. Unfortunately, he usually called in at the pub first.

She heard the door and he came in. He swayed and bumped into the door frame.

'What's wrong with you? Are you pissed again?'

'No, course not. They haven't made a drink strong enough to get me drunk, love.' He grinned at her inanely and then stumbled into the table, knocking her wine glass over.

'You clumsy drunk! Just watch it!' she shouted.

'Hey, don't shout, love, you'll upset the kids; they'll think we're having an argument.'

'Well, we are, you slob, you're drinking our money away.'

'I'm not, love, it's just a few pints with the lads in the bar, you know, come here.' He caught hold of her and his mouth slobbered over hers.

'Get off me. I don't want your beery breath in my face!'

He sat down, still grinning at her. 'I'll bet you've made a cracking dinner. I want you to know how much I appreciate it.'

She looked at him and shook her head. She couldn't be angry with him for long. She hit him over the head with a tea towel. 'Well, it's a good job. I didn't marry you to be a 1950s housewife, slaving away over a hot stove while you drink in the pub.'

'I know, love, I know. You need to get a job as soon as you can when those two are a bit bigger, but in the meantime don't worry about money.'

She poured herself another glass of wine. She'd been brought up in Harrogate and trained as a nurse. She'd hadn't minded coming out here when she married Ian – she liked the countryside – but the job opportunities were limited.

'Why not? We're always a bit short on the stingy wages he paid you.'

'That's the point though: the bugger's gone, good riddance.' He smiled. 'I'll get a better deal from the next gaffer.'

Jenny looked at him, a little shocked. 'You shouldn't talk like that about someone who's been killed, Ian.'

'Why not? Stingy, moaning bastard.'

'Shush! The kids will hear you.'

'Well, he made my life a misery – never satisfied with anything. He deserved it.'

'Ian! That's horrible! And anyway, what makes you think you'll get more pay from whoever takes over?'

'It can't be much worse, can it? We're better off with him out of the way. Look, is dinner ready? I'll set the table and get the kids to wash their hands.'

'OK. Five minutes.' She took a drink of her wine. His attitude to the murder of Sandy Fraser had unsettled her. Maybe it was because he was a bit drunk, but that callous reaction was not like him. For a dark moment she found herself thinking back to Friday night. Ian had got back from the bar at the Dog and Gun by about ten thirty and they had gone to bed. Surely he hadn't got up and gone out to . . . ? No, she would have heard him. She was a light sleeper. She always heard him if he got up in the night. Jenny took another sip of wine. No, she was being silly; Ian would never do anything like that. Nevertheless, she found herself thinking that she would be very happy when the police found Alan Green, or whoever it was that had killed Sandy Fraser.

Shortly after Steph left her caravan, Liz Smith made a call on her battered old mobile.

'The police have been round . . . Yeah I knew this would happen, bloody police . . . I didn't tell them any more than I had to . . . Oh, they always side with the Establishment . . . I told that policewoman that . . . Yeah, I did . . . Anyway, bugger alibis, they can't pin anything on us, but I'll bet they'd like to . . . No, I agree . . . Yep . . . Bye.'

Liz smiled as the call ended. She was engaged in a war, a war that had been raging ever since she'd become involved with the fight to protect animals when she was a teenager. She'd learned early on that the people whom she was struggling against – hunters, shooters, factory farmers – were not going to change their views by persuasion. It was going to take force; hence she'd begun her campaign of disruption of hunts and shoots, and daubing graffiti on the walls and gates of chicken farms.

She went over to a small wardrobe. The doors were covered in posters showing gruesome scenes of animals being killed or confined in tiny pens. She reached up and took down a scrapbook from the top of the wardrobe. She kept a record of her exploits: newspaper cuttings, photographs of the groups she worked with. She took pride in the fact that she'd been arrested several times and even served a short prison sentence. This was her life now and she was devoted to this noble cause. She'd left home as a teenager and gone to join a group in London. She had no contact with her family any more.

Liz turned the pages of yellowing cuttings and blurry photographs. Some people would say she was a fanatic, an extremist. She didn't care. She felt her life had a purpose beyond the empty conformist tedium of a conventional existence: a job, a car, and a house in the suburbs.

When you were involved in a war, there were going to be casualties. She hadn't been entirely honest with that young detective when she'd said that people were also animals, and that she would never be violent towards them.

If people were torturing and killing animals, you had a duty to defend the animals. She had been involved in protests where people had been assaulted.

Liz reached the end of her record, a blank page in the scrapbook. She would have to put in something about recent events. After all, it was something to celebrate that a major enemy of innocent birdlife was now dead.

~

Ian Davis had finished lunch and was having a quick nap on the sofa before returning to work, when there was a knock on the front door. Jenny went to the door, which led straight into their living room, and opened it to reveal a man and a woman she didn't recognise.

'Is this the home of Ian Davis?' asked Oldroyd. 'We're police officers investigating the murder of Alexander Fraser.' He and Steph showed their identification.

Jenny felt faint with the shock; it was as if her worst nightmare was coming true. Had her husband really been involved in this murder?

'Yes,' she tried to say, but no noise came out of her mouth. 'Come in.'

'Are you OK?' asked Steph, concerned at Jenny's white face and shocked expression. 'It's just routine questioning of anyone who knew Mr Fraser.'

'Come in,' Jenny repeated, feeling some relief. 'Come on upstairs, you kids. Ian!' She put the Lego and the wooden train track into a box and ushered the children upstairs, much to their dismay.

Davis woke up when Jenny shouted at him, and was startled by the presence of the detectives whom he recognised from the inn. However, he soon composed himself. He'd sobered up and had been expecting this. He remained seated on the sofa during their introductions.

'We need to ask you some questions about the murder of Mr Fraser,' said Oldroyd. He and Steph sat on chairs; the floor and most of the surfaces were covered in odd bits of toys, jigsaw puzzles, crayons, pencils and half-finished drawings.

'Fire away,' replied Davis, yawning.

'I'll come straight to the point,' continued Oldroyd. 'You worked as a gamekeeper for Mr Fraser and you didn't have a very good relationship with him. Is that true?'

'Yes. It's no secret that he and I didn't see eye to eye. He was very demanding; nothing was ever good enough. He was always picking me up over summat. It gets on yer nerves after a bit. And he was a tight git as well. He never paid me what I deserved for doing that job. It's hard work, out in all weathers up on t'moors. Of course he knew nowt about what's involved, just expected everything to be in order when he wanted it to be.'

'So, did you feel bad enough to want to harm him?' Oldroyd understood the resentment of the skilled worker instructed by an ignorant boss.

'To be honest, yes. There was many a time I felt like ramming his shotgun down his throat. Like on Friday. He was carping on to me all day: the beaters were too slow, I should've stopped them sabs from making a nuisance, on and on. And all this were in front of everybody. I could have smashed him in the face, but' – he paused and looked at the detectives – 'I didn't and I didn't shoot him later that day, either.'

'You mentioned the sabs. Were you there when one of them died in a confrontation a few years ago?'

'Yes, but I didn't see much. That bloke had a heart condition, didn't he? I don't have much time for those sabs, and I don't think you can blame Fraser for that, though he did go at him in a bloody rage.'

'OK. You were in the bar at the Dog and Gun on Friday night, weren't you?'

'Yes, there were four of us: me, Peter Gorton, Alan Green and Wilf Bramley.'

'And you saw Mr Fraser?'

'We did. Him and his shooting-party mates were gathered there all dressed up for their posh dinner. Fraser always puts on this Highland dress crap, kilt and everything – makes a right idiot of himself. We could hardly stop ourselves laughing.'

'So I presume they all went into that private dining area to eat?'

'They did, and we stayed in t'bar. We were glad to get rid of 'em.'

'What time did you leave?'

'Not long after half ten. I walked straight back here, and Jenny and me went to bed about eleven.'

'Did you see anything or anybody when you left the inn?'

'No. It was quiet.'

'Did Alan Green leave at the same time?'

'No. Wilf did, but Alan and Peter were still there when I left.'

'I'm sure you've heard that Alan Green has been identified by a witness as the murderer and he's gone missing?'

Davis shook his head. 'Yeah, but I can't believe it. Alan was just an ordinary bloke, did some gardening and stuff. I heard him say he wasn't fond of Fraser. He'd done some jobs for him and Fraser took a long time to pay him, but I can't believe he would have killed him over that. There must have been a mistake.'

'How long have you known Alan Green?'

'Since he came here a few years ago. I can't remember just how long he's been around now, but he's a good bloke, fits in well; likes a drink and a natter in t'bar.'

'Do you know where he lived?'

'Pateley, wasn't it? I don't know. He didn't live in t'village.'

Oldroyd looked at the young man on the sofa. He seemed like a normal rural worker struggling to support his family. He was an unlikely suspect, even if he didn't get on with Fraser.

'What will you do now that your boss is dead?'

'Me? Carry on where I am, I hope. I was just saying to Jenny, t'next owner o' t'moor can't be as bad as Fraser, so I'm hoping things will improve.'

'So you admit you had a reason to want Mr Fraser out of the way?'

Davis realised he'd fallen into a trap and scowled. 'OK, yes, I've already said as much, but I didn't shoot him.'

'Do you possess a shotgun?'

'Yes. It's locked up in a cupboard upstairs and all the paperwork is in order.'

'We'll have to take that away to be checked.'

Davis went upstairs to get the shotgun and, when he returned, Oldroyd thanked Davis for his time before he and Steph left.

Outside, he turned to her. 'You head off back to the inn, take the gun. It needs to go to forensics to see if it's the kind of gun that was used. They don't get much information from shotguns though. I'm just going to pay a quick visit to that artist Dexter told us about.'

'OK, sir.' Steph began to walk across the green, looking a little menacing with the shotgun, to join Andy and Potts, who were looking at statements and conducting further searches in and around the inn. So far, nothing further of interest had turned up.

~

Miriam Fraser looked out of the narrow, mullioned windows of the manor house at the garden and the fells beyond, which were illuminated by sunshine. It was a beautiful view that had been one of the factors in persuading them to buy the house several years ago, but now it was unable to stimulate any joy in her. Everything felt flat. The house was quiet and seemed empty, cold and oppressive. The phone rang. It was her daughter Henrietta.

'Yes, darling, I'm fine . . . well, as good as I can be . . . Yes, I'm looking forward to you coming tomorrow . . . That's wonderful . . . Any idea what time you'll be here? No, don't bring anything, just yourself . . . I know . . . OK, then . . .'

She chatted for a while longer, but when she put the phone down everything was quiet.

Henrietta would be here soon to help her arrange the funeral. She would be around for a while. Her son would also come to stay later, but then he would go and she would be by herself again.

She couldn't tell her daughter what she really felt: that she was frightened of the future. Would she end up a lonely, isolated old woman in this house? Everything had been fine when she and Sandy had moved here, away from all the people they knew in the city, because they had each other, but without him things were going to be very different.

Why hadn't she foreseen this? Maybe she should move, but where to? She couldn't go too near her children; who knew when they might move and leave her by herself again? But it would be so much easier to be near one of them.

Miriam was also worried about money. What she'd told the police was true: Sandy had controlled all their personal finances and always told her not to worry. But she had the impression that there were problems. She knew he'd sometimes not paid his bills promptly, and he was always very anxious to arrange as many of those shoots as possible, as if he really needed the money. What if he'd incurred debts that he hadn't told her about? She might have to sell the house to pay them off, and then where would she end up?

Getting agitated, she went into the kitchen to make herself some tea and to distract herself from painful thoughts. She took the drink back into the sitting room. Clouds had moved across the sky, blotting out the sunlight. She shuddered in a moment of loneliness and gloom.

Theirs had been a traditional marriage: she had given up her job as a legal secretary and followed her husband's career. Sandy had organised everything and her role had been to look after the children and support him. Now she felt anger at how ignorant he'd kept her about so many practical aspects of their life. It made her feel weak and helpless.

She would feel better when her daughter arrived, but she was still frightened about what they might find when they looked into Sandy's affairs.

She looked at a photograph on the mahogany table, of Sandy in his Highland dress. What had he been up to? Why had someone wanted to kill him?

～

The guests at the Dog and Gun were getting restless. They were confined to their rooms and the dining areas and short walks near the hotel until Oldroyd decided that the police had acquired sufficient information and the guests could be released. He was expected to give this permission by the end of the day.

Meanwhile, Henry Saunders and James Symons were in Symons's room, passing the time by playing chess. They had acquired a set from the lounge. Saunders was very disgruntled and agitated.

'I hope we can get away from here soon. I mean, we're all very sad and shocked about Sandy's death and so on, but some of us have work to do and I have to get back to London. I have important meetings tomorrow and the phone reception here's rubbish, so I can't contact anyone. I'll have to ask to use the landline.'

'Check,' replied Symons, removing one of Saunders's knights.

'Blast!'

'Calm down, old boy, you're not concentrating. There's nothing you can do about it. We've just got to sit it out. It won't be long now; they've got no reason to detain us any longer.'

'No, but you never know with the police. They're always checking and double-checking and asking you to go over things again.'

'That's how they work, grinding away at the same material looking for a lead, especially in a case like this. But they don't always get there.' Symons smiled.

'What do you mean?' asked Saunders.

'The public have watched too many crime dramas and read too many crime novels in which the police always catch the culprit. In fact, there are lots of murders that are never solved. It's a myth that justice will always be done in the end. There might not be such a thing as the "perfect murder", whatever that means, but the police can't always find the solution and catch who was responsible.'

'I think we probably persuaded them that Rawnsley didn't do it. Where is he, by the way?'

'Sulking in his room I think. I haven't seen the silly man since breakfast,' replied Symons, while concentrating hard on the chess game.

'They seem to think this Green character is responsible,' said Saunders, still considering his next move. 'Apparently that girl behind the bar saw him do it. It's a bit weird, but it does look suspicious the way he's disappeared.' He decided to move a bishop to clear a path for one of his rooks.

'Possibly. But I still fancy it was one of those "sab" people or whatever they call themselves – capable of anything, in my opinion. I told the police what I thought about them. By the way,' Symons continued, changing the subject as he moved his queen into a threatening position, 'what do you think will happen to the grouse moor now that Sandy's gone?'

'I've no idea. I can't think that Miriam will want to keep it. Oh! I'd forgotten about poor Miriam. I really ought to look in and pay my respects before I head off. Blast! That's going to keep me here for longer.'

'I thought I might put an offer in if it comes up for sale.'

'For what?' Saunders was distracted as he considered the implications of his opponent's move.

'For the moor.'

Saunders looked up, rather surprised. 'Really?'

'Yes. I've always fancied owning my own grouse moor. It will consolidate my position as a prominent Yorkshire landowner.' Symons chuckled.

'Isn't it a bit, sort of, early to be talking about that? Sandy's not even buried yet.'

'Well, old boy, the early bird and all that. Maybe you could mention it to Mrs Fraser when you call in.'

Saunders was now quite shocked. 'James, don't you think that would be insensitive at a time like this?'

'Not really, she might be quite pleased that there's someone ready to take the grouse moor off her hands who can pay cash. After all, I've heard rumours about Sandy.'

'What rumours?'

'Ah, you see, you're away in London so you're not tapped into local gossip about your friend and mine.'

'Well, what are people saying?' Saunders moved his rook out into a place where he hoped to mount an attack on Symons's king.

'Just that Sandy's finances were, well, not very sound. It may be that his widow has debts to pay off.'

'The police were asking me about that. I told them that I wasn't aware that he had any money worries. Anyway, even supposing he had, surely you can't see that as an opportunity to advance yourself?' He looked at Symons, and for the first time noticed that his blue eyes were very cold.

'And you a banker,' said Symons. 'I'd have thought you'd have known that the world rewards those who seize their opportunities.' He suddenly moved a knight that had been lurking at the edge of the board. 'Checkmate, I'll think you'll find, old boy.' He grinned at Saunders, who felt a shiver run through him.

~

Oldroyd easily found John Gray's studio down a short lane off the green. It was in a small extension to a cottage and there was a sign outside saying 'Nidderdale Art'. The word 'Open' was displayed on the door, so Oldroyd went in. Inside, the walls were hung with watercolours in the style he'd seen at Tony Dexter's barn, and there were racks of prints, some available at a reduced price. In a corner, Oldroyd saw a man working at an easel.

'Good afternoon,' he said.

The man turned round. He had long greying hair tied back in a ponytail, and a straggly beard that was also grey. He was wearing a paint-smeared checked shirt and old corduroy trousers.

'Hello, please feel free to browse round and ask me if you need any assistance,' the man said, in a standard RP accent. Then he turned back to the easel and began to hum a tune.

Oldroyd persisted. 'I do want to have a look at your paintings, but I would also like to ask you a few questions.' The artist turned round again. 'I'm Chief Inspector Oldroyd, and I'm investigating the murder of Alexander Fraser. Are you John Gray? If so, I understand you knew the victim.'

Oldroyd presented his ID, and Gray put down his paintbrush and got up from his chair. Oldroyd could see that he was working on a dales landscape scene.

'Yes. I am John Gray. It's a nasty business. Please sit down. Can I get you a herbal tea?'

Oldroyd declined.

'To answer your enquiry: yes, I did know Sandy Fraser, but not well. He used to come here quite regularly, and he was always very complimentary about my work. His daughter also used to come in when she was visiting from London. He bought an original watercolour and some prints. He asked if he could pay in instalments, and I didn't want to say no as he was a local. It hasn't been easy for me to establish myself here. You need to get recommendations from local people. He was a bit slow with his payments, but he got there in the end. So if you're looking for motives, I'm afraid I haven't got one.'

'So you didn't know anything else about him?'

'No. He owned a grouse moor, didn't he? Got wealthy people to pay to come and shoot birds. Very unpleasant. What did Oscar Wilde say, "The unspeakable in full pursuit of the uneatable"? That was fox hunting. I suppose in this case they do eat the game. I hope they get the shot in their mouths!' Gray laughed.

'You're not the only person in the village who dislikes blood sports. I presume you know Liz Smith and Tony Dexter?'

'I've met Tony Dexter, he bought some prints from me. Is Liz Smith the caravan woman? Animal-rights activist?'

'That's right.'

'They're both much keener than I am in opposing these things. I just find it very distasteful, but I'm not an activist; too much of a coward. I wouldn't go to prison for my beliefs, I'm afraid.'

'No. I just want to ask where you were on Friday evening. We're asking everyone who knew Mr Fraser.'

'Here, Chief Inspector. I live in this cottage and I let out one of the bedrooms to a bloke called Vic Moore. He's come up here to escape from the city for a while.'

'Was he here on Friday night?'

'Yes. We could vouch for each other. We get on fine and we often share meals together, which we did on Friday evening.'

'Do you have a shotgun?'

'What on earth would I do with one of those, Inspector? I'm creative, not destructive.'

Oldroyd laughed, concluded the interview and spent some time looking at the paintings. He identified a couple of moody studies of windswept scenes high in the fells that he liked, but decided to go away and think about it for a while. He established that Gray had a website and thought he would show Deborah and discuss it with her before making a decision.

As he walked back across the green to the inn, he looked up at the fells and wished, as he often did, that he had the ability to paint a scene like that. But maybe there was another way he could capture the landscape and convey his deep feelings for it.

He also wondered, again not for the first time, whether he might move out to one of the dales someday, maybe when he retired, and settle in a pretty village like this. Many people did, including the victim in their current case. It was tempting in many ways, but much as he loved this landscape, part of him still needed the larger towns and cities for what they could provide in terms of culture and social interaction.

He always came back to the same conclusion: he was fine where he was at the moment.

~

Gideon Rawnsley was indeed, as Symons had said, sulking in his room. He didn't feel like socialising any more, particularly with Saunders and Symons. He was still embarrassed about his behaviour on Friday night and he was also afraid that he would find it difficult not to convey his pleasure at Fraser's demise, and that would create suspicion.

Rawnsley lay on the bed sipping from a glass of water – no more alcohol – waiting impatiently for the go-ahead to leave and make the journey home. He went over possible ways to mitigate any damage he'd caused. He hadn't expected that they'd be held for so long, and he urgently needed to get back and do something to counter any bad publicity that might occur as a result of his involvement in this unfortunate event.

In the luxury-car trade, your reputation was everything. He didn't want anything negative about his relationship with Sandy Fraser to start circulating among his regular customers. He intended to send out an email to them, informing them of Fraser's death and paying tribute to him as one of Elite Cars' most loyal and valued customers. That should strike the right note and prevent unpleasant rumours from gaining hold. Yes, that would do the trick; then he would be in the clear. Even though he'd lost a customer, that customer had been troublesome in a number of ways. It was a relief to know that certain problematic issues had died with him.

A smile came to Rawnsley's face. He'd decided what to do, and he could now make a fresh start.

~

Sheila and Rob Owen were sitting in the living room of their private flat at the back of the inn. It felt very strange to have little to do; the skeleton service being provided by the bar and kitchen could run without them. Paradoxically, it was a break from the intense stress of running the inn – something they welcomed, even though they were losing some business.

They'd been watching a film to take their minds off the trauma of recent days. It had just ended, and Rob got up to make some tea. Sheila yawned and lay down on the sofa. Rob came back with the mugs.

Sheila yawned again. 'God! I feel so lethargic. I could lie here all evening,' she said.

'It's doing you good. You were exhausted after all the work you've put in recently, and the shock at what happened.'

She sat up and sipped her tea. 'Is everything all right down there, do you think? It feels weird not to be supervising everything.'

'They're all fine. They're only doing basic food for everyone. The restaurant's not open to the public. All the staff are keen to help. They know you've had a shock.'

'That's so good of them, but we can't have this going on for too long, can we? We're losing money.'

Rob sat down. 'I know, but I don't think it will be long now. That DCI seems a reasonable bloke. He won't keep us shut down indefinitely for no good reason.'

'No. Do you think our reputation will be damaged?'

'I can't see why. It's not as if people have died from food poisoning, or there's been a fire because we breached the regulations. Someone was shot outside the inn. We can't control that. If we were in the inner city, people might be wary, but here, they know it's a freak incident. You know what the public are like. We might get an influx of ghoulish types wanting to see where Fraser was shot.'

She laughed and gave him a hug. 'You're always so optimistic! So good for morale.'

'Yes, well, we'll survive it all, even if we've temporarily lost a good contract. I'm sure whoever takes over running the grouse moor will want to patronise us too. There isn't really anywhere else to go.'

'To be honest, I was getting heartily sick of Fraser.'

'I don't blame you. That last salvo against your cooking was completely out of order. Anyway, he's been taken care of now.'

She pulled away from the hug and looked at him. 'What do you mean?'

'Well, I'm not having a man upsetting my wife like that, so I'm the one who took a contract out on him.'

She spluttered with laughter. 'Rob! That's not really funny when someone's been murdered!'

'Why are you laughing, then?'

She hit him playfully as he collapsed into laughter himself. They had a brief pretend fight but the laughter subsided because, however distasteful and unsettling the thought was, it couldn't be denied that their lives would be easier now that Sandy Fraser had gone, as long as they could fill the gap financially.

Rob was very pleased to see her so relaxed. He was determined that she should remain like that, so there were certain things about Fraser she would never need to know.

～

It had been a long day, but there was still one interview to do: with the farmer Wilf Bramley. Oldroyd and Andy ended the day as they had begun, labouring up a track out of the village – but in the opposite direction from Dexter's barn. Rob Owen had told them where Bramley's farm was: halfway up the fellside in the direction of Pateley.

'Lovely view, sir,' observed Andy as they gazed down the length of Nidderdale.

'Absolutely,' replied Oldroyd, as he followed the sweep of the dale with its pattern of drystone walls and farms dotted around the hillsides. He looked up the track. They were walking towards one such farm: small, stone-built with a barn attached and stone tiles on the roof. There was a tree behind the farm, planted long ago to provide some meagre shelter. The fell rose steep and dark behind the isolated building, up to the moorland tops.

It reminded Oldroyd of the iconic Top Withens on the moors above Haworth: the now-ruined farmhouse which had almost certainly been the model for Wuthering Heights in the eponymous novel by Emily Brontë. This one was far from ruined, however, and Oldroyd always admired the sheer grit with which farmers eked out a living in such hostile circumstances. The winter conditions, with wind, rain and snow, must be hard to endure, especially with the sheep living out on the hillsides. He'd heard many stories of farmers having to dig sheep out of snowdrifts in the worst weather.

As they got closer to the farm, they noticed that one field near the house seemed to be full of vehicles or machinery. A closer inspection revealed tractors of various colours, sizes, ages and states of repair. Some had been there so long that grass had grown through the rusting wheels and bodywork. Not many seemed to be in working order and some were half dismantled. There was a huge pile of old tractor tyres and engines in one corner of the field.

'I think we can safely say that Mr Bramley collects tractors,' observed Oldroyd, wryly.

Andy found it beyond comprehension. He shook his head as he looked at the field of rusting metal carcasses. 'Bloody hell, sir, I've never seen anything like this. I know people collect some funny stuff, but tractors!'

'Well, I'm sure they mean a lot to him. He's probably worked with them all his life. It's nice that you can see them here in the fields. It's not like the musical instruments those collectors had in that case we investigated in Halifax. They were all hidden away, remember?'

'I do, sir, but at least they were worth millions. What do you think this pile of crap is worth?'

'Oh, that's not the point, is it?' Oldroyd threw up his hands in mock despair. 'It's the sentimental value and probably a fascination with the different designs and so on.'

'It beats me, sir. I mean, I remember collecting Pokémon cards, and I had a friend who collected football stickers . . . but we were just kids. You grow out of it.'

'Obviously, not everybody does and—' They were approaching the farmyard and there was suddenly ferocious barking from at least two dogs. 'Oops! I think we're going to get the traditional welcome at an isolated farm. Let's wait here. He'll know from this early warning system that someone's here.'

Oldroyd was right. It wasn't long before a voice was heard shouting at the dogs. 'Bob! Ben! Shut thi bloody noise! Get in there! Go on!'

The barking subsided and Wilf Bramley appeared at the gate. He looked at them suspiciously. 'Yer not reps, are yer? If y'are just tae thi hook – ah don't want nowt.' He turned away.

'Mr Bramley? We're police officers: DCI Oldroyd, and Detective Sergeant Carter. We'd like to ask you some questions about the murder of Sandy Fraser.'

Bramley turned back to see Andy and Oldroyd brandishing their warrant cards. His brow furrowed. 'Oh, reight. Well, ah know nowt abaht it, so yer wastin' yer time.'

'Well, if we could just come in and talk to you. I also want to ask you about your fine collection over there.' Oldroyd pointed to the tractors.

Bramley's face lit up. 'Oh aye, well, come on right in then. Ah'll put t'kettle on.'

Oldroyd smiled at Andy, who shook his head at his boss's wiliness as they followed Bramley, who called back: 'Never mind abaht t'dogs. Ah've put 'em in t'shed.' He led the way into a yard flagged with ancient cobblestones. There was a tall narrow shed with a door, which Oldroyd suspected was an outside toilet, and two cows in a pen were leaning over a gate drinking water from a trough.

Bramley opened the back door and they went into the kitchen, which was a bit on the rough-and-ready side but very cosy and comfortable. It was clear that little had changed in the farmhouse for generations. There was an ancient Rayburn warming the kitchen, some dusty sofas up against the walls, and a large, bare wooden table. The kitchen units were not fitted, and the peeling Formica worktops reminded Andy of some of the hipster cafes in Leeds. Bramley grabbed a blackened kettle, filled it with water at a solid-looking porcelain sink, and slammed it on to the hot plate.

'Sit thisens dahn then.' He indicated the sofas and they all sat down around the table. 'Ah'm mostly here by misen these days. Ah lost me wife five years since. Me son comes up to help me but he lives down in Pateley. Me daughter moved to Leeds – she's a nurse. There's not much for t'younger folk round here if they're not farmin'.'

Andy looked around the isolated, old-fashioned farmhouse, thinking that he too would have wanted to escape pretty quickly from here once he'd hit his late teens. The kettle whistled and steam billowed out from the spout. Bramley spooned loose tea into a big brown teapot and stirred it up. He rummaged in a tall wooden cupboard and produced a half-empty packet of ginger snap biscuits. He put the packet on the table.

'No, I'm sure the old way of life is a struggle for you, Mr Bramley,' said Oldroyd. 'Anyway, we've come to ask you about Mr Fraser, who I understand was your landlord, and also what you can tell us about the evening of his murder.'

'Aye, just a minute.' Bramley put a milk bottle and a dirty sugar bowl on the table. He poured dark brown tea into three discoloured mugs. 'Help yourself to sugar and a ginger biscuit.' He put three spoonfuls of sugar in his own tea, took a drink of it and wiped his mouth on his sleeve and continued. 'Ah wor in t'Dog that neet – that's what us old uns call t'pub. There were a few others there: young Ian Davis, he's a gamekeeper; Peter Gorton who runs t'shop; and that Geordie chap who's been here a while now . . . Alan . . .'

'Green,' prompted Oldroyd.

'Aye, that's it. We were all just havin' a quiet pint and all those posh shooters started comin' in dressed up to t'nines and drinkin' gin before their fancy dinner.'

'So I imagine you all said one or two things about them?' suggested Oldroyd, who noticed Andy struggling with the strong tea and with Bramley's broad Yorkshire speech.

'Hmm . . .' muttered Bramley. 'Aye, we did, but nobody likes 'em, swaggerin' round showin' off their brass. And they show other stuff off as well, accordin' to that lass behind t'bar.'

'Kirsty Hemingway?'

'Aye.' Bramley told them about Jeanette finding the man naked.

Andy smiled and perked up at hearing about that incident, despite not following all the details of the story.

Oldroyd laughed. 'So did you see Mr Fraser?' he asked.

'Aye.' It was Bramley's turn to smile. 'He came in with his kilt on – reckons he's got summat to do wi' a Scottish clan 'cos he's called Fraser. He looked a reight silly bugger.'

'I understand he's not popular, either.'

'No, you're right there. Ian Davis wor havin' a go at him and Alan Green wor sayin' what a stingy sod he is.'

'I see. What about you?'

'Ah've no time for 'im. He's t'worst landlord ah've ever 'ad, and ah've 'ad a few over t'years. T'problem is, t'land my farm's on is owned by t'same estate as t'grouse moor above t'village so Fraser's been my landlord since he came, worst luck. Mr Wilson who owned it before, he wor a real gentleman – never hardly put me rent up. He knew ah couldn't afford it, but this chap, well . . .' He stopped, shook his head, took another drink of his tea and snapped a ginger biscuit in half.

'So did you dislike him enough to wish him harm?'

Bramley looked at Oldroyd and frowned. 'Aye, well, ah know what you're gettin' at. Did ah bump 'im off? The answer's no.'

'Do you own a shotgun?'

'Aye. What farmer doesn't? You've got to keep t'crows and t'pigeons at bay. Rabbit makes a good stew an' all. Ah've got a licence and ah keep t'gun locked up.'

'OK. I'll have to send another officer up to look at that later. How well did you know Alan Green?'

Bramley frowned. 'Alan? Well, ah only saw him in t'pub, but we 'ad some laughs. Wasn't he a gardener or summat? He was sayin' that night that Fraser never paid properly for t'jobs he did for him. Why are yer askin' me?'

'Alan Green has been identified by a witness as the murderer, and now he's disappeared.'

'Alan Green?'

'Yes. Kirsty Hemingway saw the murder from an upstairs window at the inn.'

'Kirsty the barmaid?'

'Yes.'

Bramley shook his head. 'Well, that's a funny do. But if yer think it was Alan, why are yer quizzin' me?'

'We have to keep our options open. Kirsty Hemingway might turn out to be wrong, so we have to consider everyone who had a motive to kill Mr Fraser.'

Bramley grunted. 'Aye, well yer wastin' yer time. Ah'm too busy to be goin' round shootin' folk.'

'OK. Did you ever hear Alan Green threaten violence against Mr Fraser?' asked Andy.

'No, as ah said, he agreed with all of us that Fraser was keen with his brass, but he never threatened to do owt abaht it.'

'Do you know anybody who might have wanted to do Mr Fraser harm?' continued Andy.

Bramley finished his tea and put down his mug. 'No. Put it this way: nob'dy liked t'chap, but ah can't see anyone shootin' him.'

'Very well,' said Oldroyd, getting up. 'Thank you for the tea and biscuits.' Andy also stood, leaving his mug half empty, although he'd enjoyed the biscuits.

'Aye, now, before yer go, yer were asking abaht t'tractors?' Bramley had a big smile on his face.'

'Oh, yes,' said Oldroyd, who'd forgotten about the tractors and now wished that Bramley had too. But there was no chance of that.

The farmer marched the two detectives out to the field that held his collection. Andy groaned in despair.

'This one here belonged to me dad,' Bramley said, indicating a small rusty vehicle, on parts of which the traditional red paint was still visible. 'It's a David Brown VAC 1C Cropmaster. They were made at Meltham near Huddersfield, you know, but this model was only made for six years, between 1947 and 1953. They didn't used to have cabs – oh no! Farmers were tough old buggers, out in all weathers.' He went on to the next without a pause. 'Now, if you want to see one wi' a cab, look at this: it's a Ford 5000 1968 – absolute classic. Not much left of t'cab though.'

To Oldroyd and Andy, it looked like an utter wreck.

Oldroyd tried desperately to think of a way of escaping, but the flow of information from Bramley was unstoppable. And so they had to wait until every machine had been identified and its history and special features had been described. This included a steam-powered traction engine and an early-model tractor without rubber wheels, which must have been excruciating to drive along the uneven country roads.

Finally, they were able to say goodbye to a very happy Wilf Bramley, who beamed with pride and satisfaction as he insisted on shaking hands with them. They were silent for a while on the walk back, exhausted from the battering of information they'd received.

'Well, sir,' said Andy, at last. 'I don't really suspect him of being the murderer.'

'No. Neither do I,' replied Oldroyd.

'But for goodness' sake, sir, if he needs to be questioned again, could you please send someone else? If I have to go back there and he starts going on about his tractors, I think I'll get into one of them and drive over him!'

They laughed together as they walked down the path, back towards Niddersgill.

Three

Gollinglith Fleet
Crookrise Crag
Oughtershaw Side
Healaugh Crag

Early next morning, Inspector Gibbs sat in his office at Pateley Bridge station feeling puzzled and unsure about exactly what to do next. The attempts to track down Alan Green had not yet proved successful. He and his team had made enquiries in a number of villages and hamlets around Pateley Bridge, but no one seemed to have heard of the man. This was odd, because in a rural community like this, anonymity was hard to maintain, particularly if you were a gardener and odd-job man and therefore knew a lot of people. It seemed that he was paid cash in hand for all his jobs, so it was hard to trace a bank account – if he had one.

Gibbs got up and walked over to the window, which commanded a view of the road bridge over the River Nidd. He could see people talking in little groups, and a window cleaner who waved to a farmer going over the bridge in a tractor. Two people were having a conversation at a petrol station. How could you lose yourself in a place like this? He began to wonder whether Green was actually who he said he was.

Was he at all active in the town and the surrounding area, or had he come to Nidderdale with the intention of targeting only Niddersgill and Fraser? He had done jobs for a number of people in Niddersgill, but apparently nowhere else. He must have a base somewhere, but it could just be a basic bolthole where he lay low. Did he travel in from further afield? That didn't tie in with the absence of a car. Walking or cycling from the Pateley area to Niddersgill was one thing, but living any further away would not be practical.

Gibbs shook his head; he was a dogged character but this was a frustrating case. He'd been brought up in the dale and knew every inch of it. They would search every barn if necessary. They would also have to mount a 'Have you seen this man?' campaign.

Unfortunately, as they had no photograph of the suspect, it would have to be an identikit-type picture based on what people who knew him remembered of his features. At least they were a little more sophisticated in terms of computer graphics than they used to be. If all that still yielded nothing, they would have to accept that he'd fled the area leaving no trace, or that he had an accomplice who was hiding him. Gibbs would have to alert other forces and instigate a watch at airports and seaports. But if Green was anywhere on his patch, Gibbs was determined to flush him out – because only then could they begin to answer the further puzzling question of what he'd had against Fraser that had made him kill the man.

However, it was not all gloom. His research into the death of the saboteur had yielded material of more interest, and he'd sent a report to DCI Oldroyd. It was possible that they had uncovered a promising lead.

~

As Gibbs dealt with his frustration at not making more progress in the search for Green, Andy, Steph and Oldroyd met in Oldroyd's office at Harrogate HQ. Gibbs had sent two more officers from Pateley to help DC Potts monitor the crime scene in Niddersgill, while the investigating team reviewed what they knew. Coffee and chocolate biscuits were available but, as everybody was on some kind of health drive at the moment, the latter remained untouched. Andy gazed at them longingly, but he was under orders from Steph to lose weight, so he had to resist.

Oldroyd had adopted his customary position, sitting back in his desk chair with his hands behind his head and his eyes partly shut while he listened to what the others were saying. He saw that his two detective sergeants had laptops with them – an inevitable change, he supposed, from the old leafing through sheaves of paper, and probably an improvement. However, he was happy to remain only half engaged with the digital world, whatever derision he had to endure from his daughter and others of her generation.

'Anything interesting come in?' he asked.

'Yes, sir,' replied Andy. 'It seems that Fraser was in a bit of financial trouble. He'd run up debts and he had a big bank over-draft. Apparently, he had no significant savings.'

'Hmm, I suspect he took on more than he bargained for with that grouse moor. He had no experience of managing anything like that and he'd never been a businessman. He was a retired judge who'd had his salary paid every month.'

'No wonder he struggled to pay his bills with people like Rawnsley,' observed Steph. 'But does that help us in any way? Does it mean there could have been more people with a motive because they were owed money?'

'Maybe. One of his biggest debts could have been to the Dog and Gun. We couldn't find any payments to the Owens over quite a long period, but he must have run up a substantial bill for his shooting parties.'

Oldroyd whistled. 'Did he indeed? I wonder why they never told us that? In fact, Sheila said he always paid.'

'Maybe they knew it made them possible suspects, sir,' said Steph.

'You're probably right. People get scared, don't tell the truth and then get themselves into deeper trouble. If they were involved, they must have been in league with this Alan Green or whoever actually shot Fraser. I can't see how either of them could have done it and then got back up to their flat without being seen by Saunders and Symons.'

'Unless they were in on it too, sir,' suggested Andy.

Oldroyd shook his head. 'And then we get back to the big conspiracy theory and you know what I think about those. Anyway, let's run through the rest of the suspects, now we've had time to think about things. What do you make of Kirsty Hemingway? Do we believe her?'

'If we don't, sir, it makes things much more complicated,' answered Andy. 'It would mean she was covering for someone by trying to incriminate Green.'

'She could be honest and just mistaken,' added Steph. 'But surely Green's disappearance is the clearest indication that she's telling the truth.'

'I agree. The latest from Inspector Gibbs, by the way, is that they still haven't tracked him down.'

'He could be dead, sir,' observed Andy. 'Felt guilty and topped himself or was silenced after he played the hitman.'

'Not impossible, but you're making it sound more like the world of city gangsters. I don't think downtown Pateley Bridge is that edgy and dangerous.'

They all laughed at this image.

'What about the last three to see him?' continued Oldroyd. 'His shooting pals?'

Andy began: 'Rawnsley we know had an argument with Fraser, but being late with your money for a car seems a flimsy reason to be murdered. Saunders the old school friend and Symons of the local gentry don't appear to have had any motive.'

'They had the best opportunity, though,' said Steph. 'As they knew when Fraser had left the inn and were on hand to kill him. It could very well be Saunders and Symons were working together. Maybe one of them impersonated Alan Green, and somehow Green found out he was going to be framed for a murder and bolted?'

'Hmm, impersonation – that's making me think a bit,' said Oldroyd, leaning back with his eyes shut. 'But do you have any evidence for your theories, imaginative though they are?'

'Not much, sir,' said Steph, smiling. 'I think we're floundering, aren't we?'

'Maybe a little at the moment,' conceded Oldroyd. 'What about our two activists?'

'I think Liz Smith would be capable of violence in some circumstances. She's very passionate about her beliefs and angry with people who do what she considers evil things. Fraser was a classic example of the type of person she hated: upper-middle-class, arrogant, contemptuous of her views. There's also the issue of getting revenge for the sab who died on the moor. She has no alibi for Friday, so I would place her high on the suspects list. She could have been involved with Alan Green in some way.'

'And Tony Dexter, Andy?'

'No alibi, again. Disliked Fraser but didn't come across as the volatile type. We haven't ruled out collusion between the two who opposed Fraser's grouse shooting. By the way, DC Potts went round to see Theresa Rawlings, and she verified that the postman, Eastwood, was with her on the Friday evening, and he didn't leave until after Fraser was shot. Of course, we've only got her word for it, but we've no reason to suspect her or Eastwood of anything at the moment.'

'OK,' said Oldroyd, who appeared to sink down even deeper into his chair. 'There's one more thing to add. Going back to the issue of the sab who died, I've had a report from Bill Gibbs. He confirmed all the medical details and that no one could be held responsible for the man's death, but the potentially interesting thing is that he was a man called Sam Cooper, and his brother Greg is a sous chef at the Dog and Gun.'

'Someone with a real motive,' said Steph.

'Sir, I remember that name,' said Andy. 'Wasn't he the one who was on late-night duty at the inn on the night of the murder?'

'You're right, Andy. Well remembered, and that is interesting. It gave him the opportunity. This could lead somewhere and I hope it does, because somehow the rest of it doesn't seem to amount to very much. You may be right that it'll all be over when Gibbs flushes out Green, but I'm uneasy. What was his motive and why is it proving so difficult to find any trace of him?'

'Maybe this Greg Cooper employed him as a hitman?'

Oldroyd frowned sceptically. 'Well, I suppose it's possible. It does seem as if Green only undertook jobs here in Niddersgill. It's as if he came to the village with a purpose and now he's done what he needed to do, he's gone. But where did he stay during that period? Gibbs can find no one in Pateley who knew him or had any jobs done by him. I think we need to look carefully into Fraser's past to see if Green's name crops up. My hunch is still that, if it was him, he shot Fraser on his own behalf. He must have had a grudge against him about something that happened a while ago, maybe before Fraser retired here.'

'Why didn't Fraser recognise him, then, sir? Green did jobs for him, didn't he?' asked Steph.

'That's a very good question. It could have been a long time ago,' said Oldroyd thoughtfully. 'We'd better get back out there; we obviously need to speak to this Greg Cooper and to the Owens again. You stay here, Andy, and get people working on Fraser's past, and also see if you can turn up any Alan Greens in the London and Leeds areas, which is where Fraser spent his career.'

'There'll be quite a lot of those, sir.'

'Yes. Start with ones that have any criminal connections. Steph, you come with me up to Nidderdale. We'll speak to the Owens and we'll have a look at Fraser's possessions and papers and see if they can tell us anything. I think his widow might have recovered a little from the initial shock now.'

'OK, sir.'

Oldroyd's phone rang. It was Tom Walker. 'Jim, you'd better get back up to Nidderdale as quick as you can. Someone's rung in from that inn . . . Dog and Gun, isn't it?'

'Yes.'

'Well, apparently the bloody press are swarming all over asking questions. Typical, isn't it? It probably took them two days to find out where Niddersgill is. They haven't got the slightest interest in places like that until something juicy happens, then they don't mind trampling all over and making a nuisance of themselves when the poor locals have already had their peace shattered.'

'We were just about to leave anyway, Tom, so don't worry.'

'Excellent. You're good at talking to the hacks, and no doubt Watkins'll be watching to see if anything is reflecting badly on the force. That's the only thing he bloody cares about of course—'

'OK, Tom, we're off now,' Oldroyd cut in, as he sensed a rant beginning: the two things Walker hated most were the press and the chief constable. 'Better get a move on,' he said to Steph. As they got up to leave, he turned to Andy. 'And you keep off those chocolate biscuits!' He wagged his finger. 'I've counted them. You need to keep on track if you're ever going to be as fit as I'll be soon with my running.'

'Blimey, sir,' said Andy. 'At this rate we'll soon be cheering you on in your first marathon.' Steph and Oldroyd laughed as they went out.

~

It was a quiet Tuesday morning in Peter Gorton's shop in Niddersgill, but then most mornings were quiet. Gorton didn't mind. He'd bought the shop in order to move out of the city into semi-retirement, and he'd never expected to make a lot of money. The newsagent part kept him ticking over, and locals popped in to buy bits and pieces they'd forgotten in their weekly grocery shop in Pateley Bridge. Things were clearly extra quiet because of the fear that still hung over the village, although Gorton had noticed one or two people who looked more like reporters than tourists wandering around.

He was arranging a display of confectionery in front of the counter when the door opened and Wilf Bramley came in. He was dressed in his usual dirty moleskin trousers, an old jacket and a woolly hat.

'Morning, Wilf.'

'Morning, Peter, gi' me twenty o' me usual.'

Gorton passed the cigarettes across. Bramley handed over the money with a gnarled hand.

There was only one topic of conversation for people in the village at the moment, and Wilf was no exception. 'It's a reight bloody carry-on is this business, in't it?'

'It is.'

'Somebody shot outside t'Dog, bloody hell! There's never been a murder in this village before, ah can tell you, not in ma time, anyroad.'

'No, I'll bet there hasn't. It's a funny do.'

'And it were not long after we left?'

'No. I suppose we were some of the last people to see him alive.'

'Bloody hell!' repeated Wilf, shaking his head. 'Anyway, let's hope they catch t'bugger who did it before he does someone else in.'

'They're saying it was Alan Green.'

Wilf shook his head again. 'Ah know, but ah can't believe that. Ah know he were a comer-in, like, but he were a good bloke. Ah've had some laughs with him at t'Dog. Ah've 'ad t'police up at t'farm. They'd clocked ah didn't like that bugger Fraser but ah told 'em ah didn't bump 'im off and ah don't think Alan did either.'

'Apparently Kirsty Hemingway says she saw him do it, but there's something strange going on. It's not like Alan at all, but he has gone missing.'

'Maybe he's been bumped off an' all. It's a funny do, as yer say. Anyway, ah'd better be off.' Bramley left the shop still shaking his head at this monstrous thing that had disrupted the peace of the village. 'Morning,' he said to a woman who was just coming in. It was Miriam Fraser.

Gorton hadn't expected her and he wasn't sure what to say. 'Oh, Mrs Fraser! Good morning. I'm . . . I'm sorry about Mr Fraser.'

'Thank you,' she replied, trying to smile. She looked very pale, and the hand that held her purse was trembling. 'I've just called in for some milk. My daughter's arriving soon.'

'Oh, that will be nice. Look, I'll just get you the milk.' He came from behind the counter and went over to the fridge. 'Do you want semi-skimmed?'

'Yes, thank you.'

He brought the milk over and she counted out the money. Gorton struggled with what else to say. 'If you need any help with anything,' he said after a pause, 'you've only to ask.'

'Oh, thank you, that's very kind.' She looked at Gorton. 'We were married for nearly forty years. It's a long time to know someone.'

'It is,' replied Gorton, as he opened the door for her and watched her walk slowly back up the lane to the manor house.

∼

Just as Tom Walker had warned Oldroyd, and Gorton had seen, a number of reporters had arrived in Niddersgill and were trying to ask questions of anyone who was prepared to speak. Murder in a country village was always good material, and the press loved bringing out the clichés: 'Horror in a Sleepy Dales Village', 'Peaceful Village Rocked by Savage Murder' and the like.

The journalists were not, however, finding things particularly easy-going, as the villagers generally resented the intrusion from these rude and prying individuals.

When the detectives arrived, Oldroyd immediately let it be known that he would speak to the press in the bar of the Dog and Gun. Much better to get it over with now than arrange something back at HQ. Oldroyd addressed the reporters while sitting on a stool and leaning back against the bar. He would have liked to have a pint of bitter next to him, but that would have created the wrong impression.

'The deceased is Mr Alexander Fraser. He's a retired judge who lived in the village for a number of years and owns a grouse moor. He was shot on Friday evening at around midnight outside this inn, and died almost immediately. We have a witness to this murder, and we also wish to speak to a Mr Alan Green, a local handyman and gardener.'

'Is it true that the suspect has disappeared, and that you can't find any trace of him?'

Someone in the village had been talking, thought Oldroyd. 'It's true that we haven't found Mr Green yet, but we are confident that we will. Of course, it is important to emphasise that anyone with information about him or any aspect of this case should come forward. It is also important to note that, while Alan Green is the principal suspect, we cannot rule out other possibilities.'

'Could this be the work of animal-rights protesters, Chief Inspector? We understand there have been some recent clashes up on the moors between the shooters and people trying to sabotage them. Also the victim was involved in an incident a few years ago, wasn't he – when someone died? Could this be a revenge killing?'

Oldroyd was impressed that someone had been doing their homework.

'That is a line of enquiry we are pursuing but we have no hard evidence yet. While it is true that there have been more conflicts in this area between these groups, there have not been any cases in which the situation has become violent. I repeat that there is no evidence, as yet, to suggest that the animosity which some protesters no doubt felt towards Mr Fraser may have escalated to the point of taking his life.'

Steph smiled as she looked on. The way Oldroyd handled these press conferences with fluency, sharpness and the occasional humorous put-down was one of the many things she admired about him. He was always too good for the reporters.

'Could the suspect be hiding nearby, and could he strike again?'

Oldroyd was expecting this, which was a standard question when a murderer was 'on the loose', as reporters were fond of saying. The problem was always that they wanted to inject some drama and fear into the situation, as this made a better story, while the police wanted to calm things down and reassure the locals.

'It is normal for us to warn local people to be alert in situations like this,' he began. 'We have no evidence that the suspect is some deranged killer, and we have no indication that he may strike again. However, it is also true that we are not sure about his motives and that he has not been apprehended. A sensible approach, therefore, is that people should remain cautious, although there is no reason to panic.'

A bald-headed reporter wearing dark glasses and chewing gum, whom Oldroyd had seen many times before, asked the next question. He worked for one of the more sensationalist tabloids.

'Could this Fraser character have been eliminated by a hit-man? It sounds like a professional job to me. Could he have been involved with the criminal fraternity?'

Here we go, thought Oldroyd, and he smiled. He enjoyed defusing outlandish ideas such as this.

'I presume you mean that Mr Fraser must have been involved with such activities before he came to Nidderdale, as I'm not aware that Niddersgill has a particularly well-developed criminal underworld.'

This was greeted with laughter. Oldroyd continued. 'Mr Fraser was a respected judge in his professional life and has lived a relatively quiet existence since retiring here, except for some disputes over grouse shooting and one unfortunate incident in which he was absolved of blame. I think it strains credibility a little to imagine that he could also have been some kind of mobster on whom one of his enemies took out a contract. It's not a line of investigation which we're pursuing.'

Steph could barely contain her laughter. After this elegant and barbed put-down, the reporter remained silent, and others were deterred from asking similarly sensationalist questions.

At the end of the press conference, Oldroyd and Steph made their way to the Frasers' cottage. Oldroyd wanted to look through Sandy Fraser's papers and belongings to see if they afforded any clues.

'Well done, sir,' said Steph, still chuckling about how her boss had handled the reporter. 'You were on good form.'

'Thanks,' replied Oldroyd. 'It's important to stamp out some of the most outlandish ideas. Anyway, here we are. You knock on the door, as she knows you now.'

Unexpectedly, the door was answered by a woman of about forty. She made a striking figure in tweed culottes and a shirt that looked to Steph as if it were made of pure silk.

'Yes, can I help you?' she said in a brisk manner.

Oldroyd explained who they were.

'I see. Well, come in, but you'll have to be very quiet. She's having a lie-down on the sofa in the sitting room. I'm Henrietta Williams, her daughter. I arrived about an hour ago and she was in a dreadful state – very anxious and a little confused. It's an absolutely appalling business. I can't imagine who on earth would want to kill my father. He was a fine man – brilliant career, highly respected. Anyway, I'm going to have to stay here for a while. There's so much to do and Mummy just can't cope with arranging the funeral and everything. I need to take her to Harrogate to register the death and, well, there's just so much to decide and to do!' She threw up her hands as if to emphasise what a mess it all was.

'I understand,' said Oldroyd, wondering if he would welcome such breezy efficiency if he were in Mrs Fraser's position. 'We're here to look through Mr Fraser's papers and possessions to see if we can find anything relevant to the case. We may not need to speak to Mrs Fraser. I'll leave my sergeant down here with you to answer any questions you may have. I'd be grateful if you could show me to where Mr Fraser kept his documents and paperwork. Did he have a study?'

'Yes. It's just through here.' She showed Oldroyd through to a rather gloomy room at the back of the house, and then returned to join Steph in a small reception room next to the kitchen.

Oldroyd surveyed the study. There were bookshelves containing legal tomes – obviously a legacy from Fraser's career in the law – and a number of volumes about Scottish clans and tartans. His distant Scottish heritage had been important to him. There were also some books on field sports but there was very little fiction. Clearly he'd been a practical man, not one who valued fancy and imagination.

Oldroyd couldn't find any diaries or anything personal. He opened drawers in the large, old-fashioned desk and scanned through various papers and deeds concerning insurance policies and the purchases of the house and the moor with shooting rights. Everything seemed very mundane and straightforward, so he turned to the computer. There was no password to get in so he browsed through lists of folders and files. This seemed to be the usual kind of stuff: letters, photographs, admin concerning the shoots, and a number of old files about cases Fraser had been involved with in his time as a judge.

Oldroyd felt he was getting nowhere; this man seemed to have nothing suspicious in his past. There was no evidence of womanising, gambling or bitter arguments with family, friends or colleagues. They were still left with only the disputes over the grouse shooting and the fact that Fraser was in debt. Then he tried to open a file called 'P' and was asked for a password. Could the 'P' stand for 'Private'? Here, at last, was something to work with. The computer would have to go back to HQ. The likelihood was that this file concerned financial matters, and that Fraser had put a password on it to prevent anyone, including his wife, from seeing the contents. The details might prove interesting, since they had discovered that Fraser was in debt.

Oldroyd went back through to the front of the house to find everyone in the large sitting room. Mrs Fraser had woken up and was looking rather groggy. Steph and Henrietta were talking quietly. It was an awkward moment for Oldroyd. He didn't want to upset Miriam by telling her that her husband had been in some financial difficulties, but it was his duty to progress the investigation as quickly as he could, so he informed her gently about Fraser's money issues and that the computer would have to be taken away for analysis.

'Well, I hope this is strictly necessary, Chief Inspector,' said Henrietta, adopting a stern expression. 'My mother has been through a lot and what you're saying is very disturbing if it's true. I must say, it doesn't sound at all like my father to be running up debts.'

'Don't worry, Henrietta,' said Miriam. 'I've been expecting this.'

'Have you?' Henrietta looked shocked.

'Yes, I might as well get it over with. I just hope it's not too bad.'

'What made you suspect your husband might be in debt, Mrs Fraser?' asked Oldroyd.

'Sandy looked after our finances, and everything was fine for most of our marriage. Recently, I became aware that he hadn't been paying bills promptly. There were one or two phone calls which I overheard – people asking for money. He also seemed to be a little overenthusiastic about these shoots. I mean, he enjoyed them, but he was organising them for nearly every week in the season, as if he really needed the cash. So I began to wonder.' She looked at Oldroyd directly. 'How bad is it?'

'I couldn't put a figure on it, Mrs Fraser, and it isn't my place to do so. You will have to consult your solicitor. We know that he owed Mr and Mrs Owen at the Dog and Gun quite a substantial sum, presumably because he hadn't paid for all the hospitality related to the shoots. Were you aware of any conflict between them and your husband?'

Miriam shook her head and sighed. 'No, I wasn't. It's sad that he was struggling with this and never told me. I think the problem was that he paid too much for the grouse moor. Buying this house was OK, but the moor was too much. He'd always dreamed of shooting on his own land, but I think he overstretched himself. Sandy wasn't really a businessman.'

'Why do you think he didn't tell you?' asked Steph.

'I think he was probably ashamed. Like my daughter says, it was unlike him to incur debts. He would have justified his silence by thinking that he didn't want to worry me, but I picked up the clues that something was wrong. He obviously didn't expect to die when he did, so I imagine he believed that he would get back on his feet eventually.'

'I'm sure you're right,' said Oldroyd, 'but we'll know more after we've looked at the computer.'

'And now I think that really is enough for one day, Chief Inspector.' Henrietta stood up, indicating that she wanted the interview to be brought to an end. Oldroyd was happy to agree. They needed to return to the inn to talk to Greg Cooper and the Owens again.

∽

At Pateley Bridge police station, Bill Gibbs's frustration continued. There was still no sign of Alan Green, and Gibbs had abandoned the search, convinced that his quarry was no longer in the vicinity. The puzzling questions of his motive and how he had managed to maintain such a low profile in the area remained unanswered.

Gibbs was particularly disappointed because he had such respect for DCI Oldroyd and wanted to create a good impression. He had hoped to make the breakthrough by capturing Green, but his part of the investigation had gone so quiet that he had reluctantly turned his attention to other work.

It was a quiet day, and Gibbs was at his orderly desk clicking through some files in a desultory fashion, when DC Potts came rushing up to his office.

'Sir, a report has just come in,' he said, clearly excited. The desire for progress in the murder case at Niddersgill was felt throughout the station. 'An unidentified person has been spotted behaving suspiciously by a reliable witness. Apparently they were wearing a balaclava on their head and seemed to be looking around warily as if they didn't want to be seen.'

'Where was this?'

'A great place to hide sir: How Stean Gorge.'

'Oh, bloody hell! Right, let's get up there.'

~

'Greg Cooper, Chief Inspector? Can I ask why you want to speak to him? He'll be hard at work in the kitchen preparing for this evening.' Rob Owen looked very concerned.

'We understand Mr Cooper's brother died after a clash with Mr Fraser on the moors a few years ago. We need to question him about that.' Oldroyd and Steph had found Rob Owen in his small office near reception.

'Really? I didn't know that.'

'The man who died was called Sam Cooper.'

Owen put his hand to his mouth and shook his head. 'God, yes. I remember that now, but I never made the connection. It's a fairly common name in these parts.'

'So Cooper never mentioned his brother's death?'

'No, he didn't. He wasn't here when it happened.' Owen was clearly worried, realising that this did not look good for his chef. 'I'll go fetch him.'

'We'll be in the residents' lounge.'

Shortly after Oldroyd and Steph had settled themselves again in their makeshift office, a man appeared. He was tall, in his early thirties, and dressed in a chef's white double-breasted jacket and checkered trousers.

'Mr Cooper?' began Oldroyd.

'Yes.' His tone and expression gave nothing away.

'Please take a seat.'

Cooper perched stiffly on a chair.

'I'm sure you know why we want to see you.'

'I presume it's because of my brother.'

Oldroyd's sharp grey eyes examined the man's face. 'Yes. We know how your brother died, and that a number of people held Mr Fraser responsible. What are your feelings about that?'

Cooper sighed and screwed up his face, which conveyed his feelings for the first time. He seemed to be very reluctant to revisit this topic. 'OK. I don't like talking about this as I'm sure you can understand.'

'Certainly. We're not here to pry into your private feelings, but in a murder case like this we sometimes have to ask difficult questions.'

Cooper nodded and seemed reassured that he was talking to sensitive people. 'I think I'll find it easier to just go through it and explain things.'

'Sure, go ahead.'

'Sam was a few years younger than me. We were brought up in Leeds. He was a lot more academic and always interested in politics. He went to university and we were all proud of him. He was the first person in the family to go. While he was there he got involved with these animal-rights people and started to go on marches. He told me all about it, but I was training to be a chef and learning the standard repertoire. There was a lot of meat involved. Anyway, we disagreed but it didn't come between us.

'Sam went into teaching, and I became a commis chef in Harrogate. Then he got involved with the sabs. I told him he was going too far. I was worried about his safety if he was attacked, or what would happen if he was arrested. He would probably have lost his job. Then . . . you know what happened.'

'Were you still in Harrogate at the time?'

'Yes.'

'And how do you feel about what happened?' Oldroyd asked again.

Cooper took a deep breath. 'It was devastating. My parents will never recover. They blamed Fraser; that was only natural. If I'm honest, I can't really say I think it was his fault. The doctors said that Sam's heart could have packed up any time. It's just that niggling feeling that you wonder if it would have happened if he hadn't been chased like that. Fraser was a big bloke and I'm sure he could be very intimidating. Sam was running to escape. So . . .' Cooper shrugged.

'Did you harbour any harsh feelings towards Mr Fraser? Anything which would make you want to cause him harm?'

'No. I certainly didn't murder him, if that's what you're getting at.'

'You were on late duty here that evening. Can you tell us what you did?'

'There's not much to do. It's just a question of waiting until all the residents have gone to bed, and then checking that everything's secure and in order around the building. We have a little staffroom next to the kitchen and I was in there watching television. I locked the front door just after eleven. I noticed that there were still people in the residents' lounge so I went back to the staffroom. I may have dropped off for a while; it had been a long day. Then I heard a bang which seemed to come from the front of the building. It was after midnight. I went to investigate and saw Rob and two of the shooting party running out of the door so I followed them. Fraser was lying on the ground and there was a lot of blood around. Rob tried to revive him. There was nothing I could do and I noticed one or two residents coming out of their rooms so I went back and tried to reassure them. Then Rob went in and called the ambulance.'

'When the shot was fired, you were in the staffroom.'

'Yes.'

'But there was no one with you?'

'No.'

'And what happened then?'

'When we're on night duty, those of us who live out don't go home. There's a small bedroom for us to stay in. I stayed around for a while until the police and ambulance arrived, and then I was so tired I went off to bed.'

Oldroyd considered all this for a moment and then continued. 'Some people might think it odd that you came to this inn to work when your brother had died nearby, and the man many held responsible for his death was a regular patron.'

'I can see that. Basically, it was too good an opportunity to miss. This place has such a good reputation, and it was a promotion for me. I kept quiet about the whole business with Sam. I don't think anybody here knew I was his brother, even if they knew what had happened to him. I know what you're thinking: I came here to get revenge. If I'd wanted to do that, there were far better ways of damaging Fraser. I could have poisoned his food or wine or something. And, before you ask, I've never possessed a shotgun.'

'OK, Mr Cooper, that will be all for now. Please return to preparing for tonight.'

'What did you make of him then, sir?' asked Steph, when Cooper had returned to the kitchen. 'It still seems very suspicious to me that not only is he working here near to Fraser, but he's on duty the night he was murdered.'

'Hmm, yes, it looks incriminating, but in a way too obvious. If he was the killer, he's almost drawn attention to himself.'

'He had the opportunity to go outside, impersonate Alan Green, kill Fraser, return to the kitchen and change back into his normal clothes.'

'But then we're back to the fact that Green's disappeared, and to conspiracies and so on. We'll have to see what the Owens have to say next.'

~

Greg Cooper went straight back to the kitchen, where a number of inquisitive faces greeted him. Rumours had been passing around the staff ever since he'd been called in to the interview.

'Everything OK, Greg?' asked Harry Newton quietly, as he prepared a sauce.

'Yes.' Greg looked around the room. All the staff were there except Sheila. Maybe it was better if he said something now. 'Look,' he announced, 'Fraser was involved in my brother's death – so the police think I had a motive for killing him. But I didn't. That's all there is to it, OK?'

People nodded and looked a little embarrassed. Nobody said anything.

With a sigh, Greg got back to work. It was a painful business and he hadn't been entirely honest with the police. It was impossible for him not to believe that his brother would still be alive if Fraser hadn't chased him. Since he'd been working in the village and had observed Fraser's arrogance and sense of superiority, he'd hated him even more.

∼

Ian Davis was back at work for the first day since the murder. The atmosphere was strangely muted as he and his team of four men drove up to the moor in a jeep. The usual banter and liveliness was absent. There was silence in the vehicle until they arrived at one of the bothies.

'OK. Let's get on with it then,' announced Ian, trying to sound cheerful. 'We've got to check t'feeders and t'traps. And make sure no dead birds were missed last Friday, that just encourages t'vermin.'

The men got out of the jeep and stood around sullenly with their heads down, scuffing their boots on the ground.

One of them, looking a bit nervous, approached Ian. 'We were all just wondering what's going to happen now, you know, after . . .'

He didn't complete the sentence. Ian looked at them. They were all youngish men in their twenties and thirties who came in from Pateley Bridge. None of them had a permanent contract like him. They were paid on a casual basis and got more hours of work when there was a shoot because they also acted as beaters. He frowned. People didn't realise how difficult it was to find work in rural areas. If they lost their jobs with the estate it would be very hard for them, and some might have to leave Nidderdale and try to find employment in the cities. Some had young families who would be uprooted. He tried to sound optimistic even though he was concerned about his own job.

'OK, I know you're all worried, but th'only thing we can do is carry on. This grouse moor in't going anywhere, and whoever ends up owning and running it'll need it to have been properly maintained. They'll also need workers, and who better than us 'at know it really well?'

There were glum mutterings of 'Yeah' and 'Suppose so'.

'What about t'shoots, though? Are they still goin' to happen?' asked another member of the team.

'I don't know yet. T'next one isn't until next week, but th'estate needs t'brass, doesn't it? So somebody'll have to take over from Fraser. They can't afford to cancel 'em all.'

'Are we goin' to get paid for last week?'

'Why not? I don't think Fraser wa' bankrupt. You've got a reight to that money. Look, we've just got to get to work and show 'em they need us, reight?'

The men looked at each other and some shrugged their shoulders.

'Aye, reight enough,' said one, and they all got themselves ready to work.

Davis sighed inwardly with relief. He'd managed to quell the discontent for now, but there would be a lot more disruption before this matter ended.

~

At the Dog and Gun, Rob and Sheila Owen received the detectives in their private flat. All four sat on sofas in the lounge, which overlooked a small, untidy patch of private garden. The Owens did not have much time for gardening.

'OK,' said Oldroyd. 'I'll come straight to the point. We believe that Sandy Fraser owed you money, maybe a considerable amount. Can you confirm that?'

Sheila looked puzzled and shook her head. 'No, Chief Inspector, I don't think—'

'Yes, it's true,' interrupted Rob, looking sheepish.

'Rob.' Sheila turned to him.

'I'm sorry, love, I didn't want to worry you – you've got enough stress running the kitchen. I thought I should take responsibility for the financial side of things, even if it got difficult.'

'But how much?'

'Forty thousand.'

'What?!'

'He hasn't paid for any of the shooting events for quite some time.'

'But how have we managed?'

'We've got an overdraft at the bank, but don't worry, we'll manage.'

'Rob, what on earth—?'

'I'm sorry to interrupt, Mrs Owen,' said Oldroyd, 'but I must ask your husband some questions.'

Sheila sat back on the sofa and closed her eyes.

'I assume this debt was a source of conflict between yourself and Mr Fraser.' Oldroyd's expression was very direct and his grey eyes were piercing.

'Yes, of course, but I didn't kill him, Chief Inspector.'

'Why did you allow him to build up a debt like that?'

Rob sighed. 'It happened gradually. He started by paying part of the bill and promising the rest later, and it escalated. He was always so nice about it and I always believed I could trust him if he gave his word.'

'But you found that you couldn't?'

'I suppose so.'

'Suppose!' shouted Sheila.

'Look, love, just remember how important he was to us when we first got the contract. Those shooting parties brought in a huge amount of revenue: the lunches, special dinners, overnight accommodation.'

'Apparently they didn't!'

'I know, but we couldn't afford to lose him as a customer. We were trying to build up a reputation here for some of the finest food in the area and the best accommodation. You know how difficult it can be, especially in winter. We weren't really established. It might be a bit different now, but back then we needed the money that we got from those autumn shoots. I was sure that he would pay up in the end.'

'Or did you finally decide that the only way to get your money was from his estate after his death?' asked Oldroyd.

'No,' said Rob firmly, while running his fingers nervously through his hair. 'How would that have worked? If he was struggling financially, his estate may not have had the money to pay off all his debts, so we would never have got it.'

'Maybe,' said Oldroyd. 'But you must have been very frustrated with him and also worried about how you were going to manage, being owed so much.'

'It was a difficult thing to balance.'

'Did you confront him?' asked Steph.

Rob chose his words carefully. 'I made it clear that his credit couldn't continue and he said he understood. He was always so apologetic about it. It was difficult to get angry except when he made criticisms like he did about Sheila last Friday. I thought he had a shocking nerve to say things like that when he owed us money.'

'What did he say?'

'He criticised Sheila's cooking. He could be very demanding and arrogant, but he was hardly in a position to say things like that.'

'So did it make you angry enough to want to harm him?'

'No, definitely not. You've got the wrong idea. Only recently he promised me that he would be able to pay soon. He said he'd accessed another source of money.'

Oldroyd's ears pricked up. 'Did he? And did he give you any details?'

'No. But I didn't think I had any choice other than to believe him.'

'Huh,' grunted Sheila.

'Right. We'll leave that there for now. There is another matter I want to clear up. You said earlier that you didn't know that Greg Cooper was the brother of the man who died on the moor.'

'That's right. We didn't know, did we, Sheila?'

'No,' muttered Sheila, clearly too angry to properly respond.

'Did you ever see him behave strangely or hear him say anything negative about Fraser?'

'No, I didn't. Greg is an excellent worker. Isn't he, Sheila?' Rob was still trying desperately to engage his wife.

'Yes.'

'On that night when you went out and found Fraser lying there, how long was it before Cooper appeared?'

'Not long. I seem to remember he wasn't far behind us.'

'OK.'

It was Rob's turn to ask a question. 'Chief Inspector, can we fully open up the inn again soon? We have bookings and we're losing money.'

'Yes, I don't see why not. We've done all we need to do here,' replied Oldroyd.

He saw how relieved Rob was at this news, but Sheila still had a face like thunder. There was going to be a hell of a row when he and Steph left.

~

At Harrogate HQ, Andy was working hard. Ever since he'd arrived from London some time ago, he'd developed a deep respect for

DCI Oldroyd and always wished to impress him. This was never easy, as his boss was a man who possessed an uncanny ability to solve the most intractable and baffling cases. Nevertheless, Andy always hoped he could uncover some piece of information that would prove vital in an investigation. Here was an opportunity.

His search for the fugitive had proved fruitless: there were too many Alan Greens and it would take months to contact them all. There was also, of course, the strong likelihood that the man the village of Niddersgill knew as Alan Green had adopted that name as a false one to conceal his real identity, which would really make the search fruitless. So Andy had turned his attention to Sandy Fraser and read about his life and career. He'd been born in London to a family with well-defined Scottish ancestry. He had been sent to a boarding school in Scotland and then read Jurisprudence at Melrose College, Cambridge, a college with Scottish connections. Following this, he was called to the bar and entered chambers in London, rising over the years to become a High Court judge. There were details of his marriage, his children and his interests. Shooting had been his primary hobby for many years, mostly on Scottish estates owned by relatives. It was an unremarkable portrait of a member of the Establishment and revealed nothing of note that could be seen in relation to his murder: no public conflicts, divorces or clashes with authority.

Andy turned to a more detailed record of Fraser's professional life. He'd learned from working with Oldroyd on difficult cases that if a motive for murder was not obvious in the present circumstances, there was nearly always something dark from the past which was intruding into the here and now. Random murders by psychotic serial killers, contrary to media-fuelled popular images, were rare. And here at last he discovered something unusual and interesting, although he was not sure there was any connection to Fraser's murder.

Fraser had been the judge in a very high-profile robbery case ten years earlier, towards the end of his career. The Drover Road robbery had made headlines in the media for several weeks, the trial extensively reported on. A gang had broken into a warehouse on an industrial park not far from Heathrow Airport and got away with ten million pounds' worth of money and diamonds. They held the staff inside the warehouse at gunpoint and threatened to shoot them if they didn't reveal the combination numbers of the secure vaults. Matthew Hart, Patrick Wilson and Philip Traynor were arrested three months later.

This was where things got interesting, in Andy's eyes. Hart turned Queen's evidence and received a light sentence in return for destroying the alibis of the other two and divulging all the details of the plan. When passing judgement, Fraser had remarked that Hart, in addition to helping the police, had shown remorse for his actions, while the others, by pleading not guilty, had not. He gave Wilson and Traynor twenty-five-year sentences – which was thought by some commentators to be harsh, given that violence had only been threatened and nobody had been hurt during the robbery. Hart returned his share of the loot, but the others would reveal nothing, so most of what was stolen was never recovered.

Andy enjoyed reading dramatic accounts of daring crimes and the trials that followed, even if it felt like a busman's holiday. One thing that always fascinated him was how clever many of these criminals were. The planning and ingenuity that went into their schemes was amazing. If they'd used their intelligence in a socially acceptable way, many of them could have secured excellent jobs. But the lure of quick money proved irresistible, even though they must have known the odds were against them; it was a form of gambling.

This case seemed to be the only one in Fraser's career that had made the headlines.

Andy got up to make a coffee and failed to resist the temptation to eat just one chocolate biscuit. He smiled to himself: well, when the cat was away . . . !

When he got back to his desk, he continued to examine aspects of Fraser's life and career, but he found himself drawn back to that Drover Road robbery even though he doubted its relevance to their enquiry. Maybe it was just the lure of the colourful and dramatic story. The events in London's criminal world were so far away from a little village in Nidderdale that it seemed crazy to expect to find any connection. However, his boss was always encouraging him and Steph to listen to their instincts. These might prompt you to continue with a line of enquiry before any hard evidence was uncovered. If you had a feeling about something or bells were ringing in your head, it was often a sign that you had subliminally made a connection before you were conscious of it.

Could this case be important to their investigation? It was worth further research.

~

'Well, it's a good job Andy's not with us today. He had enough of caves in that business over in Burnthwaite.'

Oldroyd was driving his old Saab at a fair speed through the ever-narrowing lanes towards the upper reaches of Nidderdale, and they were now about five miles north of Niddersgill. Steph was with him. The fellsides were closer and steeper, with glimpses of the wild country at the head of the dale. They'd been back in the Dog and Gun when the call came from Gibbs about the sighting at How Stean Gorge, and now they were on their way to join him at one of Yorkshire's curious beauty spots.

'Mind you,' continued Oldroyd, 'I would have enjoyed telling him about How Stean: "Yorkshire's Little Switzerland", as it's called, and—' He suddenly stopped and turned to Steph. 'Sorry, I'm mansplaining again. You were brought up round here, so you'll have been to How Stean.'

Steph laughed. Like Andy, she was used to Oldroyd's enthusiasm about Yorkshire, which admittedly did sometimes spill over into mini lectures. But it was a minor fault. 'It's all right, sir. I'm used to you by now. I do remember coming once to the gorge when I was little, and then to do outdoor pursuits when I was at high school. We abseiled down some of the cliffs and did some river walking. It was great.'

'I remember going there when I was a boy in the 1960s,' Oldroyd said. 'We discovered it when we were driving up the dale. A lot of these places weren't well known in those days. It was misty and raining and it seemed so remote, magical and scary, like something out of Tolkien. There was a ruddy-faced farmer with a big moustache taking money for the car park, and then we went over this bridge and looked down! It was terrifying. And right on cue, here we are.'

Oldroyd had been driving up a steep narrow road with high hedges at either side, and then the sign for How Stean Gorge appeared and he turned a sharp right into the entrance.

Gibbs was waiting and came to the car window. 'Hello, sir. Probably best to go over the bridge and park in the bottom end of the field. I'll update you then.'

'Fine,' replied Oldroyd, and he drove slowly over a bridge that looked as if it were spanning a stream or small river, which indeed it was, except that the water was a dizzying seventy feet below at the bottom of a narrow gorge, formed long ago by the collapse of a cavern.

Oldroyd parked up, and he and Steph walked back over the bridge. Gibbs came to meet them.

'Have you found anything?' asked Oldroyd, with a sense of urgency. Perhaps they were making some progress at last.

'No sir, not yet. We had a call from someone working in the cafe.' Gibbs pointed over to a building which had recently been refurbished with a glass viewing platform stretching over the gorge. 'The cafe worker was here very early to start preparations for the day and there was no one else about. From a small window in the kitchen she could see into the gorge, and this figure wearing a balaclava came out of Tom Taylor's Cave, looked to see if anyone was watching, and then walked off on the path downstream.'

'Good Lord!' exclaimed Oldroyd. 'Such goings-on in Nidderdale! What on earth's happening to the place? Have you had a look round down there?'

'I've had a couple of officers go through the cave with torches. The thing is, that cave is one the public go through. It's an easy route – ends up in the car park in the field. I can't see that anyone could really hide in there; there must be some branch off the main cave.'

'Not hidden caves again,' muttered Oldroyd, shaking his head and remembering again the dramatic case he'd worked on with Andy and Steph over in Wharfedale. 'Mind you, it would make a good place to disappear to for a while if you came and went at quiet times.'

'If it is Alan Green, sir, what do you think his long-term plan is? He can't be intending to stay in a cave for very long,' said Steph.

'True, but he might be waiting until he thinks everyone's off guard and then make a run for it, or he may be waiting for help to arrive. What do you think, Bill?'

'I agree with you both. It feels like something temporary, but it may be a kind of bluff: he thinks we've assumed that he's left the area but in fact he's hiding here under our noses. Then, as you say, he'll slip away when things have cooled down.'

'Right, well, no harm in going to have another look. After all, the legend is that Tom Taylor the outlaw hid in there, so it would only be history repeating itself.' Oldroyd rubbed his hands at the prospect. Steph smiled because she knew this was really Oldroyd taking the opportunity to do a bit of dales caving.

Gibbs got torches for them all and they went back over the bridge and through the field to the top. Here, there were steps by the base of a large tree, descending to a cave entrance. Two sheep watched them curiously from a hillock, probably wondering why any creature would be daft enough to go into that darkness. The path went steeply down into a cavern and on into a passage with a high roof and wide ledges at either side.

Oldroyd savoured his return to the strange underworld: the cold earthy smell of mossy rocks near the entrance, with the green fronds of ferns clinging to the wet walls.

Further into the tunnel the light faded, but their torches illuminated the familiar stalactites on the roof, which was ribbed like the belly of a whale. There was the sound of running water and they sloshed through shallow pools as they walked along the bottom of the cave.

They continued to rake the cave roof with their flashlights in the forlorn hope of spotting another cave, and they also looked around for signs of human activity. The tunnel was not long, and soon light ahead of them indicated that they were nearly through. A boardwalk took them the last few yards. They exited the cave halfway down the gorge.

Oldroyd looked down into the stream as a bird fluttered past. It was a dipper that landed on a stone and performed its characteristic bobbing movement.

'Well, I enjoyed that, although we weren't ideally dressed for it,' said Oldroyd, as he noticed their waterproof jackets were covered with dirt and Steph's hair had been streaked with mud.

'Never mind, sir, all in the course of duty,' laughed Steph.

'Yes, unfortunately it didn't tell us very much. We know these cave systems are incredibly complex, so he may have found a hidey hole somewhere off the main passages.'

'Yes, sir,' agreed Gibbs. 'What I'm going to do is set a watch tonight. We've been quite low-key here . . . no uniforms or marked cars . . . so with a bit of luck, this person won't know the police have been here. When he returns, he'll hopefully lead us to his den, wherever it is.'

'Good plan,' said Oldroyd, glad that his days of taking part in such cold and weary vigils were past. 'It's strange, if he did choose this cave which the public walk through. You'd think he'd have chosen somewhere more remote.'

'That could be a useful cover, sir,' replied Gibbs. 'No one expects anyone to hide in there.'

'True. Anyway, tell me how you get on. It will be a big step forward if we can catch Green,' said Oldroyd. 'Let's go for a drink in the cafe, and have a quick catch-up.'

They followed the gorge path as it crossed a bridge over the water and then wound back up to the entrance and the cafe. A group of schoolkids in helmets was abseiling from the road bridge under the supervision of an adult leader. Inside the cafe, Oldroyd went over to the glass floor.

'Well, I haven't seen this before, it's so long since I've been up here.'

'Me neither, sir,' said Steph, and she walked on to the glass. 'Fabulous view down the gorge.' Oldroyd followed her and immediately regretted it; he found the sensation of standing seventy feet off the ground – apparently in the air – very disconcerting, and his legs turned to jelly. He moved back off quite rapidly and Steph laughed.

'What's wrong, sir? You can't fall, you know.'

Oldroyd blew out air and shook his head. 'I know, but it's a weird sensation, isn't it? I've never stood on anything like that before.'

'You should go to the Grand Canyon in America. They have an amazing one there: apparently you're four thousand feet up above the river.'

'Good God!' said Oldroyd, who felt sick at the thought.

'Some friends and I did a bit of a tour round some of the national parks a few years ago. We hired a camper van. It was great fun!'

'I must be losing my head for heights in my old age. Anyway, what do we think of what we've found today?'

Gibbs had brought over three mugs of tea, and they sat at a table well away from the glass floor.

'Well, sir,' said Steph, 'you say you didn't find anything in Sandy Fraser's papers apart from something which probably proves what we already know: that Fraser was in debt. I can't say I think there's anything suspicious about Mrs Fraser or her bossy daughter. Greg Cooper must be on the list of suspects but you were very doubtful that he could be the murderer.'

'Yes. Did you find Rob Owen's account of why he tolerated Fraser's debts convincing?' Oldroyd said.

'Yes, sir, but I'm not sure that his wife did! I wouldn't like to have been him when we left.'

'Me neither, and I agree with you, although we can't eliminate Owen entirely. There is a motive there now: he was owed a lot of money.'

'He must have had an accomplice on the night, unless he performed one of those illusions, sir.' Steph's eyes twinkled mischievously as she reminded Oldroyd of another case they'd worked on together. 'Owen was in his room in the inn when the alarm was raised.'

'Mmm, well, maybe we need to reconsider all that,' said Oldroyd, but he didn't really think Rob Owen was a strong suspect.

There was a pause. Although it had been an interesting morning in many ways, it hadn't actually yielded very much. Oldroyd turned to Gibbs, who had been listening to the update and was now finishing his tea.

'If this business with the cave doesn't prove to be anything significant, do you have any more leads on Green . . . or on anything else, for that matter?'

'No, sir,' replied Gibbs, laconically. 'It'll be back to square one.'

~

'Look, it's good news. The chief inspector said we can open up again.'

'It's not good news that you've kept the fact that we're owed a lot of money from me.'

Sheila was confronting Rob in the privacy of their flat. She was drinking a gin and tonic to try to calm herself as Rob paced up and down. It was more gin than tonic.

'OK, I'm sorry, but I didn't want to cause you more stress. You get enough running that kitchen as it is.'

'Don't you think it causes me stress when I'm made to look an idiot in front of the police?'

'I didn't see that coming. The point is, we'll get the money back from Fraser's estate, I'm sure of it.'

She gave him an odd look. 'Will we? Have you been checking that? It sounds as if you've planned it that way.'

He gave her a furious look. 'What the hell do you mean by that? Are you accusing me of arranging for Fraser to be bumped off?'

'What am I supposed to think? You've obviously been keeping the fact that we've got a big overdraft at the bank from me. Was this your solution?'

'Oh, I've had enough of this. I need to check that Greg's OK after the police spoke to him. I'm going!' Rob marched out and slammed the door behind him.

Sheila drank the rest of her gin and tonic, and burst into tears.

∽

Oldroyd had finally given permission for the people who'd been held at the Dog and Gun to leave Niddersgill. Saunders and Symons were outside the inn with their cases, preparing to drive off.

'This is not before time, I can tell you,' grumbled Saunders, as he placed his case in the boot of his Audi. 'I've missed a whole workday up here, and no proper phone reception either. They'll be going mad at the office. I hope Jeremy's stepped into the breach. Anyway, I'll be straight on the phone when I get down to Harrogate.'

Symons gave him one of his inscrutable smiles. 'Calm down, old boy, you're not indispensable you know. I'm sure the wheels will still be turning without you.'

'True enough, but it's decisions, James, investment decisions – they have to be made all the time. If you get it wrong it can be serious. Where's Rawnsley, by the way?'

'Oh, he skulked off as soon as we got the word, still ashamed of himself I think,' replied Symons.

Saunders shook his head. 'Yes. Anyway, must dash.' He held out his hand and Symons took it. 'What can I say in this situation?

134

It's been good to see you again, but better circumstances next time, I hope.'

'Hear, hear. Safe journey back, then,' Symons said.

'Thanks. And you.'

Saunders got into the car, started the engine, reversed out of the space, skidded forward on the gravel and shot off down the road to Pateley.

Symons chuckled to himself as he continued his own much more relaxed departure. He eventually set off in his vintage sports car, and, as it was another clear and sunny day, decided to drive up the dale and take the road that reared steeply out of the village of Lofthouse, then crossed over the lonely moors to Masham in lower Wensleydale.

When he reached the top of the moors, he heard bangs and saw puffs of smoke. Shoots were taking place in this vast tract of moorland, which stretched in an arc encompassing the heights above Nidderdale, Wensleydale and Wharfedale. He smiled as he reflected on how he might soon be the owner of one of these grouse moors. It could prove to be a very useful earner and would increase his prestige.

The moorland summit levelled out and revealed panoramic views in every direction over the heather, which still retained some of its purple flowers. As was so often the case in Yorkshire, there were unusual sights in the landscape if you looked closely enough.

Down a shallow valley, he caught a glimpse of a round tower: a folly built in the nineteenth century. Standing above a line of crags further on was an eerie-looking structure. It was a high tower in two long sections with a gaping space between them, and it looked like something from an alien landscape or part of a futuristic space-ship. It was actually a sighting tower built to survey the line of a water aqueduct.

Symons was familiar with all these landmarks, but in truth the appeal of these landscapes lay, for him, in their monetary value. Henry Saunders might be a successful London banker, but there was still a lot to be said for the quiet and steady acquisition of land as a path to increasing wealth and status. The more Symons owned, the more he was respected and deferred to in these rural communities. He'd managed his financial affairs very prudently over the years. He received considerable sums in rent from tenant farmers on his land, and had amassed enough capital to consider extending his estate. Now that Fraser was gone, he had the opportunity to possess his first grouse moor, establishing him even more solidly as a key person in the fabric of local life.

The car descended into Wensleydale, past the blue expanse of Leighton Reservoir, and reached the small market town of Masham where a market was in full swing in the large square. Symons turned left and headed further up the dale. He felt that he was entering his domain, as he lived in a fourteenth-century fortified manor house on the edge of a village. This had been in his family for generations. It was absurdly big for just him and his wife now that they had no children at home, but it enhanced his standing considerably.

As he neared the village he caught sight of the squat turreted tower of his residence, built as a defence against marauding Scots. These historical links were all part of the engaging diversity of a local dignitary's identity, he mused, as he turned the car into the large entrance yard of the manor house. It was all very important to him, and he would do whatever it took to protect and enhance his position.

~

Symons had been quite correct to say that Gideon Rawnsley had skulked away from Niddersgill. Once everyone had been released from the inn by the police, he had swiftly bundled his things together and left without a word to anyone. He never expected to return to the Dog and Gun, nor did he want to see Symons and Saunders again.

There was no disguising Rawnsley's relief as he drove down the dale on his way back to Ripon. He was glad that he would no longer be invited to occasions like the shoot, where he could be sneered at by upper-middle-class public-school types for being engaged in trade. He knew that Fraser had only invited him in order to keep him sweet: Rawnsley had allowed him such generous credit.

Sandy Fraser had always been a difficult person to deal with. He had played the role of the wealthy man, buying top-of-the-range vehicles, but actually getting any money from him had not been easy. He was the kind of customer about whom you felt ambivalent: you didn't want to lose them, but sometimes they seemed more trouble than they were worth. Now that Fraser had gone, Rawnsley realised he was glad of the fact. The hassle of dealing with the man had outweighed his value as a customer.

At Pateley Bridge, Rawnsley turned left and followed the road to the north-west of Brimham Rocks, across the moor, past the edge of Fountains Abbey and into Ripon. He lived on the Harrogate side, so he drove through the city past the big market square, then down the hill with the beautiful minster on his left. It felt good to be home. He would call at his house briefly to drop off his things and then go to work. He smiled; things had worked out very well in the end.

～

In the afternoon, Oldroyd and Steph went to interview Peter Gorton, the last of the group who had been at the bar with Alan Green and had witnessed some of the events on Friday. After this, there was no one left in the village who could provide any useful information about what had happened that night.

They found Gorton behind the counter in his shop. Oldroyd noted with approval the wide range of Gorton's stock, including some local produce such as jars of honey and some luscious apples. There was even a section selling craftwork produced by local people. Oldroyd liked to see local shops surviving in small communities.

He introduced himself and Steph, and then asked Gorton what he remembered about Friday evening.

'It was a fairly ordinary night in the bar,' Gorton said. 'The usual people were there: Alan, Wilf . . . Ian came in later. I'm sure you've spoken to them all.'

'We have. Everyone except Alan Green,' replied Oldroyd.

'The shooting party were there, and Fraser came in wearing his kilt – that caused some laughter.'

'He wasn't popular, was he?'

'No, and neither were those obnoxious types in his shooting parties. Actually, we were wondering that very night how the Owens put up with them and some of their behaviour, but of course they were very lucrative – if Fraser paid them.'

Oldroyd smiled. In the light of what they now knew, that was a shrewd observation by Gorton.

The man continued. 'He could be haughty and anyone who had any money dealings with him said he was mean, and I've heard he didn't pay his bills on time. I had no problems with him or his wife, but then they only came in here to buy things like milk and newspapers. I don't think it helped that he was a posh "comer-in". The previous owner of the manor house and the grouse moor was a local man. I'm a comer-in myself, but I'm a bit more ordinary.'

'So, tell us what happened at the end of that evening.'

'The bar slowly emptied. Ian and Wilf went home, leaving Alan and myself. We were finishing our last pints. Then Alan said goodnight and left.'

'Did he seem different or odd in any way?'

'No, just his usual jolly self. I was the last person in the bar. I remember the inn was quiet. Then I left, walked over here and went to bed. It would have been about ten past eleven.'

'Did you see or hear anything unusual?'

'No.'

'How long have you lived in the village?' asked Steph.

'Nearly four years. You soon get to know everybody when you're doing this job. And all the gossip. But I'm sorry, I haven't heard anything that would be useful to your investigation.'

'A pity,' replied Oldroyd. 'Did you know anyone who might have had a motive for wishing to harm Mr Fraser?'

Gorton shook his head. 'No. Ian Davis didn't like working for him. Alan Green did some jobs for him and said he was a mean sod, but I couldn't imagine either of them killing Fraser, despite what Kirsty says. We've all heard about her seeing Alan Green with the gun. Could she have made a mistake?'

'Possibly,' said Oldroyd.

'There were also those animal-rights and green campaigners: Tony Dexter and Liz Smith. Fraser got on their nerves too, but again I can't see them committing murder.'

'No,' said Oldroyd wearily. Gorton was only repeating what everyone else had said. There was no new information. He decided to wind up the interview.

'I'll let you know if I hear anything over the counter,' said Gorton as they left.

'Thanks,' said Oldroyd. He was too tired and frustrated with the lack of progress to warm to Gorton's little attempt at humour. 'Well, it's been another day in which we've pretty much drawn a blank, apart from a few unconvincing leads,' he remarked with a sigh, as he and Steph walked back to the inn. He was looking down at the ground and slouching along.

Steph had known Oldroyd a long time, and knew that he was susceptible to dark moods on occasion. 'Cheer up, sir. We'll get there in the end. We always do, don't we?'

Oldroyd smiled. 'I suppose so, but there's always a first time. Anyway, let's call it a day and hope for some inspiration tomorrow.'

'You usually regard a difficult case as a challenge, sir. What's wrong this time?'

'Yes I do, I do. I don't know. I can't seem to get my head round this one. I think I'm missing something.'

'You'll crack it, sir.'

Oldroyd laughed. 'Well, it's good to know that my team have such faith in me. Yes, you're right. I have to practise what I preach and be patient. Let's get back to Harrogate. I'm going to have a relaxing evening watching a film with Deborah.'

'Sounds good, sir.' Steph smiled to herself. It seemed she'd said the right things and succeeded in boosting her boss's mood.

∾

Rob and Sheila Owen were making up after their row. Sheila sat on the sofa, still looking jittery but not drinking alcohol any more. She'd stayed in the flat all day but had now calmed down. Rob was sitting next to her and stroking her hair.

'I'm sorry I said that about you planning Fraser's murder,' she said. 'I don't know what came over me. I was stressed out with what's happened and the police coming back. I didn't know what to think. The whole thing was just overwhelming. When you said all that about Fraser not paying his bills, I thought for a terrible moment they suspected you, and then I wondered about it myself.' She shook her head to dispel the memories.

'Don't worry – it did look suspicious and I should have told you. You had a right to know. I was treating you like a child. The thing is, you're the most important person in this place.'

'Rob! That's not true, it's a team effort.'

'Yes, but you're the key person. If it wasn't for the reputation we've got due to your food, we'd be nowhere. I was trying to shield you from any financial worries so you could concentrate on what you do best.'

'Rob, that's a lovely thing to say, but keeping things from people like that isn't good, is it? Because when they find out, they feel deceived and angry.'

'I know, and I'm sorry, too.'

'Come here.' Sheila pulled him to her and they kissed. 'I don't think you're a murderer.'

They sat together for a while, feeling more relaxed than at any time since the murder. Eventually, Sheila looked at her watch. 'Now look at the time. I'd better get down to the kitchen.' She got up, her mood seemingly more positive. She had thrown off her recent lethargy.

Rob was pleased that she seemed to have regained her enthusiasm, and followed her back into the inn where he was due for a stint on reception.

∼

That evening, Oldroyd and Deborah were sitting on the sofa in Oldroyd's apartment watching a film.

'Well, I enjoyed that,' announced Deborah as the drama finished and she took a sip from her glass of wine. 'I'm glad they got back together in the end. I'm a sucker for a romantic ending. How about you? Jim? Oh, here we go again. Jim! Wake up!'

Oldroyd snorted, started and sat up. 'What? Oh dear!'

'I asked you if you liked the ending.'

He ruffled his hair and yawned. 'I have to confess I didn't see it.'

'What was the last thing you saw?'

'When there was that fight in the hotel and the police were called.'

'That was ages ago! You must have been asleep for nearly an hour! Great company you are. I thought you were quiet because you were absorbed in the action.'

'Sorry,' said Oldroyd, looking sheepish. 'It's been a tiring day.'

'Maybe,' said Deborah thoughtfully, 'but that's not the only problem. You've got nothing but work to occupy your mind, so when you're not there your brain packs in. You're getting stultified. You need something creative to balance all this struggling with puzzles – something where you can relax, go at your own pace.'

'I like my music.'

'Yes, but that's passive. You need something where you can engage your mind in a different way and produce something.'

'Such as?'

'Well, you're a literary type, aren't you? But you've never told me about any writing you've done yourself.'

Oldroyd looked up, interested. 'No, that's true. I was thinking yesterday when I went to see that artist bloke in the village that it would be nice to portray the dales landscape. I can't paint, but I could do it in words. Actually, I used to write a lot of poetry when I was a teenager; mostly dire stuff about the meaning of life or soppy romantic sonnets about some girl I was in love with.'

'I'll bet they liked it.'

'Maybe. I wrote some poetry at university too, but it's so long ago that I'd almost forgotten about it. It's the same old story: once work took over it was fascinating but time-consuming and it pushed everything else out.'

'Well, it sounds to me like it's time you took it up again. I think it'll be very good for you. You told me what your sister said about retirement and she's right. If you don't develop interests in the next few years, you'll leave the job with a vacuum inside you. Work will have taken everything.'

Oldroyd nodded. He felt a sense of discovery. 'You know, I think you're right, about both things. I do need something outside work, and why not return to writing poetry?'

'As long as you don't write a soppy sonnet about me.'

'Oh no, you'd be worth an epic of enormous length.'

'Get away with you!' she laughed, and Oldroyd went into deep thought.

'You know, I think I'm going to write some good old-fashioned descriptive poems. I love Edward Thomas and Hardy, but there's not as much poetry about the northern landscape. One of the suspects we interviewed, a bloke called Dexter – a sort of eco-campaigner and writer – he said he wrote landscape poems and I felt a little pang of envy. I didn't give it much thought at the time but now you've brought it up it sounds exciting.' He felt himself becoming more animated. This felt like the perfect hobby, marrying his need for stimulation and his love of the landscape. 'And I'd want to incorporate some dialect words. We were investigating a case a while back – a body turned up in a pothole, and I found an old book with some nineteenth-century dialect verse about caving in the dales. They were very evocative, those poems.'

Deborah smiled. It seemed she had achieved her purpose.

In Nidderdale it was another fine night. There was a full moon which kept disappearing behind clouds as they moved steadily across the sky. How Stean Gorge was quiet except for a breeze rustling the trees, the occasional night calls of birds, and the sound of the stream at the bottom of the ravine. It was deserted except for three shapes crouching around the entrance to Tom Taylor's Cave halfway down the gorge. Water dripping from the cave roof could be heard falling into pools and echoing in the darkness.

DC Potts and two of his colleagues had been given the job of keeping watch on the cave. They were dressed in black as a camouflage in the darkness. It was tedious work and the September night was getting rather chilly. It was after midnight.

'Bloody hell,' whispered one, blowing on his hands. 'I wish old Gibbs would come and do a stint himself, then he'd know how bloody boring this is.'

'What then?' replied Potts. 'If he found out how bad it was, he wouldn't want to do it again, and we'd get it just the same. Anyway, I expect he did plenty of this when he was a junior officer, and he's now enjoying giving it to his minions to do.'

'Too right,' said the third man. 'I can't wait till I move up the ranks and I can make some other poor sods do the donkey work.'

'Well, you won't, unless you do a good job now.'

'Is this bloke likely to be armed?'

'I doubt it,' replied Potts. 'That would draw attention and it would also be very difficult to manoeuvre in the cave, as we assume there's some kind of narrow, well-concealed entrance to his hiding place. He also wants to come and go as carefully and quietly as possible. We have the element of surprise: we'll overpower him easily, assuming he's by himself – and I think that's highly likely.'

They fell silent for a while. A sheep bleated in the distance and a dipper sped upstream, its white breast the only visible part of its body. The rocky sides of the gorge were black and menacing. They seemed to imprison the officers waiting below.

'How long do you think we should stay if there's nothing happening?' said one, shifting his position to avoid stiffness.

'A while yet,' said Potts. 'No one's going to come unless they're pretty sure that there's no one around, and that means the dead of night.'

At that moment, the black fluttering shape of a bat passed at speed just over their heads and disappeared into the cave.

'Bloody hell, that was another! Spooky little things, aren't they? I wouldn't—'

'Quiet!' whispered Potts urgently. 'I can see something. Everybody to the hiding places.'

One man moved swiftly into the mouth of the cave and crouched behind a rock, and another stepped off the path and hid at the back of a bush. Potts went behind a tree, from where he could peep out and see what was happening. A figure was walking slowly and quietly up the path by the stream towards them. Potts saw the glow of a small torch. As the person got nearer, Potts saw that they were wearing a balaclava. It was clearly the figure that had been identified by the witness. When they reached the mouth of the cave, Potts shouted, 'Go!'

It was over in seconds. As the three detectives pounced from different directions, there was no escape for the newcomer. Potts produced a torch of his own, ripped off the balaclava and shone the light on their face.

'Shit!' he exclaimed, and threw the balaclava on to the ground. 'Ryan Gomersall. I might have bloody known.'

'I haven't done nowt.'

'Oh really? Well you must have done something, then.'

'Eh?'

Potts was frustrated and disappointed. 'OK. You'd better show us where you're hiding the stuff, because if we have to find it ourselves, you're in big trouble. We might even arrange for you to have a little accident. Poor man, he fell into the stream in the dark and knocked himself out. It was his own fault for coming here in the middle of the night. It's a dangerous place, How Stean Gorge, isn't it?'

'You wouldn't.'

'Don't push us.' He came close to Ryan's face. 'Now, where is it?'

~

At the moment of Ryan Gomersall's apprehension, Kirsty Hemingway was standing at the same window as she had on the night of Sandy Fraser's murder. She had recovered sufficiently from that trauma to be sharing her bed with Harry again, but the shock had disturbed her sleep patterns. She felt some weird compulsion to look through that window and down to the scene of the crime.

All the hotel lights were off and it was much darker than on that fateful night. Was it only four days ago? It felt like four months.

As the moon came out from behind the clouds, she could just make out the place where the confrontation between Fraser and his killer had taken place. She shuddered and turned away. A cool breeze came through the window and ruffled her thin nightshirt. She didn't believe she would ever forget the sound of that shot and the sight of the blood splattering on to the ground. Even worse was the image of Alan Green's face: not angry or threatening, but smiling at her – yes, smiling.

She glanced over to the spot again, half expecting to see that eerie face. The smiling face of a murderer. It was the stuff of nightmares and ghost stories. Suddenly she shut the window and rushed to join Harry in bed, cuddling up to him for warmth and reassurance.

Harry woke up. 'What's wrong?' he mumbled.

'Nothing, go back to sleep.' Harry looked at her, then closed his eyes and almost immediately began snoring. The long hours in the kitchen were exhausting.

Kirsty lay there for a while listening to the wind in the trees and imagining that all sorts of horrible things were out there. There was no news from the police investigation, and they had not caught Alan Green. She had the feeling that further unpleasant things could happen in the village, and the idea kept her awake for some while longer.

Four

Bracken Pot Wood
Outgang Hill
Darnbrook Cowside
Greenhaw Hill

Oldroyd did not sleep well that night, despite his relaxing evening. He found himself turning over the details of the case in his mind and, when he did drop off, he woke up again very early in the morning. He decided to get up and go into Harrogate HQ early.

His appearance caused some raised eyebrows, as he was not known to be an early riser. Unfortunately, his efforts went unrewarded as Gibbs rang with the bad news that the mystery figure at How Stean Gorge was not the person they were looking for.

'Turns out it was just a drug dealer, well known to us, with plenty of form. He was using the cave to hide his stash. He's a young local chap and knows the area. He'd managed to find a small opening in a dark corner high up in the cave, which led to a small chamber ideal for hiding illegal drugs wrapped tightly in plastic bags against the damp. Those caves never cease to amaze me – there's always something new to discover, isn't there?'

'Yes, I know all about that,' replied Oldroyd, remembering yet again the dramatic case he and his team had investigated in the potholes of the limestone area of the western dales.

He was disappointed with this news, but not particularly surprised. He'd not been convinced that Green would hide in a cave. Green had gone – disappeared, almost as if . . . as if what? An idea was forming in his mind, but as yet he couldn't define it.

'Right. You may as well continue a low-level search for Green, but I think you're right: he's fled the area. I assume you've put out information to other forces with the description such as we have?'

'I have, sir.'

'Good. Well, why don't you follow up on firearms licences? Did Green have a licence for the shotgun he used to kill Fraser? If it was him. Has anyone reported any guns missing or stolen? It might tell us something.'

'Yes, sir. That was next on my list.'

Oldroyd rang off and then sighed. Gibbs was a stalwart and dogged officer, and Oldroyd knew he'd given him an almost pointless task. The truth was that they were struggling. He comforted himself by remembering that it was still early days, but nevertheless this case had a strange feel and it had so far completely defeated them.

∼

Henry Saunders was relieved to be back in London and at the desk in his plush office. He sighed as he looked out of the window at the towering office blocks of the City. The grouse moors of Nidderdale and the shocking events of Friday evening already seemed very remote. He felt a sense of relief. The truth was he had made a rather fortunate escape and nobody had suspected anything.

Saunders had a senior position in a venerable old firm of merchant bankers, which paid him handsomely. His wealth had been well known to everyone including Sandy Fraser. Saunders frowned at the memory. Sandy: his old friend from school. They'd always got on very well, as he'd told the police.

But what he didn't tell them was that Sandy had changed in recent years; he'd become much more money-conscious. Saunders shook his head. He knew what the problem was – it wasn't difficult to work out. Sandy had overstretched himself buying that big estate: land like that didn't come cheap. Of course, Sandy would never talk about it, that was bad form. He always conducted himself in a gentlemanly way, even when he'd started to blackmail Saunders.

It was all done in such a discreet and charming manner. It had begun with a chance encounter. Unbeknown to Saunders, Sandy had been down in London, and they'd bumped into each other in a restaurant in Islington. Unfortunately, Saunders had a woman with him who was not his wife. Sandy had seen them behaving rather intimately together before he came over to their table, and Saunders had been forced to introduce his old friend to his mistress. A glance had been exchanged between the two men which confirmed that Sandy now had power over his old friend.

Not long after that, Sandy came to his office and asked him for money. Of course, he was very apologetic and nothing was said directly about the encounter in Islington.

'We all want to keep everything running smoothly, don't we, old boy?' he'd said, and Saunders knew what he meant. He didn't want his marriage to be ruined, so the upshot was that he had regularly handed over quite substantial sums of money to Sandy. The conceit was that the payments were only loans, but both knew that there would never be any repayments. Luckily Sandy never asked for more than Saunders could afford. He was careful not to push things too far.

After the murder, Saunders had decided that this sordid business needed to be kept out of the investigation, and so he'd denied any knowledge of Fraser's money problems. He didn't think they would be able to link anything to him as he'd always made sure that the payments were made in an anonymous manner. He'd had no difficulty in maintaining a confident demeanour when lying to the police.

So that was that. He smiled. Sandy, his old friend, would not be asking for any further payments. He turned his attention back to his desk and to the task, as he'd explained to Symons, of making decisions. The decisions, if correct, that would bring in yet more money.

~

When Andy and Steph arrived at work, they found their boss sitting in his office deep in thought.

'Morning, sir,' said Andy. 'We don't usually find you here so early.'

'No. I couldn't sleep. The pressure must be getting to me. I've just had Gibbs on the phone; that business in How Stean Gorge turned out to be a false trail, a local dealer hiding his supplies.' Oldroyd sat back in his chair and yawned. 'That means we're back at the beginning again: no sign of Green; lots of other people with possible motives but nothing very convincing.'

Steph put the coffee on, but there were no biscuits. She had recently noticed that they became depleted in her absence, and so now she had made them available strictly for special occasions only. They were locked in a cupboard and Steph had the key. Her male colleagues needed to be protected from themselves!

Andy tried to introduce something positive by reporting on his research of the previous day. 'Do you remember the Drover Road robbery, sir?'

'Yes, that was over ten years ago, wasn't it? It made a big splash in the press. It was very well planned and daring if I remember rightly. I don't think they ever recovered the money, did they? Why do you ask?'

'Fraser was the judge in the case.'

Oldroyd raised his eyebrows. 'Was he now?'

'Yes. I was researching Fraser's career yesterday while you were up at that gorge or whatever it was, and that was by far the most famous case he was involved in. I can't find any link with his murder but I keep wondering if it might be important somehow.'

'How do you mean?'

'Well, the sentences that Fraser handed out were pretty stiff, given that no one was hurt, so that could have caused those convicted to be angry and resentful.'

'So that would be a powerful revenge motive for killing him,' said Steph, handing round the coffee.

'Thanks,' said Andy. 'Yes, but there's a big problem with the idea.'

'Go on,' said Oldroyd with interest.

'Well, of the three, Matthew Hart was given a new identity through witness protection and a light sentence, so he doesn't have any grudge against Fraser. Philip Traynor hanged himself in jail four years ago, and Wilson's dead, too.'

'What happened to Wilson?'

'Another bit of drama. This was in Manchester. He'd been in prison there, but escaped during a prison transfer. He managed to get away from the security officers as they were trying to get him into a van. Anyway, there was a chase through the streets and he ended up falling in the river and was drowned.'

'I vaguely remember something about that. So those who might want revenge on Fraser are not alive to seek it?' asked Oldroyd.

Andy shook his head. 'No, sir. It doesn't look like it.'

'What about their families or their friends in the criminal world?' asked Steph.

'That's what I was thinking,' continued Andy. 'But it's a bit far-fetched, isn't it?'

'Hmm. I don't know,' replied Oldroyd. 'The families and friends never got those men back, and I do remember there were some questions asked about the sentences at the time. Those families would have blamed Fraser, thinking that Traynor killed himself because he couldn't face the long sentence. And then Wilson died trying to escape from it . . . Yes, it's all conjecture without much evidence, but I think it's worth pursuing. Let's face it: we don't have much else at the moment. See if you can find out more and let's see what emerges.'

'Right, sir.' Andy went back to his computer in the general office.

'Revenge for something like that would be a powerful motive for the murder, wouldn't it, sir?' said Steph.

'Yes. Far more convincing than any of the motives we've heard about so far. I think we've only scratched the surface of this case, but at least Andy's found something interesting. It's probably a good idea if you stay and help him with the research. There's not much else to do – we're in the doldrums.'

'Right, sir.'

'I'm going back up there. I'll call on Bill Gibbs and then I'm going to do a Holmes walk.'

Steph laughed as she went to join Andy in the office. This was her boss's code for ruminating on the difficulties of a case while walking in the countryside.

∽

At the top of Evershaw Fell on the opposite side of the dale from Fraser's grouse moor, armed men were gathering and the shotguns were about to start blasting again. Land Rovers were parked on a nearby track and beaters were moving into position. They were all being watched by figures lying very low and still in the thick, deep heather.

'Wait until they get into position at the butts,' whispered Liz Smith to the other three sabs hiding near to her. They were all dressed in camouflaged clothing. One was taking furtive glances behind them.

'The beaters are over there – they're going to drive behind us and to the left.'

Several hours before anyone else had arrived, the sabs had placed themselves in a position between the route of the beaters and the butts. Their aim was to disturb the grouse before the shooters were ready, and before the beaters could deliver them up in batches to be shot. Once they'd sent the birds up into the air, the grouse wouldn't return to that patch and the shoot would be ruined.

Liz was watching the men in their expensive jackets and trousers as they separated into small groups and took their places at the butts.

'Right, they're ready – the bastards!' she hissed. 'Joe, what's happening behind?'

'They're starting to move.'

'OK.' Liz waited a few seconds and then shouted: 'Go!'

At this signal, all four sabs stood up and ran in different directions, shouting, hooting and waving their arms around. Grouse sprang up all around them and flew away from the target area. Their cries filled the air, but this noise was soon joined by angry shouts from both shooters and beaters. The latter began to chase the sabs, who zigzagged across the heather to the right and left, trying to outrun their pursuers. Liz was being chased by a burly bearded man who was not very fast. She could have escaped but she caught her foot on a tough heather root and fell over heavily. She tried to scramble to her feet, but her ankle was painful and wouldn't bear her weight. In a few seconds the man was on her, dragging her to her feet and forcing her arm behind her back.

'Get off me, you bastard!' she screamed. 'You're going to break my arm.'

'I'd like to break more than that, you meddling bitch,' said the man from between gritted teeth. 'We've seen you here before – I'm sick of the lot of you. This time we've got you. You'll be done for trespass.'

'Trespass, my arse. You'll be done for assault, more like, if you don't let me go.'

'Aggravated trespass. You're coming to the Land Rover with me and we're calling the police.'

'We have to trespass to save the birds you want to slaughter.'

'Do you now? Who says you have the right?' He tightened his grip on her arm. Liz thought about kicking and struggling, but it was pointless; she couldn't run away with her ankle in this state. Sullenly, she allowed the beater to lead her, limping, over to where the Land Rovers were parked.

A large group of angry beaters and shooters had gathered there. Another sab, a slightly built eighteen-year-old called Max, had also been caught by two beaters. Blood was streaming from his nose and mouth and he was being virtually dragged along, bumping across the heather. The others had escaped.

'Let him go, you bloody cowards!' shouted Liz. 'He's only a boy.'

'He's old enough to break the law and be a bloody nuisance like the rest of you,' called back one of the beaters. 'Here, you, stand still!' Max had started to struggle and the beater hit him over the head with his beating stick.

This provoked fresh outrage in Liz. 'You bastards! Don't worry, Max, I'm a witness. Just like you lot, isn't it? Blood sports – anyone's blood. Look at his face! I can't tell you how glad I am that one of your type got what he bloody well deserved last Friday! Especially as he had blood on his hands too.'

This in turn offended a group of shooters who'd come over from a nearby butt to see what all the fuss was about. 'Are you referring to the murder of Sandy Fraser?' asked one, looking at Liz with withering contempt.

She glared at him. 'Don't think we've forgotten about Sam Cooper.'

The shooter loomed over her, still holding his gun. 'Well, not only is that in extremely bad taste, but I think the police might well be interested in what you've just said. You clearly hate us enough to do something extreme.'

'You can say what you damn well like to the police,' replied Liz, as she was bundled into the Land Rover. 'I'm already a suspect and I told them we fight to stop killing – we don't do it ourselves.'

The shooter came to the window, his face red with anger. 'Don't take that high-and-mighty position with me. You're nothing more than a common criminal, trespassing on people's land and interfering with lawful activities. You ought to be—'

Liz didn't hear any more as the vehicle set off. She sat in the back with her arms around young Max, who was stunned and silent, and tried to wipe the blood from his face with a tissue. The men in the front said nothing. She smiled. Two of them had been caught, but the shoot had been successfully sabotaged so it was mission accomplished. Often you had to suffer for what you believed in. As for her opponents: she meant what she'd said about Fraser. Sometimes bad things had to happen on the way to achieving a higher good.

⁓

As the Land Rover passed through the village, Jenny Davis watched it go past. She was talking to David Eastwood, who was on his rounds. His red van was parked by the green.

'I'm sure that was Liz Smith in the back of that Land Rover and it belongs to the Evershaw Fell shoot. I'll bet she's been up there with her cronies making trouble and they've caught her. Good for them. That lot are always making trouble for my Ian.'

'It looked like her. I wonder if they're taking her down to the police station. She'll kick up a right fuss.'

'Yeah, well, maybe she won't be so keen to be a bloody nuisance in future if the police give her a good talking-to.'

'I wouldn't be so sure. Anyway, you're looking very nice today. I like that skirt.'

'Thank you.' Jenny was well aware of Eastwood's reputation and always remained aloof from his flirtatious comments.

'He's a lucky man, your husband.'

'He knows that. Would your wife like to hear you say that? Never mind Theresa Rawlings.'

Eastwood laughed nervously and saw that he wasn't getting anywhere. 'OK, well I'd better be getting on – good to see you. A pretty face always brightens up a man's day.'

She still didn't respond positively, so he hitched up his postbag and headed off to a row of terraced houses across the green. The nerve of the man, thought Jenny as she continued on her way to the shop. Some people had no shame.

She enjoyed popping over to Gorton's shop. When you had a hungry young family you often ran out of bits and pieces before the weekly shop in Pateley, and it was a chance to meet and chat with people.

As she opened the door, a bell sounded and Gorton appeared behind the counter. 'Morning, Jenny, what can I get you?'

'A carton of orange juice and a tin of baked beans, please. I'm always running out of beans. The kids love them on toast with cheese on top.'

'Sounds good to me. When can I come to your place for tea?'

Jenny laughed as Gorton went to get the milk and beans. Then: 'They've arrested that Ryan Gomersall again,' she said.

'Have they?'

Jenny continued as she handed over the money. 'Yes. I had a call from our Anne this morning. She lives down in Pateley. Her husband Mark was in the pub last night with a mate of his who's in the police. News travels fast round here.'

'You're not kidding,' said Gorton.

'He's always been in trouble, that lad, ever since he was a teenager. Apparently a team of police arrested him in How Stean Gorge during the night – he was hiding drugs there.'

'Good lord! They must have had a tip-off.' Gorton frowned, and then looked thoughtful. 'I wonder . . .'

'What?'

'Why would they mount a night operation like that just to catch a local bloke hiding some drugs? Maybe a person was seen at How Stean and the police thought it was Alan Green. They might have been disappointed to find it was Ryan.'

Jenny shivered. 'Oh, I don't know, you might be right. It gives me the creeps that there's a murderer on the loose. I just hope they catch him soon and it's all over and done with. At least Ryan Gomersall wouldn't kill anyone. Anyway, must be off. Bye.'

As she walked back to the cottage, she felt gloomy again. She knew it was silly to suspect Ian, but she would never be able to rest completely until the murderer had been found. She thought about her conversation with Gorton. It had brought everything back to her again, and now another thought came to her: it seemed odd that Gorton knew so much about that police operation. What was going on there? Or was she imagining things?

She shook her head. In this tense and suspicious atmosphere, your imagination could easily run away with you.

~

After making a brief visit to Pateley Bridge station to encourage Gibbs, who had found no reports of stolen shotguns, Oldroyd put on his walking boots and headed down the path at the side of the River Nidd to the village of Glasshouses, where he was pleased to see the huge mill complex being converted into apartments. The weather was holding and it was a clear, still day, with some remnants of early-morning mist at the top of the fells.

Oldroyd crossed the river in bright sunshine and followed a path upwards across the green fields with their dark gritstone walls, and entered Guisecliff Wood. This was a stretch of ancient woodland that clung around a steep and long stony edge: the eponymous cliff after which the wood was named.

This was one of Oldroyd's favourite places in the dale. It contained many unusual features, from Bronze Age rock art to an unexpected and beautiful tarn hidden among the trees. In spring it was dense with bluebells and the sound of birdsong. Today it was full of the melancholy quiet of early autumn but no less beautiful, as the first leaves fluttered down from the trees and the colours of the foliage started to become more varied.

Oldroyd walked up through the woods and followed a twisting path until he reached the top of the ridge. He found a spot to sit from where he had a wonderful sweeping view of the dale from Gouthwaite Reservoir, beyond Pateley, down to the outline of Brimham Rocks. He was intending to think about the case, as he'd told Steph, but was also taking this opportunity to make a start on his new hobby: writing. He took out a notebook and a couple of Ordnance Survey maps, then he looked out over the magnificent scene. Descriptive poems celebrating landscape were common, but difficult to write without resorting to clichés. He got out the maps and saw how many unusual names for fields, summits, woods, rocks and moorland there were in the dales area. It was a wonderfully evocative language. You could feel its Viking age and its Yorkshire eccentricity and strangeness.

He started to copy some of them down in his notebook and realised he was writing a poem, just by arranging the names in verse form and creating a rhythmical pattern that was also very alliterative:

> Crutching Close Laithe
> Yarnthwaite Barn
> Hawkswick Clowder
> Pikesdaw Barn
>
> Stony Nick Crag
> Low Dowk Cave
> Dumpit Hill Moss
> Swinsto Cave
>
> Tommy Hill Pasture
> Outgang Hill
> Darnbrook Cowside
> Greenhaw Hill
>
> Numberstones End
> Lumb Gill Wham
> Seavey Crook Bank
> Lower Wham

When he read it back, he realised that he'd liberated the poetic potential of the names, and those four stanzas were just a start! It was exciting, and he spent the next hour or so constructing a long poem that read like an incantation celebrating the places of the moors and dales. It was very absorbing. Deborah was right: this creative activity was going to benefit him.

He was still immersed in his composition when he heard a voice behind him. 'Chief Inspector? Is that you?'

He turned to see Tony Dexter smiling at him. He was dressed in boots, walking trousers and a jacket. He held a pair of binoculars.

Oldroyd stood up. 'Yes, Mr Dexter. You've stumbled on me at an off-duty moment. I was just enjoying the view from here and doing a bit of writing.'

'Really?'

'Yes, and you must take a bit of credit. When you talked about your poems the other day, it inspired me to do some writing myself. I've always intended to but I'm sure you know how work can get in the way.'

'Oh, I do, Chief Inspector. I used to have a very time-consuming job, and I went through some difficult times.' He looked into the distance and frowned, as if contemplating some painful memories. 'It's very hard to concentrate on writing or any other creative activity when you're feeling stressed.'

Oldroyd showed him part of his poem. 'It feels a bit of a cheat,' he said. 'You know, just using place names.'

'Well, I don't know,' replied Dexter. 'I think it's very effective. After all, you're only using the names like you would any other parts of the vocabulary to construct a poem.'

'I suppose so.'

'Look, I'm walking across to the folly, do you fancy coming along? Don't let me interrupt you if you're still writing.'

'No,' said Oldroyd. 'I was about ready to leave.' He put the maps and notebook away and the two men walked along the top of the cliff, Oldroyd noticing that, in places, there were some sheer drops down into the woods below. You had to keep to the path and watch your step.

The folly to which Dexter had referred was Yorke's Folly: two stone columns built in the early nineteenth century as a work-creation project by the eccentric landowner John Yorke, of nearby Bewerley Hall. There had originally been three columns, but one blew down in a gale in Victorian times. The remaining structures looked out over the dale and formed a strange local landmark.

Oldroyd and Dexter reached the site and sat on a bench behind the folly.

'They're clearly made to look like a Romantic ruin,' remarked Oldroyd, as he traced parts of the structures that falsely suggested they'd once formed an arch.

'Yes,' replied Dexter. 'I suppose it was part of that landscape trend for creating faux-Romantic ruins which they thought enhanced the landscape. Have you seen Hackfall?'

Oldroyd had indeed visited that extraordinary collection of follies, grottoes, cascades, lakes and a fountain built in the eighteenth century in the Ure Gorge in Wensleydale. He felt he had much in common with Tony Dexter, and they chatted for a while about Yorkshire landscapes and history as they walked back down through more woods.

'Have you seen the ice house with the cave spiders?' asked Dexter as they were passing through a wooded area which had once been part of an estate attached to a large house. Oldroyd had to confess that he hadn't, so they took a diversion from the path up to the structure set into the hillside. From the door, there was a short stone-built tunnel to the huge cylindrical brick-lined chamber where the ice had been stored. Dexter pointed out the large

European cave spiders, *Meta menardi,* their white egg sacs hanging from the roof of this tunnel. Oldroyd was fascinated.

'It's amazing how they live in this dark and wet place, isn't it, and manage to find enough food?' he said, and Dexter agreed.

Their walk eventually concluded back in Pateley Bridge.

'Well, it's been very pleasant, Chief Inspector.'

'It has indeed,' replied Oldroyd. 'Do you need a lift back to Niddersgill?'

'No. I have my van here. I may see you again up there in the village. I'm glad you enjoyed the ice house and the spiders. Don't forget it; it's a special place.' Dexter walked off with a wave and Oldroyd watched him go. It had, of course, not been strictly professional to spend time with a person who remained a suspect in the case, but Oldroyd tended to ignore those kinds of rules if he felt like it.

In this case he felt justified because when Dexter had described the ice house as a special place, he'd looked at Oldroyd very directly in a meaningful way.

Was he hinting at something that he couldn't or didn't want to spell out?

~

John Gray was at work in his studio in Niddersgill. His latest canvas showed a wide panorama of the windswept top of the dale with the ancient village of Middlesmoor hugging the high fellside. But he was painting without enthusiasm. The truth was, he was getting a little tired of painting local landscapes in order to make a living. He'd always known his stay in a comparatively remote rural village would be temporary, that he'd want to return to the city after a while. He was starting to feel that it would not be long before his work was done out here, and he would need a change: a change of environment and a change of subject for his art.

He stopped for a moment and looked out of the window, which commanded a view of the fells. He loved the wild upland scenery, but restlessness was part of his nature. He was ready to return to the anonymity of an urban environment, at least for a while.

His reflection was interrupted by the sound of the door opening. Henrietta Fraser entered the studio.

'Ah, John! Nice to see you again.'

'Yes, Henrietta, come in – you've not been up here for a while.'

'No, and obviously it's not in the best of circumstances now, as you'll appreciate.'

'Of course. How is your mother?'

'Oh, as well as can be expected, as they say. It was a terrible shock.'

'It must have been. Please send her my regards.'

'Thank you. I will.' She turned towards the paintings on display in the gallery section. She always visited Gray's studio when she was in Niddersgill and often bought something to take back with her to London.

'It's such a relief to come over here, I can tell you. My mother needs a lot of attention and after a while . . .' She shook her head. 'It wears you down. I needed a break.'

'You know you're welcome here any time.' Gray enjoyed Henrietta's infrequent visits. He felt she was a more discerning customer than many of the tourists who wandered into the studio.

'You have been busy,' she remarked as she walked through the gallery. 'When was I last here?'

'It was Christmas I think.'

'Yes, and I love that snowy winter scene.' She stopped by a painting that depicted the barns, walls and fells of Nidderdale dusted in snow below a heavy grey sky.

Gray got up and went over to talk to her about it and others in the collection. She ended up buying the winter scene.

'I know exactly where I'm going to put it. I have the perfect spot in my hallway,' she said enthusiastically, as Gray wrapped up the framed picture. Henrietta lived in a Georgian terraced house in London.

'I hope you're happy with it.'

'Oh, I know I will be. My father loved your paintings too.'

'Yes.'

'They're still on the walls. My mother likes them.'

'Good. I'm glad about that.'

Conversation flagged a little. Gray was a little embarrassed, remembering that her father had been a difficult customer.

'Well, I'll be off. See you again before too long, I hope.'

'Yes, bye for now.'

Henrietta left clutching her package and Gray, shutting the door behind her, felt a little relieved. He'd considered telling her that he might well not be in Nidderdale for much longer, but had decided against it. However, he felt more than ever that he needed to end his time in the village and move on.

∿

'Get off me!' shrieked Liz Smith, limping badly as she was frog-marched by two burly beaters into the police station at Pateley Bridge. Max, blood oozing from his lips, stayed in the Land Rover guarded by another man. He was still dazed and quiet. Bill Gibbs was talking to the station sergeant as the group appeared. He and his small team had been slogging their way through details of gun licences. It had been very boring and fruitless. He actually welcomed some action.

'OK, let's just calm down,' said Gibbs. 'Let her go.'

The beaters released their hold. The one who had chased her down said: 'This woman was caught trespassing on a private moorland area and behaving in a way which could have caused danger to individuals involved in a lawful activity. We have another trespasser outside in the Land Rover.' The words sounded rote, like a passage he'd been taught to recite.

'Rubbish!' exclaimed Liz. 'The only creatures in danger are those beautiful birds, and from your bloody guns. We never do anything to put people in danger. Who do you think you are anyway, forcing me to come here against my will? You're not the police.'

'It's a citizen's arrest.'

'Citizen's kidnap, more like! Why haven't you brought Max in? I'll tell you why, because he was beaten up and you don't want them to see how violent you are.'

Gibbs, and officers at the station, had dealt with this issue many times before. He was familiar with the two sides of the game-bird shooting controversy and the enmity between them. He addressed the beaters first. 'OK. You can make a statement to the sergeant here, but I warn you: don't take the law into your own hands. You can report a crime if you think one has been committed, but you cannot physically restrain people like this, however angry you are. How was what they were doing endangering you and the shooters?'

'They hid in the heather and sprang out. We could have fallen over them.'

'That's absolute crap!' exclaimed Liz. 'Bring Max in and we'll see who was a danger to who.'

'He got those injuries when he fell over and then he started to attack us.'

'You lying bastard!' shrieked Liz.

Gibbs intervened quickly. 'Right, that's enough.' He addressed the beater again. 'I'm going to send an officer out with you to your vehicle to see if anyone needs medical attention. We'll see what he says about how he got his injuries and we'll take it from there. And remember what I've said.' The beater looked sheepish, realising that it might have been a mistake to bring the sabs to the police station. He went out with a PC.

'Ms Smith – in here, please.' Gibbs indicated his office. They both went in and he shut the door. 'Sit down. That's a bad limp you've got. I take it they didn't twist your ankle?'

Liz remained sullen. 'No. I fell over a heather root.'

Gibbs sat behind his desk and looked at her. It wasn't the first time he'd interviewed her about an incident like this.

'You're never going to stop doing this, are you?'

'No. Why should we? It's a cruel, brutal sport and it needs to be stopped.'

'We've had this conversation before, haven't we? It's not illegal and you are trespassing on those moors.'

Liz shrugged.

'They could bring a civil action against you or even one for criminal damage if they can prove anything.'

'Let them try. We only disrupt them, we never damage anything.'

Gibbs sighed. 'OK, but you're playing with fire, and one day someone's going to get seriously hurt.'

'Someone already has.'

'Who?'

'Fraser got what was coming to him.'

Gibbs frowned. 'And what do you mean by that, exactly?'

Liz smiled. 'Nothing, except he got what he deserved. He lived by the gun and he died by it.'

'That doesn't sound very non-violent to me.'

'He was a violent man himself. You remember Sam Cooper? None of us have been shedding any tears.'

Gibbs looked at her closely. She was clearly very angry and it made him wonder what she might really be capable of in the pursuit of her cause.

~

The next day, Oldroyd drove down the M1. Despite the lack of progress in the Nidderdale case, he was taking time off and going to his daughter's degree ceremony at Oxford. His sister Alison was with him. Louise had managed to arrange guest accommodation for them at her college. The M1 was a motorway he detested, with its heavy traffic and its never-ending roadworks with queues and speed restrictions. At least the purpose of the journey was a good one.

Alison asked Oldroyd about Louise's plans. 'So she's doing an MSt this year?'

'Yes, but I don't know what she intends to do after that. If I know her, she probably doesn't have any idea.'

'Does it matter? I think people of our generation were too quick to enter jobs and professions and stay there for life.'

'Like me, you mean?' laughed Oldroyd.

'Yes, a good example. Young people now try different things and do more travelling. Look at Louise, she's worked in the women's refuge and she's been backpacking round the Far East.'

'And she's paid nothing into a pension scheme,' said Oldroyd facetiously.

'No, but it's very limiting if you're planning at the age of twenty-three for when you're in your late sixties.'

'Some people say there'll be a crisis when the young generation get old and they've nothing to live on.'

'Maybe, but hopefully society will have changed by then, in ways we can hardly imagine.'

'With universal income and stuff like that?' said Oldroyd.

'Why not? We can't go on with our present economic model that is creating huge inequality and destroying the earth into the bargain.'

'I hope you're right. But I get the impression that she's doing a Master's because she can't think of anything else to do. She's very capable, but somehow I can't see her as an academic. She'd never conform to the systems and she'd be forever in conflict with the hierarchies over gender equality, environmental issues and so on.'

'That's what I like about her. She's not afraid to speak out. She'll find her niche eventually, you mark my words.'

Oldroyd smiled. 'Probably. She's so different from Robert and always has been.'

His son had done a degree in engineering at Birmingham, and now lived in the Midlands with his wife Andrea. His was a very conventional life compared to that of his sister.

'You wouldn't want her any different than she is. And it's good, by the way, that you're still coming down to Oxford for this, despite being involved in a tricky case. I can remember the time when you would have sacrificed family events to concentrate on your work.'

Oldroyd winced at the memory. It was the reason his marriage had broken down. Those years of neglect couldn't be changed, and he wondered how many more men of his generation had missed their children growing up due to an obsession with their job. He shook his head to rid himself of gloomy thoughts. Onward and upward, as the saying went. He was starting to change in a number of ways under the influence of Deborah, who was reinforcing the things his daughter and his sister had been saying for some time.

To be honest, Julia had also said the same things but he hadn't listened to her.

'Our personalities are so complex and shifting,' continued Alison.

'I'm not looking forward to Julia being there,' said Oldroyd. 'It's going to be awkward.'

'Maybe, but you'll handle it. Remember, you're there for Louise so we don't want any unpleasantness. Jim?'

Oldroyd had lapsed into a reverie about the past and wasn't listening. He suddenly became more alert as he saw warning lights flashing ahead.

'Oh, not more bloody roadworks! We'll never get there.'

~

At Harrogate HQ, Andy and Steph were hard at work researching the Drover Road robbery, so far without a great deal of success. As Oldroyd had suggested, they were attempting to trace any relatives or close friends of the two men who had received long sentences: people who might have had a grudge against Fraser. Steph was concentrating on Philip Traynor, who'd killed himself in prison, but there was no trace of any family except for an ex-wife who'd divorced him several years before. They'd had a son together who would now be about twelve. Traynor had pages of form, including membership of a number of gangs, and he'd done time for a series of offences.

Steph sat up in her chair and stretched her back and neck.

'Oh, I'm not getting far with this,' she said as she yawned. 'I can't see anyone who would be prepared to take revenge against Fraser on Traynor's behalf.'

'It's a long shot, isn't it?' said Andy, who was working on the computer next to hers. 'I think the boss knows it but he's desperate for a break like the rest of us. I don't envy poor old Gibbs up in Nidderdale, checking on shotgun licences.'

'No. The only thing about Traynor which I find puzzling is why he killed himself. It's not usual for hardened criminals to top themselves like that. They know the game and if they're caught they know they're going down.'

'Something must have got to him. Maybe, as the boss suggested, it was the long sentence.'

'Yes, he had a son who he might have missed seeing, but – I don't know – it doesn't feel right to me. I'm going to look into that with the prison authorities. How about you?' said Steph.

'Like you, no luck with tracing any family for Wilson. He seems to have been a loner. I think we're wasting our time with that approach. I think there are interesting questions about these two characters themselves, never mind any families and friends. Why did Traynor kill himself, and how did Wilson manage to escape like he did?'

'I agree – why don't you contact the prison where Wilson was kept, see if you can find out more?'

'OK, I will. It would be great to present the boss with a breakthrough.'

Steph smiled. 'You always want to impress him, don't you.'

'I suppose so. But he's somebody you feel you want to impress, isn't he?'

'I know what you mean, so let's have a coffee and then get on with it. It might be me that finds the crucial information – I'll race you!'

'No way,' said Andy, reaching over and switching her computer off.

'Andy! Stop it! I might have had things I hadn't saved. Right, no biscuit for you today!' laughed Steph. Andy, however, grabbed the key to the cupboard where the biscuits were stored from her drawer, and she had to chase him round the office to get it back.

~

'God! I thought you weren't going to make it!' Louise looked extremely relieved to see Oldroyd and Alison as they finally arrived at the entrance gate of her college. Oldroyd hardly recognised her, as she was formally attired in the female Oxford academic dress: dark skirt, white blouse, black tights and shoes. She had a black ribbon around her collar and her hair was tied back.

'Sorry, love,' said Oldroyd as he gave her a hug. 'It was the blasted traffic; we set off in good time.' He knew the delay would cause her to be anxious, and would trigger reverberations from the years when she was growing up. During that time he'd missed so many of her activities and performances because of work.

Louise hugged Alison. 'Is that true, Auntie Alison?'

'It is – you'll have to let him off. Anyway, we're here, and it's so wonderful to see you.' There was a special bond between niece and aunt for many reasons, not least because Alison had no children herself.

'Come on,' announced Louise. 'There's a reception in the Dorrington Rooms before lunch. Mum's already there, I left her talking to one of my friends' mothers.' They walked through the porters' lodge, around the manicured lawn of the front quad, and down a passageway to another quad where the ornate door to the Dorrington Rooms was open.

Oldroyd felt nervous as he entered the dark, wood-panelled room. He knew that he would see Julia and, as usual, he didn't know what he was going to say to her. His wife was the only person who could render him inarticulate.

Smartly dressed waiters with trays of glasses containing red or white wine stood at either side of the door, and he and Alison took a glass each. The room was already pretty full with a buzz of conversation. Young people in academic dress mingled with groups of parents. Oldroyd saw the elegant figure of his wife, dressed in a copper-coloured knitted dress and matching light wool coat. She was chatting with another woman and sipping a glass of white wine.

She turned and saw him, but continued with her conversation. It was only when she saw Alison that she excused herself and greeted her sister-in-law warmly.

'Well, you look wonderful, Julia, it's so nice to see you,' said Alison.

'And you too!' exclaimed Julia.

Then she turned to Oldroyd. 'Hello, Jim.' She gave him a peck on the cheek, which he returned.

'Hi,' said Oldroyd. Everything went quiet for a few seconds.

'People are moving into the hall, we'd better follow,' said Louise. 'You can take your drinks with you.'

They walked across the quad and up some stone steps into the dining hall. This long room had an ancient ceiling with wooden beams and there was a large fireplace. The walls were lined with portraits of college rectors and benefactors going back to the college's origins in the fifteenth century. Wooden benches stood on both sides of sturdy wooden tables set with heavy silver cutlery and plates bearing the college crest. Name cards rested by each plate and, to his dismay, Oldroyd found he was sitting next to Julia. Obviously the college staff didn't realise that Mr and Mrs Oldroyd were separated. Oldroyd immediately started to eat his bread roll while Julia was talking to Alison. Louise, sitting opposite, was in conversation with a friend next to her. As he munched, he tried to think of what he might say to Julia when the inevitable moment arrived.

When the smoked-salmon starter came, Alison turned to speak to the person next to her and Julia turned to Oldroyd. 'Well, Jim, I hear you're in a new relationship. How's it going?'

He'd not expected this, and dropped his knife on to his plate with a clatter.

'Very well, thanks. Deborah lives in Knaresborough – she's a psychotherapist.'

'That's interesting. I hope it works out for you.' He noticed that she broke eye contact when she said this. Was she upset about it?

'Thanks. How about you and . . . Peter, isn't it?' Quite a while ago, Julia had turned up unexpectedly at his flat in Harrogate and asked him for a divorce. She was in a relationship with Peter, an art teacher at the sixth-form college where she worked. He'd agreed, but had heard nothing about it since.

'No, that was over a while ago. I'm just on my own again.' She smiled at him.

He'd not expected this either and it unsettled him. He didn't know what to say.

'Oh, right.'

'It's a shame Robert couldn't make it,' continued Julia. 'Couldn't get the time off work. We would have been together as a family again. It's been a while.'

'Yes.' This was very disconcerting. It wasn't like her to get nostalgic for their past family life. She had usually criticised him for overworking and not spending enough time with her and the children.

'And how's work?'

He was glad she'd changed the subject. 'Oh, you know, the usual. Challenging.'

'Are you on that case in Nidderdale where that man was shot outside the pub?'

'That's the one.'

'Well, be careful. I always used to worry when you were on cases where firearms were involved.'

'Yes . . . I will.'

The main course of duck à l'orange, sautéed potatoes and green beans arrived, and Oldroyd was thankful for the distraction. He enjoyed the duck, and the chocolate tart that followed, despite his feelings being rather shaken.

Julia started to talk to the person next to her and he was happy to remain quiet and eat while conversations went on around him. There was also a good pinot noir. Food and drink were always excellent compensations when things became strained and difficult.

After lunch, Louise went off to prepare for the ceremony, and Oldroyd, Alison and Julia walked the short distance through the courtyard of the Bodleian Library to the Sheldonian Theatre.

Again, Oldroyd found himself sitting next to his wife, this time in the gallery of the semi-circular building, as the ancient ceremony, conducted mainly in Latin, took place. It was moving to see their daughter take her degree and get her gown and mortar board. He saw that Julia was having a little weep, and he felt he had to console her by putting his hand on hers. His hand was eagerly accepted and she smiled at him through her tears.

On the way out, they talked about Louise and the different phases of her growing up. Normally Julia would express bitterness about how he'd been such an absent father, but on this occasion she spoke about nothing but positive memories. The general bonhomie remained as they all posed for photographs together and then went for a walk in the University Parks. Oldroyd was glad that the atmosphere was so convivial, but it left him with uncomfortable feelings of a different kind.

∽

Back at Harrogate HQ, Steph and Andy were still working hard to find out more about Wilson and Traynor, two of the Drover Road case criminals.

Steph had contacted Durham Prison, where Traynor had killed himself. The records had revealed little, but she was able to speak on the phone to the prison officer who'd been in charge of Traynor immediately before his death.

'Did he seem depressed?' asked Steph.

'No. If he had, he'd have been on suicide watch,' the officer replied in a strong north-east accent. 'I remember he was very angry, though.'

'What about? Did he think his sentence was unfair?'

'He didn't say anything about that. I remember him shouting something like, "That bastard's not getting it", and he threw things around his cell in a temper. He was a violent man, but he turned it inwards in the end, you know: strangled himself with his sheets tied up to the bars on the window.'

'Who do you think he was talking about, and what was "it"?'

'I've no idea, and he'll not be telling us now, will he?'

Meanwhile, Andy contacted the authorities at Strangeways prison in Manchester, and spoke to an officer who had been involved in transporting Patrick Wilson the day he escaped from custody.

'How did he manage to get away from you?' asked Andy.

'We think he'd managed to make some kind of picklock from a hairpin or something and opened his cuffs. It's not easy; he must have known what he was doing. We kept that low-profile – things like that make us look daft if the press get on to it, but these things happen.'

'I know. So you pursued him?'

'We did. He had the advantage of surprise – he suddenly slid the cuffs off, pushed an officer aside and bolted down the street. He headed towards the River Irwell and we didn't get near him until he was at the river's edge. There was an old pipe bridge and he managed to climb on to it and tried to get over the river. We told him to stop, it was dangerous, but he carried on. When he was halfway across, he slipped and fell into the water. It'd rained and the river was high and fast-moving. He surfaced once but then he disappeared, and that was the last we saw of him.'

'Who identified the body?'

'What?'

'His body. Did one of you identify him, or was it a relative?'

'You've got your facts wrong there, mate,' replied the officer. 'Wilson's body was never found. He's still technically missing, presumed dead.'

~

That evening at the Dog and Gun, the Owens were back at work and the restaurant and accommodation bookings were picking up again. It was going to take a lot to compensate for the loss of Sandy Fraser's shooting parties, thought Rob Owen as he looked at the reservation book at the reception desk, but they would manage. At least they wouldn't have the cash-flow problems associated with Fraser. Maybe they needed to create some interest in the inn: some speciality food evenings or wine tastings. Such was the reputation of the food that they'd never needed such promotions before, but perhaps times would now become a bit more challenging. It could work out well in the end, Rob thought optimistically. It might have been a mistake to rely too heavily on the shooting parties for their autumn revenue.

He heard footsteps and looked up. It was Harry Newton on his way to the kitchen. 'Harry!' he called, and the young man stopped and turned.

'Yes, Mr Owen?'

'How's Kirsty?'

'Oh, she's a bit better, thanks. Less agitated during the day now, though she's still spooked by what she saw and it stops her getting to sleep. Last night she was looking out of that window again and . . .' He stopped, realising he'd said too much. How did he know she was looking out of the window?

Rob laughed. 'Well, I hope you tucked her up in bed if she got scared again.' Harry's face went bright red and Rob laughed even harder. 'Go on, you big oaf. Don't think we didn't know that you two were getting it on. Just be discreet about it, OK? It mustn't interfere with your work at all.'

'No, Mr Owen, it won't. Thanks.' He managed a weak smile and then hurried off to the kitchen, realising that his brother's warning had made him overcautious.

Rob made a few notes about certain ideas he'd been considering, and then went into the kitchen himself to see how Sheila and her team were getting on. He stood quietly just inside the door, and was pleased to see her bustling away and calling out orders to people as if the horrors of nearly a week ago had never happened. He smiled as he looked at her. She was usually at her happiest and most fulfilled when she was working in the kitchen, but now he wasn't sure how much of her cheeriness was an act.

Rob went on to the bar, where he was due to put in a shift. Here, too, he was pleased to see that things seemed to be getting back to a semblance of normality. The first diners of the evening were eating in the restaurant area and some of the usual characters were at the bar.

'I can't believe it's not even a week yet since all that kicked off,' said Ian Davis. 'Mind you, I can't say we've missed th'old bugger – t'job's been a lot easier without him.'

'You shouldn't speak ill of the dead,' said Vic Moore, laughing. 'But I can imagine it's a lot better without him on your back all the time.'

'Too right it is,' replied Davis, taking a swig of his beer.

'Ah take it t'police haven't found owt yet?' asked Wilf Bramley, dressed in his usual faded tweed jacket and corduroy trousers.

'I don't think so,' said Moore. He saw Rob Owen behind the bar. 'Rob!' he called out. 'Have you heard anything from the police?'

Rob was drying glasses and shook his head.

'No. As far as I know they're still looking for Alan, and from what I hear they've spoken to nearly everyone in the village about what they heard or saw.'

'Apart from me.' Vic grinned. 'I wasn't here that night and I never had anything to do with Sandy Fraser, so I'm not a suspect like the rest of you.'

'Get lost,' said Davis. 'Anyway, you could be t'dark horse.'

'What do you mean?'

'Well, it's always t'person you least suspect, isn't it? In these murders on t'telly.'

'And what would my motive be?'

'Fraser maht've been knockin' off yer wife,' chipped in Bramley.

'I'm divorced. And he'd be welcome to her, I can tell you that.'

'Aye, well, Fraser maht've been t'reason why yer divorced,' continued Bramley, to general laughter.

'No, I'm afraid it's much more likely to be the disgruntled employer or tenant,' said Moore, pointing at Davis and Bramley.

Then he turned to Rob Owen. 'Or even the long-suffering inn-keeper who wanted rid of an awkward customer.'

'Hey, watch it!' said Rob, laughing. 'Or I'll bar you for slander-ing the landlord.'

'I still think one of those cranks were behind it,' said Davis. 'That madwoman who lives in that caravan. I hear she and some of her cronies were caught up at the Evershaw shoot, but t'police let 'em go as usual.'

'Yeah, well, she's a wild character all right,' said Rob, 'but I can't think Tony Dexter would have had anything to do with it. He's a bit of a loner I know, but he seems a mild-mannered sort of chap.'

'Well, you could say that about Alan Green,' said Vic. 'But he's the main suspect.'

'Aye.'

They all shook their heads at the baffling nature of the crime.

'Anyway . . . whose round is it?' asked Davis after a pause.

'Yours,' replied Bramley, to general laughter again.

The conversation moved on to more familiar territories: sport, the weather and the price of beer.

When Kirsty came down to work in the bar, Harry popped out of the kitchen to intercept her.

'Hey,' he said in a stage whisper and gestured outside. Then he took her to the back of the building. 'I've just been talking to Mr Owen – they know about us.'

Kirsty put her hand to her mouth and giggled. She looked round, but they were alone by the staff entrance to the bar.

'What did he say? I'll bet he wasn't bothered, though, was he?'

'No, he was fine; just said to be careful about it and not let it interfere with our work.'

'I told you. How did he know?'

'Well . . . I let something slip. He asked me how you are, and I mentioned that you were looking out of that window again, and of course I couldn't have known that unless I was . . . there in your room.'

'You idiot!' laughed Kirsty.

'He also said *they* already knew, not just him.'

'How? I'll bet Jeanette's been blabbing – wait till I see her! She's as bad as you!' She put her arms around him. 'Anyway, it's all good. We don't need to be so secretive any more.'

'No.' They kissed, and then Kirsty broke away. 'Better get back or we'll get into trouble!' Harry laughed, as they went back into the inn with light hearts.

~

As Andy and Steph were driving home to Leeds with Steph at the wheel, they were feeling satisfied with what they'd discovered through their research.

'I think there's every chance that Philip Traynor was talking about Matthew Hart when he referred to "that bastard", and what he didn't want him to get was his share of the loot,' began Steph. 'Remember, only Hart returned his share to the authorities, but what if somehow he got to know where Traynor had hid his? That would add insult to injury: not only did Traynor have to serve a long sentence, but the man who betrayed him got his hands on his money. The anger and despair could have been enough to push him over the edge. God, this queue's long tonight!'

They were in a long line of traffic snaking up the hill to the traffic lights at Harewood. On their right they caught a glimpse, through the woods, of the ruins of the medieval Harewood Castle.

'But how would Hart have found out where Traynor had hidden his share?'

'Maybe Traynor had told him things when they were still fellow members of the gang; enough for Traynor to believe that Hart would be able to work out where it was.'

'OK, you could be right. But I'm not sure it has any bearing on the case.'

'We don't know yet.'

'True, and any bit of information is useful, as we've been getting nowhere. The fact that Wilson's body was never found is very interesting.'

'It's unlikely that he actually survived.'

'But not impossible, and it raises the possibility that Wilson could be alive and involved in the murder of the man who sent him down. Do you think we should contact the boss?' Andy was quite excited by his new theory.

'No. He's down in Oxford for his daughter's graduation and I don't think it'll go down well if we bother him with work. We'll wait until he gets back.' She yawned. 'I'm tired after all that computer work – I don't know how some people sit doing that all day. I don't fancy cooking . . . I know, let's go to Caravanista by the Corn Exchange, I just love their hummus and falafels.'

'You're on.'

~

Oldroyd lay in bed in his guest room at Louise's college. It was a student room, currently unoccupied, as it was still three weeks or so before the start of term. A wardrobe, bookcases and desk – all empty at the moment – waited for the student who would live in the room for a whole academic year beginning in October.

It was impossible for Oldroyd not to reminisce about his own time as a student. He vividly recalled sitting at such a desk writing essays, sometimes until the small hours. He also remembered the times towards the end of his first year when he had smuggled Julia into his room so they could spend passionate, if uncomfortable, nights together in the narrow single bed.

Feeling wide awake, he got up and looked out of the window, which afforded a view over the rooftops and spires of Oxford. It was not very late, but the city was in its student-vacation quiet period, without the noise of drunken, cavorting students passing through the narrow dark streets.

Julia was on his mind; and the feelings she evoked were confusing, and even a little disturbing. They'd separated by mutual consent several years ago. He had gone to live in Harrogate while she stayed in Leeds with Louise and Robert. For a while after this, he'd hoped they would get back together again. They'd met regularly, usually in Harrogate, to discuss their children's progress and any problems they were having, but when they'd left home these meetings had slowly dried up.

It had taken him a long time to accept that their relationship was over, even when she asked for a divorce. Eventually he'd managed to move on. Now he had met Deborah, and they had a really good relationship.

But . . .

His thoughts were interrupted by the deep bell in Tom Tower at Christ Church College striking eleven.

What was he to make of Julia today? The idea of divorce seemed to have been forgotten, and she wasn't in a relationship any more. Moreover, she seemed to be hinting strongly that she still cared for him: telling him to be careful, taking his hand, smiling; no recriminations from the past, only happy memories of family life.

It had continued right through until the evening, when they'd all had a meal together at the Turf Tavern, hidden beneath the walls of New College. She'd sat talking to him in an animated and interested way, and she'd kissed him briefly on the lips when they finally split up and went to their separate guest rooms in the college. He felt that if he'd pushed it, he could have gone to her room with her.

He shook his head at the memory. It was made all the more unsettling by them being in Oxford. They shared so many memories of their time together as undergraduates. How could he not have tender, nostalgic and, yes, romantic feelings about being here with her again?

If this had happened before he'd met Deborah, he would have welcomed it. He'd never wanted to separate from Julia in the first place; he'd always thought of her as the love of his life. But now! He lay down again, but without much hope of sleeping, and sighed. He had enough stress with this difficult case; he didn't want his private life to become complicated again.

∽

Next morning, he went into the college hall for breakfast very early, hoping to avoid Julia.

More recollections of his time at Oxford came to him as he sat on the wooden bench drinking tea and munching toast and the sun came through the ancient windows.

Then he walked on a familiar route across the High, down to Christ Church Meadow, along the banks of the Thames to the confluence with the Cherwell, and back to the Botanic Garden.

It was a pleasant morning but, unfortunately, everywhere he went brought back memories of his time in Oxford with Julia.

He returned to Louise's college, watching out for his wife. He didn't want to see her by himself again. Luckily, Alison was chatting to the porters at the lodge. She turned and saw him.

'Jim! Where on earth have you been? Julia's gone. She's off to London to stay with some friends for the weekend. She was disappointed not to see you again.'

'Yes, well, that's the problem. Look, fancy a coffee? Any sign of Louise?'

'She texted me to say she'd meet us for lunch before we set off.'

'Right, come on then.'

Over coffee he explained what had happened and how unsettled it had made him feel. Alison listened as sympathetically as ever.

'I'm sure I wasn't imagining it,' he concluded. 'I got a completely different set of messages from her than what I'm used to. She wasn't cold and aloof as she has been for so long – no sarcastic comments about me and work and stuff like that.'

'Hmm, I can see why you scarpered this morning.' Alison smiled as she sipped her coffee.

'What do you think's going on?'

Alison thought for a moment. 'Her relationship with her colleague is over, you say?'

'That's what she told me.'

'She's probably feeling lonely after that. Then she hears about you and Deborah, and how does that make her feel? I suspect she has pangs of jealousy; it's the first time you've had a relationship since you split up with her. She realises that she still has feelings for you. And here you are in Oxford, which must bring back many memories for you both. Really, it's not that difficult to explain, is it?'

'I don't suppose so, when you state it so clearly like that.'

'The question is, how do you feel about it, Jim? You've yearned to be reunited with Julia for a long time, but things are different now, aren't they?'

'Yes, very – it's going well with Deborah and I don't want to damage that. It's just . . . unsettling to feel that Julia's interested in me again.'

'Yes, I understand, but don't be too swayed by emotions from the past. My advice is to stay with what's real. What might happen with Julia or how she or you could feel is all vague and, while you're here in Oxford, affected by old feelings. Your relationship with Deborah is solid and actual. I'd say stick with that, but it's your decision.'

'Thanks, sis,' said Oldroyd with a smile. Alison, as the older sibling, had always been his mentor and confidante. Her advice was always very wise and he found it difficult to ignore.

He felt better as they embarked on another walk around Oxford and then met Louise for lunch. On the drive home with Alison and Louise, his feelings clarified still further as Oxford and its unreal magic slipped away.

Five

Louise collected together the things she wanted on the Sunday morning, and in the afternoon Oldroyd introduced her to Deborah and they went for a walk around the Stray. As he had hoped, they got on really well.

'She's great, Dad, I'm really pleased for you,' Louise said later, as she prepared to leave to spend a few days with two old school friends in Leeds, who were in a relationship and managing to buy a terraced house in Headingley. 'No more mooning over Mum, OK?'

'Yes, you're right.' He hadn't told her about what had happened in Oxford with Julia, probably because he knew what she would say.

'It was nice to see Oxford again. I might pay you a visit next term.'

'You're welcome. And bring Deborah. I'll be able to book some graduate accommodation now.'

'I will, and I hope it goes well. Keep me informed about the study, it sounds fascinating. Deborah will be interested, too.' For her MSt, Louise was going to write a thesis on how women's mental-health issues had been regarded and treated in the nineteenth and early-twentieth centuries.

'I will, Dad. And it'll be fine. I can't wait to get started on it.'

Oldroyd found his daughter's usually brief visits very helpful, if not always comfortable, as she challenged him and encouraged him to change in ways he needed to. He was pleased that she liked Deborah. It was unlike the normal pattern: instead of her bringing a boyfriend home for approval, he was presenting his new partner to her. When you had a daughter like Louise, he reflected, such reversals were to be expected.

∽

The three detectives all arrived at Harrogate HQ early on Monday. Oldroyd was keen to catch up with any developments, although he knew that if anything really important had happened someone would have contacted him. He felt refreshed after his break and a weekend with Deborah, including another parkrun. He had decided to follow Alison's advice and ignore the signals he'd appeared to be getting from Julia. Alison was right: how could he be sure about their meaning anyway? Since their separation he'd often found Julia's behaviour difficult to interpret. He wasn't going to spoil what he had at the moment.

Steph and Andy were eager to tell their boss about their findings. They met in his office and Oldroyd listened intently to their accounts.

'Good work,' he observed, when they were both finished. 'So it's possible that Wilson is alive?'

'It's a long shot, sir, but no body was found. He would have had to survive falling into that rapidly moving water and, if he got out, what would he do then with no money, nowhere to go or anything?' replied Andy.

'He may have had people waiting somewhere near as part of a plan,' said Oldroyd.

'So if he did escape, sir, do you think he played a part in the murder?' asked Steph.

'Well, he certainly had a motive to kill Sandy Fraser given the sentence he handed out. The question is: in what way could Wilson have been involved?'

'Maybe Alan Green was one of Wilson's criminal friends, and Green acted the part of the hitman? We know he was a relative new-comer to the village and we haven't been able to find out anything about him. The name could obviously have been false, and now he's disappeared back to his criminal haunts in London or wherever,' suggested Steph.

'It's plausible,' said Oldroyd. 'It would have meant that Fraser might not have recognised the man who was planning to kill him, which would have been a risk if Wilson had come up here himself.' He shook his head. 'I don't know. Something doesn't feel quite right. Why did it take Green so long to do it? According to every-one, Green was around for some time before the murder. He got to know people in the pub and in the village.'

'I suppose it was a kind of cover. No one was expecting him to do it. Most of the villagers still don't believe that Green did it, do they?'

'True. The problem is, despite your good work, we're no further on. We still need to catch Green to find out the answers. If Wilson is alive we've absolutely no idea where he is.' He turned to Steph. 'So your theory is that Traynor was thrown into despair because he thought Matthew Hart was going to take his share of the loot?'

'Yes sir. I'm not sure what bearing it has on the case, but it's a bit of extra information.'

'You're quite right. It might turn out to be important in the long run. Anyway, I've got to go and see Superintendent Walker.

Could one of you contact Bill Gibbs and see if he's come up with anything about missing shotguns, or any leads in the search for Green?'

'I'll do it,' said Steph. She shook her head and frowned at Andy as Oldroyd left the room. Their investigation was still in the doldrums despite the new information.

~

DCS Walker was sitting behind his desk as usual, wearing a worn and shiny suit: the only one Oldroyd had ever seen him wearing. He was good at his job, but hated the managerialism and business culture of the higher echelons of the police force. Oldroyd suspected he missed being involved in the nitty-gritty of police work.

'So, how's it going up in Nidderdale, Jim? I take it you haven't had a breakthrough yet?'

The two officers were on first-name terms in private. 'No, Tom. I'm afraid it's a tricky one. The main suspect, identified by a witness, has disappeared, and we don't really know what his motive was. We've identified a number of people in the village who might have had a reason to kill the victim, but we can't link any of them to the crime.'

'Well, it's the kind of conundrum you specialise in working out, isn't it?'

'I suppose so, but progress is frustratingly slow.'

Walker grunted. 'I sympathise. I've had Watkins asking me how the investigation is going. It's only just over a bloody week since it happened. He'd know how difficult it is if he'd ever done much police work himself. As it is, he expects bloody miracles, and he's jumpy as hell because the victim was a local bigwig. I know he'll be coming back soon asking if the investigation needs fresh thinking and someone who can "transcend the structural assumptions in the current investigative model" or some such drivel. Don't worry, I won't move you off the case. I know you always get there in the end.'

'We do our best, Tom. I have an excellent team and we're working hard. If we can find this Alan Green, the suspect, I think he would be able to answer many of our questions and then we'll crack it. It could turn out to be quite simple in the end.'

Unfortunately, events were shortly to prove Oldroyd wrong.

~

It was seven o'clock on the Monday evening and the soft September light was fading. The nights were drawing in, thought Peter Gorton as he made preparations to close his shop. He went outside to bring in his display stands: a rack of garden plants and a few hardware items.

He'd been open for twelve hours. It was the only way to make any kind of profit. His wife helped a little but she was disabled with arthritis, and so couldn't do too much. Gorton didn't mind; he enjoyed the social contact with all his regular customers, which was so different from his previous job. He found village life wonderfully relaxing after spending most of his working life in a stressful environment in the city.

The village was quiet. He saw Jeanette Brown crossing the green, presumably to start a shift at the Dog and Gun. He called out and waved. She waved back. At that very moment, a figure emerged from the shadows in the narrow lane at the side of the shop. Gorton turned and recognised the person.

'Oh, hi. You're just in time. I was about to close up for the night. I—'

He got no further because the newcomer produced a shotgun, raised it and shot Gorton in the chest. The explosion resounded around the village, and a shocked Jeanette, who'd seen it all, screamed. The killer looked across at her and then walked off quickly back down the lane carrying the gun.

Jeanette, still screaming, ran the short distance to the inn. People who had heard the shot appeared at the door.

'Quick! Peter Gorton's been shot!' Jeanette was almost hysterical. She pointed. 'Just outside his shop. I think he's dead, there was a lot of blood.'

'Did you see what happened?' It was Rob Owen who took hold of her, as she appeared to be about to pass out.

'Yes. It was Vic Moore.'

'Vic?!'

'Yes. He shot Peter, then he looked over at me and ran off down that lane at the side of the shop. I'm absolutely sure it was him.' Suddenly she collapsed in Rob's arms and had to be carried into the pub.

~

It was dark in the village now. Temporary lamps had been set up by the police, and the beams shone on the incident tape hung around the shop and Gorton's body, which still lay on the ground slumped against a blood-spattered wall. A sombre Bill Gibbs was talking to a couple of his detective constables. Tim Groves was completing his initial investigation and removing his rubber gloves as the detectives arrived. Steph and Andy had only just got home when they received the call. They'd got back into their car and driven up to Niddersgill over the dark moors around Fewston and Blubberhouses, reflecting that the investigation had suddenly become more complex and urgent.

They walked over to Tim Groves.

'Ah Jim!' called Groves, as affable as ever. 'Beat you to it again, I see. You're a bit slow off the mark these days. Are you losing your grip?' The light-hearted banter between the pathologist and Oldroyd was a function of their deep respect for each other.

'I don't have a car like yours, Tim.' Oldroyd glanced at Groves's BMW. 'The old Saab trundles a bit.'

'Like its owner,' laughed Groves. He turned to the body. 'Anyway, not much to say again. Shotgun wound, close range, to the chest. He would have died almost instantly.'

Oldroyd pulled back the sheet to have a quick look. 'I see.'

'How are you getting on with tracking down the killer of our friend outside the pub?'

'Not well, I'm afraid.'

'Maybe he's reappeared. It's a very similar murder. How are you classifying them?' said Groves. Oldroyd had a habit of using acronyms to describe the circumstances of a murder, and these amused the pathologist.

'Probably VOR, for victims of revenge. I have an idea that that could well be the motive. They're not random killings.'

Groves smiled. 'OK. Well, I'll leave you to it. There was a witness, apparently. I'm sure Inspector Gibbs has already spoken to her.' He pointed over to the Dog and Gun before signalling to the ambulance staff to remove the body.

Oldroyd and Steph went across to Gibbs. 'We'll have to stop meeting like this, Bill,' said Oldroyd, and Gibbs shook his head, looking worried and harassed.

'I don't know what the hell's going on, sir. Two murders in almost the same manner in a dales village, apparently committed by different people.'

'Different? How do you know? Isn't it more likely that Alan Green has returned?'

'Not according to the witness.' He looked at his notes. 'Jeanette Brown – she works at the inn. She saw the murder and positively identified the killer as Vic Moore. Apparently he's some kind of freelance copy-editor and he lodges with an artist in the village. He's not cropped up in the investigation of Fraser.'

'That artist will be John Gray. I've been into his studio to look at his paintings.'

'Right. Well, that's all we know, but it's bloody weird. I'm getting déjà vu all the time: shotgun killing, no obvious motive, and a young woman witnesses the murder. Then she identifies the killer which is a surprise to everyone. And of course this person is nowhere to be found. What's the betting that we can't trace him? I don't get it.'

It was a clear night. Oldroyd looked up at the stars as if hoping for divine inspiration. Then he turned around and looked at the night-time village: the inn, the shop with blue-and-white incident tape, the village green. Some people were standing outside their cottages and talking in little groups.

'Let's go inside,' he said at last. Gibbs, Steph and Andy followed him across the green to the inn. Oldroyd appeared to be deep in thought. They passed Jeanette being comforted by Sheila Owen, another curious echo of the previous murder, and went into the residents' lounge which had become their office.

'The two murders have to be linked in some way, sir, surely,' said Steph.

'Well, if they're not, it's the greatest coincidence I've ever encountered. But how? That's the question.'

'All these similarities are a bit spooky, but what do you think it's all about, sir? Surely not some feud playing out between gangs in Nidderdale?' asked Andy.

'I don't know about gangs,' continued Oldroyd, 'but something connects these people: Fraser, Green, Moore and Gorton.

We've got to look harder than we already have to find out what it is. I take it you've still had no luck finding Green?' he said to Gibbs.

'No. Vanished into thin air. He obviously had an escape route and I'll bet this Vic Moore has too.'

'Well, this second murder is a game changer. Assuming the murders are linked, it's obvious now that there's much more to the whole business than we thought. It's not about one victim and who might have had a motive to kill them. It's more complicated and darker than that. It means we'll have to reassess all the motives we thought people might have had, you know, like the anti-blood-sports woman and Dexter the environmentalist, unless Gorton was a keen grouse shooter too. Also the gamekeeper and Fraser's shooting cronies who may have had motives to kill him. None of these motives apply to Gorton.'

'Do you mean we're focusing on the wrong people?' asked Gibbs.

'Not necessarily, some of the same people might be involved, but the motives may be different from the ones we've been considering. There's an undercurrent in this case, something which links these people, which we're not picking up yet. Anyway, we'd better have a word with the witness. Bring her in, Bill.'

'Right, sir.'

The detectives suffered déjà vu again as Jeanette came into the room. Like Kirsty, she was still trembling with shock. Oldroyd asked her gently to describe what she'd seen.

'I was just walking over the green to the inn when I saw Peter outside his shop. I think he was packing things up ready to close.'

'Don't you live here at the inn?'

'Yes, but I'd been to see Liz Smith. She lives in a caravan just out of the village.'

'Yes, we know. Are you a friend of hers?'

'Yeah. She's a good laugh and I agree with her . . . her campaigns. She's just had a nasty do with some of those shooters, who made her go to the police.' She glared at Gibbs.

'Never mind that now,' said Oldroyd. 'Did Mr Gorton say anything to you?'

'Yes, he called out "Hi" to me, and waved. Then, as I waved back, I saw someone come out of the lane at the side of the shop. Peter turned and I heard him say something and then . . .' She stopped as she remembered the horrifying scene, and started to weep.

The detectives waited.

'He just raised the gun and fired. There was a huge bang. Peter was pushed back against the wall and then fell down. I could see lots of blood. I screamed and the person who fired the gun looked across at me.'

'Who was it?'

'It was definitely Vic – Vic Moore. I had a good look at his face. I was so shocked that I just stood there looking at him, and then I thought he might fire another shot at me because I'd seen him. But he didn't, he just walked quickly back down the lane, still carrying the gun.'

'Are you sure it was him?' asked Steph. 'Wasn't it getting dark?'

'The sun was setting but it was a clear evening and the sun was shining on his face. I'm sure it was him.'

'What happened then?'

'I was hysterical. I ran over to the inn and there were people outside who'd heard the shot. I don't remember much after that, but Rob and Sheila have looked after me.' She began to shake, as if the recollection of the events was too much.

'OK,' said Oldroyd kindly, 'that will be all for now.' Jeanette got up and left the room.

'It's very weird, isn't it, that two young women who live and work at the inn witnessed these murders and then they were both looked after by the Owens?' observed Gibbs.

'Yes,' replied Oldroyd. 'Of course, that part really could be a coincidence. The interesting bit to me is that both murderers didn't seem to mind being seen and made no attempt to conceal their identity, which is highly unusual if you want to avoid being caught. Also, they could have worn some kind of mask or a balaclava.'

'Maybe they thought it didn't matter as they had such a good getaway route ready. I'm assuming that Vic Moore has disappeared too,' said Gibbs.

'I'm sure that's what we'll find, but at least we know where he stayed in the village. We need to get over to John Gray's cottage ASAP to check. I assume you've investigated that lane by the murder scene?'

'Yes,' replied Gibbs. 'It's just a track which leads to a footpath through the woods. The killer could easily have disappeared that way.'

'Right, let's get over to the cottage. After that, there's not much more we can do tonight. I assume you've got your DC taking statements at the inn?'

'Yep, but I can't see how that will reveal anything.'

'OK, Andy, stay and help to supervise that. The rest of us, let's go.'

～

The stars were out and there was a full moon as the three detectives crossed the village green and headed to John Gray's cottage. The moonlight was ghostly on the short path to the door. Behind the building, large trees formed a black mass. The cottage was dark and silent. Oldroyd banged on the door.

'Mr Gray, it's the police. Open up, please.' There was silence. An owl hooted in one of the trees.

'I'm not sure I like this, sir,' said Gibbs. 'Do you think he may have done his landlord in, too? He may have known too much about Moore's movements.'

Looking grim, Oldroyd banged on the door again. A light went on upstairs, followed a few seconds later by another in the small hallway. There was the sound of locks being turned and a voice saying, 'OK, just a minute.'

The door opened to reveal the figure of John Gray, wearing a dressing gown.

He peered out into the darkness. 'Chief Inspector? Is that you? What on earth's going on?'

'I'm sorry to disturb you, Mr Gray, but we need to talk to your lodger, Vic Moore. We need to question him about a murder.'

'A murder? Vic? My God, who on earth's been killed this time? I've been down in Harrogate all evening – I've only been back about an hour, and then I went straight to bed. I wondered why all those people were standing around at the inn.'

'It was Peter Gorton, the owner of the shop.'

'Peter? That's terrible. You think Vic did it?'

'He was identified by a witness. Is he in the house?'

'Well, I don't know. When I got back I assumed he was in bed.' He looked at his watch. 'It's late.' He turned back into the house and called out: 'Vic! Are you there? The police are here. Vic!' There was no response. 'That's very odd. You'd better go up, Chief Inspector. His room is the first on the right. But surely Vic wouldn't . . .' Gray looked frightened.

Oldroyd led the way upstairs. The light above the stairs was on. He rapped on the door. 'Mr Moore? Are you in there?' There was no response, so he turned the handle and went in. The room was dark and he switched on the light. There was no one inside and the bed had not been slept in. It was starting to seem as if Gibbs was right: Moore, like Green, had disappeared.

'When did you last see him?' asked Oldroyd.

'This afternoon. He was working on his laptop downstairs and I went into the studio. I left at about six. He was still there. I went to see a film at the Harrogate Odeon. It was a late showing.'

'Has he been behaving strangely recently?'

'Vic? Well, no. He's a quiet sort of chap. He's been here a couple of years now. He's the ideal lodger – pays his rent regularly, no trouble. He does his work, goes walking and he's a regular at the inn. He likes a pint or two. I think he got to know a few people there.'

'What do you know about his past?' asked Steph as they went back down the stairs.

They headed into the lounge. Gray pointed towards a chair. 'He usually leaves his laptop on that chair, but it's not there. He must have taken it with him. To answer your question: nothing. He wouldn't talk about it. I don't know whether he'd got divorced or lost his job or what. I'd advertised that I had a room to rent and he contacted me saying he just had to get away from the city and wanted a long stay in the countryside. He didn't even say which city that was, but he wanted to do his own thing. I didn't ask any more questions because I didn't think he would welcome anybody probing into his past. Ah!' Gray put up his hand and raised a finger. 'Now I remember something.'

'What?' asked Gibbs eagerly. They were desperate for any kind of information in this baffling case.

'A couple of days ago, Vic seemed anxious – said he'd had some unwelcome news and he had to do something he didn't want to do. Yes, those were his words: "something I don't want to do". He didn't say anything else and I didn't like to ask.'

'I see,' said an intrigued Oldroyd. 'Right. Well, we'll be back tomorrow to search his room, so don't touch anything. By the way, did you know Peter Gorton?'

'Not well, Chief Inspector. I only saw him in the shop.'

'Did he have any enemies? Did you ever hear Vic Moore talk about him?'

'No to both questions, Chief Inspector. It's just the same as Mr Fraser, I've no idea who would want to harm either of them.'

The detectives left and walked back to the inn.

It was too late to do anything else, so Oldroyd left Gibbs to finish things off. With Andy's help, the process of taking statements had nearly been completed.

'This is getting more and more complex and sinister, isn't it, sir?' said Steph as the three of them met in the residents' lounge, just as they had after the first murder.

'I agree. As I said, we're going to have to start the investigation again. Things now look different. What did Moore mean when he told Gray he had to do something he didn't want to do?'

'It sounds like he was being controlled by someone,' suggested Andy. 'Did that person instruct him to kill Gorton? And did the same person order Green to murder Fraser? I hate to say it, sir, but it is actually beginning to sound like gangland stuff – you know, bosses, loyalty and hitmen. And if so, it must increase the chances of Patrick Wilson being involved.'

'Possibly,' said Oldroyd. 'But if so, what did he have against Gorton? And what kind of power did he have over Green and Moore that he could get them to kill people?'

'Gangland debts? I suppose we've only got Gray's word that Moore said that about doing something he didn't want to do.'

'True, but if Gray lied, that makes him a suspect too, and things become yet more complicated. I just don't know. Anyway, we can't do any more tonight. We'd best get home and start fresh in the morning.'

Oldroyd was deep in thought as he drove along the dark winding lanes of lower Nidderdale and the lights of Harrogate became visible in the distance. Clearly, the answer lay in finding out more about the characters in this enigmatic drama. They were going to have to work hard to uncover the so-far hidden connections between these people before they could finally make sense of the whole thing.

~

Next morning, a frightened silence hung over Niddersgill. Some people were reluctant to leave their homes and some were talking melodramatically about the end of the village, a portent being the sad sight of the closed shop, which had been a busy social meeting place as well as a supplier of basic needs. Now there were no newspapers and no milk, bread or groceries of any kind. The shooting of Peter Gorton felt like a death blow, not only to him but also to the community, and the stains of his blood on the wall near the shop were a grisly reminder of the shocking violence which had now been visited twice upon this small settlement.

As if to reflect the dismal mood, the weather broke after two weeks of early-autumnal clear and sunny weather. Dark clouds formed and heavy rain fell on the whole of Nidderdale. Mist descended on the fells, blotting out the glorious panoramic views.

At the Dog and Gun, Jeanette Brown was in bed exhausted after her trauma, having suffered a sleepless night.

Kirsty was sitting by the bed and comforting Jeanette in a curious reversal of what had happened just over a week ago. She looked out of the small window of the loft bedroom. The woods opposite were just visible in the mist. The rain was drumming on the hotel roof.

'I just can't believe it,' Jeanette mumbled for the umpteenth time. 'We both saw the same thing, the same horrible thing. It's like a nightmare. What's going to happen next? I can't bear to think about it!' She turned over and buried her face in the pillow.

'It's difficult,' said Kirsty. 'I'm still nervous about going out by myself, but I'm sure the police will find out what's going on soon. That chief inspector is very clever.'

Jeanette looked up. 'Do you think so? It's more like a horror story than a crime. We knew those men who became murderers, and the men they killed. I can't make any sense of it.' Her head sunk into the pillow again.

'I know. It's awful, but at least the police will believe us now we've both seen a similar thing happen. I don't think they believed me, but now it's obvious that something weird is going on. Anyway, look, your parents don't live far from here, do they, Jeanette?'

'In Northallerton.'

'I think you should go to them for a while. Get away and have a rest. I'm sure Mr Owen will be fine about it and I can't see the police objecting. I'd have gone home too after last Friday if I didn't have Harry.'

'You're right. I can't do any work here at the moment. The thing is, if I go, I don't think I'll come back. This place gives me the creeps now,' said Jeanette.

'I know. Me and Harry are staying for a bit because he's getting good experience in the kitchen here, but in a while we're hoping to move to Leeds. I'm from Sheffield and I miss the city.'

Jeanette managed a weak smile. 'It's going well then, you and Harry?'

'Yes,' said Kirsty, smiling back. Their relationship was a ray of sunshine in a dark time.

Oldroyd and his team were back in the village by mid-morning and they met up with Gibbs at the Dog and Gun. Gibbs looked very weary. The frustrations of the case were starting to affect even his dogged personality.

'I don't know what to think, sir,' he said with a sigh. 'The two crimes must surely be connected. The murder last night is a copy of the first: victim shot, murderer disappears. Except that this time I can't imagine we'll have many suspects. Gorton had been in the village about four years and no one we've spoken to had a bad word for him. Similar story with the suspect: a relative newcomer but everyone seemed to like him too. No history of conflict between the two of them. We've made preliminary enquiries but no one seems to know anything about Moore before he came here. I'll confess I'm completely baffled. We've also done a thorough search of his room at Gray's house and the rest of the building but we didn't find anything.'

'It's a tough one all right, Bill. But we've uncovered some information which I think is going to be important.' He briefed Gibbs about what they knew of the Drover Road robbery, Traynor and Wilson.

'So you think this Wilson may still be alive? And that he had a motive to kill Fraser?'

'Yes. I know it's a long shot, but it's a lead to follow when we haven't much else to go on.'

'What about Gorton?' said Bill.

'We don't know of any link yet.'

'And this Traynor who killed himself in prison? How does all that relate to the case?'

'We're not sure yet, sir,' said Steph, 'but somehow I think it will prove significant.'

Gibbs shrugged. 'Well, OK. I have to admit it all seems a bit thin, but if you think it's worth pursuing, sir, I'm with you. But how do we progress on that line of enquiry, given that we've no idea where Wilson is, or even if he's still alive?'

Oldroyd admired his sceptical pragmatism. 'I'm not sure yet, Bill. First things first, I want to talk to Gorton's widow and see if she can tell us anything. Could you and Andy read the statements from all the witnesses and people who knew Gorton and Moore? See if anything comes up.'

'Of course, sir. As long as you don't put me on checking shotgun licences again,' said Gibbs, managing a weak grin.

'No. I promise,' said Oldroyd, laughing, before grimness established itself again. 'Steph and I have to visit the two widows,' he continued gravely. 'Not pleasant jobs, but we'd better get on with them. We've had the results of the examination of Fraser's computer. There was a file which was password-protected. It turned out to contain a list of dates and amounts of money from "H.S." He only recorded the initials. That could well have been Henry Saunders. We'll have to see if Fraser's wife knows anything. Then we'll have to speak to Mrs Gorton to see if she can tell us anything useful about her husband.' He sighed and shook his head at the prospect before he and Steph left the inn.

∾

'You're not serious.'

'I am, old boy.'

'Another murder in the village?'

Henry Saunders was astonished. It was an unexpected call from James Symons, who sounded rather more intrigued than shocked by such a dreadful event. Saunders was sitting in a cafe not far from his office.

'Who was murdered this time?' asked Saunders.

'The poor chap who ran that little newsagent and store in the village. He was shot outside the shop and apparently the killer disappeared again. It's extraordinary, isn't it? What on earth do you think is going on?'

'How would I know, James? I haven't a clue.'

'No, well at least the police can't suspect us this time. We had no connection with the man at all.'

'No,' replied Saunders tersely. He glanced through the cafe window at the busy London street.

He didn't want to be reminded about the whole business in Nidderdale. There were issues concerning him and Sandy about which he hoped the police would remain in ignorance.

'Anyway,' continued Symons, 'I think all this carry-on may give the village a little notoriety, at least in the short term, and that in turn may well bring down the asking price for Fraser's grouse moor.'

Saunders was rather disgusted by this. 'James, that's rather bad taste, especially in the circumstances.'

'Well, every cloud has a silver lining, old boy.' Symons chuckled, completely unabashed. 'Even if it's not for those directly involved. Anyway, I won't keep you. I know life is hectic for all you City types. I just want you to know that I'll be delighted if you'd join me on a shoot when I've taken possession of the moor. It'll be good to have a reunion for old times' sake, and we can remember Sandy. I might even invite that chap who got drunk and made a fool of himself. What was his name? He was some kind of car dealer, wasn't he?'

'Yes, Rawnsley.'

'He'll be good for a laugh.' Symons chuckled again.

'I must say, you seem very confident about being able to acquire that land,' said Saunders.

'Oh yes. All in good time. It's all part of the plan. Cheerio for now.'

Symons rang off, leaving Saunders shaking his head at the former's insensitive breeziness in the circumstances. To Symons, the murders seemed to afford only curiosity and an opportunity for personal gain. And what did he mean by his 'plan'? Was it just his ambition to acquire more land in the area, or was there something more sinister afoot?

~

At the Frasers' manor house, Henrietta was encouraging her mother to begin the process of sorting through her deceased husband's possessions. The death had been registered, probate applied for and the funeral arranged. Miriam was a little more relaxed but still tired after the shock. She protested that she didn't want to be bothered with any of this yet, but Henrietta insisted.

'There's no time like the present, Mummy. If you put things off they'll never get done. We're only going to start with his study and his papers. We'll just sort through them and see if there's anything important. There won't be anything personal which might upset you.'

'All right then. You've always been busy and efficient like this. Your room was always immaculate and tidy and the teachers at school said you hated any mess.'

Henrietta laughed. 'I know. I think I get it from Daddy. Look at this.'

They'd entered the study, in which everything was neatly arranged, although Oldroyd had left a few out after his search a week ago. They spent some time going through various legal documents, with Henrietta making most of the decisions about what had to be dealt with immediately and what could be deferred. After a while, Miriam said she needed a break, and went to lie down for a while.

'I'll come and make a cup of tea in a minute,' Henrietta called through to the sitting room. 'Are you OK?'

'Yes. Fine, dear. A cup of tea would be nice.'

Henrietta paused for a moment and looked around the room. Her father had some nice prints on the walls: Yorkshire landscapes and some cartoons of legal life. There was one of those caricature drawings which she thought she recognised as being the work of someone quite famous. She got up and lifted it from its picture hook, intending to see if there was any information on the back. She was surprised to find that the picture had been concealing a safe.

She placed the picture on the floor and went to the desk to see if she could find the key. Her search of the drawers revealed nothing. She thought about asking her mother, but she wasn't sure what she might find in there, so she sat down and considered the possibilities. The desk was old and solidly built, so could there be a concealed compartment?

After a patient search, she found a catch hidden at the back of the desk. When sprung, it opened a small compartment concealed by ornate woodwork at the front, and inside was a key. She rushed to the safe and opened it. There was a folder containing papers, and a large cash box which was stuffed with money. Did her mother know about this?

'Mummy,' called Henrietta, going into the sitting room. Then she saw her mother was asleep on the sofa.

There was a knock on the door, and she rushed to answer before the noise woke her mother. Standing outside were Oldroyd and Steph. This was so unexpected at this moment that she exclaimed in surprise. 'Oh, Chief Inspector! It's you! What a coincidence! Please come in, but try to be quiet. My mother's asleep.'

Puzzled, Oldroyd and Steph entered the little hallway.

'Come straight through to Daddy's study, I've got something to show you.' Henrietta indicated the safe, the papers and the money. 'It was quite by chance that I found this a few minutes ago. What do you make of it?'

Oldroyd looked at the sheets of paper, which seemed to be simple records of payments over quite a long period of time, apparently all from 'H.S.' Steph counted the money, which ran into the thousands.

He felt quite relieved to be maybe making some progress at last. 'I agree with you that this is a coincidence, but I don't think it's difficult to explain. Our examination of your father's computer showed that he'd been receiving payments from H.S. This is obviously the stash of money which he kept away from bank accounts where it could be traced. And he's kept this, a little analogue written record, as backup.'

'Who do you think this H.S. is, and why was he giving money to Daddy?'

'The most likely person is Henry Saunders, who was up here for the shoot at the time of the first murder.'

'Henry Saunders? He's one of my father's oldest friends. They were at school together.'

'Well, maybe he was giving your father money because he was in financial difficulties, but I'm afraid it looks a little clandestine to me.'

'You mean Daddy could have been getting money out of him? How? Surely not blackmail?' She put her hand to her mouth. 'But that's terrible.'

'Desperation can drive people to do unexpected things. We'll have to contact Mr Saunders and take it from there.'

Henrietta realised Oldroyd's line of thinking. 'Chief Inspector, are you implying that if Daddy was blackmailing Henry Saunders, then that might have been a motive for murder?'

'I'm sure you realise that blackmail often results in violence, but let's not jump to conclusions. We have no evidence against Mr Saunders yet and he wasn't identified as one of the shooters.'

'What could he have been blackmailing him about?'

'We have no idea.' Oldroyd decided to move things on. They had more work to do. 'OK, so we'll need to take all this as evidence. We don't need to bother your mother about it at the moment. I'm sure she knew nothing, but we'll have to check at some point.'

'Thank you, Chief Inspector.' Henrietta showed them out. She had lost all her breeziness. 'You know, it's funny how you think you know someone and then you find out that you didn't, or at least not all of them. My father was always so efficient, upright and respected, and now it seems he became involved in shabby money-grubbing after mismanaging his affairs. It hardly seems like the same person.'

'A lot of people harbour dreams, and many need them to survive,' replied Oldroyd. 'Sometimes the reality is different. Your father dreamed of living up here and owning a grouse moor. It seems he found the skills he had were not suited to the task.'

'I think you're right,' said Henrietta, and she closed the front door behind them.

～

Bill Gibbs drove back in a police car to Pateley Bridge in a sombre mood. There had now been two murders on his patch and he felt he was letting DCI Oldroyd down. The killers identified lived locally, so he should be the one who was finding them. But he and his officers had drawn a blank with Alan Green and now there was this Vic Moore character. It was baffling.

As he neared the town, still in deep in thought, he realised that the red vehicle in front of him was a postal van. As he'd been aware of following it for some time down the dale, the chances were it belonged to David Eastwood, who did the upper Nidderdale round. They had already checked at the post office, without success, to see if they had an address for Alan Green. But Eastwood might know something. He might also have delivered things to Vic Moore. It was worth a try.

Gibbs flashed his lights, which brought the van to a halt. He got out in the rain and walked over to see Eastwood's concerned face leaning out of the lowered driver's window. As long-time Pateley residents, they knew each other. 'Don't worry, David, I'm not stopping you for any problems with the car or anything.'

'Oh, right.' Eastwood looked relieved. The wipers in the van continued to swish from side to side.

'It's about these murders.' The worried look immediately returned to Eastwood's face. 'I know you do the round that covers Niddersgill. We're trying to track down a chap called Vic Moore. He lodged with John Gray, the artist.'

'Yes, I've seen him in the Dog – Alan Green, too.'

'Good. The point is: did you ever deliver any post to Vic Moore? If you can remember anything, it might prove useful.'

Eastwood thought for a moment. 'Now you mention it, I don't remember ever delivering anything with his name on. And that's a bit odd isn't it, considering he's lived here for a couple of years?'

'Maybe. And do you always do the delivery to Niddersgill?'

'Yes. I've been doing it for eight years now.'

'What about Alan Green? Did you ever come across him on your rounds?'

'To speak to, yes, but not as far as the post is concerned. He lived here in Pateley, didn't he? So I wouldn't deliver to him.'

'OK. Thanks, I'll let you get on.'

Eastwood drove off, and Gibbs got back into the police car, his hair soaked with the rain.

Another blank. But what Eastwood had said made him more convinced than ever that there was something strange about these two suspects that went beyond their apparent ability to vanish into thin air.

~

Oldroyd and Steph returned to the village and the forlorn sight of the closed shop surrounded by incident tape, with a PC on guard outside.

Oldroyd spoke to the PC. 'I presume Mrs Gorton is here?'

'Yes, sir,' she replied.

'How is she?'

'Not well, sir, as you can imagine. The doctor's been. The poor woman's disabled with arthritis and now she's got this to deal with. If you go through the shop, there's a room at the back which has been converted into a bedroom; I presume to avoid her having to go up the stairs.'

'OK, we'll go through.'

'Sir.'

Oldroyd and Steph made their way through the dark, empty shop, past piles of unsold newspapers. He knocked on a door at the back of the shop and heard a voice asking them in. Inside was the room as described by the PC, with a bed in the corner. A thin woman was sitting in a raised armchair, her feet on a footrest. She looked pale and exhausted.

'Mrs Gorton?' asked Oldroyd.

'Yes?'

'Detective Chief Inspector Oldroyd and Detective Sergeant Johnson. We won't bother you for long, but we would like to ask you a few questions.' They showed their warrant cards.

Mrs Gorton sighed. 'I presume it's about Peter?'

'Yes.'

'Sit down.' The detectives sat on a sofa opposite. 'I've already told the policeman who came everything. I've no idea who could have wanted to kill Peter. I'll never get over the shock of hearing the bang of that gun. Somehow I knew what had happened.' She closed her eyes and shook her head. 'I couldn't do anything. It takes me a long time to even get up out of the chair without help. At first I was afraid I might be next, that it could be a raid on the shop, but everything went quiet. I didn't hear anyone come in. Then I started to shout for help. It seemed a long time before someone came.'

'So your husband had no enemies, as far as you know?'

'No. I think everyone in the village liked him. Sometimes, if I was having a good day, I would come out and help him in the shop as much as I could. He was always chatting to people.'

'Did you know Vic Moore?'

'That's the man who they say shot Peter? Not really. I don't get out much. But I think I've seen him in the shop – just an ordinary man. He and Peter never had a disagreement that I knew of. I can't make any sense of it.'

Neither can we, thought Oldroyd.

'Where did you live before you came to Niddersgill?' asked Steph.

'In the cities. That's why we were keen to come out here into the countryside into semi-retirement. We moved around a bit with Peter's work and we ended up in Manchester.'

'What did your husband do?'

'He was a prison officer.'

Oldroyd looked up sharply. 'A prison officer? Did he ever work at Strangeways?'

'He did – that was his last job.'

'Did anything unusual happen while he was working there?'

Mrs Gorton frowned. 'How did you know about that?'

'About what, Mrs Gorton?'

'Well, there was a bit of an incident. Peter asked me never to talk about it – said he wanted to make a new start here and didn't want things from the past to spoil it. It doesn't matter now he's . . . not here.' The shock of this fact hit her; she stopped and began to weep. The detectives waited patiently.

'Tell us what happened, Mrs Gorton,' said Steph gently. 'But take your time.'

'I'm sorry.' She dabbed her eyes, and with an effort managed to continue. 'Peter was accused of mistreating a prisoner. He said it was all nonsense. He'd discovered the prisoner in possession of drugs and the man had gone for him. Maybe Peter was a bit too strong in fighting back. Anyway, he was suspended for a while and then they offered him early retirement. He was glad to leave – he'd had enough.'

'Can you remember this prisoner's name? It's very important.'

'Of course, it's not something you easily forget after all that trouble. It was Patrick Wilson.'

~

Andy and Bill Gibbs were just completing the humdrum job of collating the witness statements when Oldroyd came crashing into the lounge at the inn, closely followed by Steph.

'At last, I think we've got something tangible – two things actually, but I'm not sure how they're related, if they are.' He told Andy and Gibbs about the safe and the possibility of Fraser being involved in blackmail, and then what they'd learned about Gorton and Wilson. He was so animated that he didn't sit down. 'This is a link between the victims. It strongly suggests that Wilson is both alive and involved. He had the motive to kill both men: the judge who handed out his sentence and the prison officer whom he believed mistreated him.'

'How is he involved, sir?' asked Gibbs. 'We've got two different suspects for the murders. Do you think he's orchestrating his revenge from a distance? Sending out hitmen?'

'That's what Andy suggested, and he may be right.'

Andy beamed at Steph, who smiled back.

Oldroyd continued. 'He's the kind of big-time criminal who could get his dirty work done for him, and it would tie in with what John Gray told us about Vic Moore saying he had to do something he didn't want to do.'

'The problem is, sir,' said Steph, 'you said yourself that Alan Green was an odd hitman, what with him being around in the village for two or three years before killing Fraser. And now we've got the same thing with Moore. He's been around the village for quite a while, got to know people and so on, and then suddenly he shoots Gorton. It doesn't feel like a gangland hit to me.'

Andy frowned at her and, behind Oldroyd's back, she stuck her tongue out at him.

'But it's happened twice now, sir,' said Andy, defending his theory. 'As I said before, that must make it more likely that it's gang-related. Green and Moore may have been involved in crime in the past and Wilson has called on some kind of loyalty. That's how it works in gangs: once you're in, you're in for life, there's no retiring. That would also explain why Moore and Green have shadowy pasts and we can't find out much about them. They'd probably had enough of what they were doing and came up here to start a new life. But, as I say, you can always be called on by your bosses to perform a service. If Moore and Green hadn't done what they were told, then they might have ended up dead themselves.'

'That's an eloquent defence of your point of view, Andy,' observed Oldroyd.

Here, and again behind Oldroyd's back, Andy stuck his tongue out at Steph, who had to stifle a giggle.

'We need to contact the London Met,' continued Oldroyd, 'and get a full profile of Wilson: what he did, who he knew, where he lived, everything. And also tell them and the Manchester police that we think he may be still alive. The most likely scenario is that he returned to his old London haunts where he could lie low, and the Met might know where that's likely to be.'

'What about the business with Fraser and the blackmailing?' asked Gibbs.

'We've got to pursue that lead too. Henry Saunders was the most likely victim of the blackmailing. We'll start there and get him back up to Harrogate for questioning. He didn't have a motive to kill Gorton, but there's still a chance that the two crimes are not connected and the Wilson theory is wrong. So, Bill, if you can contact Manchester and we'll speak to the Met. Also, continue the search for Moore, though I think we know that will probably prove fruitless.'

'OK, sir.'

Oldroyd nodded to Steph and Andy. 'Let's get back to HQ before the press get here again. That will be soon. They must have got wind of another murder by now and we're too busy to talk to them. And by the way' – he smiled knowingly at them – 'who's the winner in your little competition to impress me?'

'Oh, I think Steph, sir.' Andy pointed at her. She pointed back.

'No sir, definitely him.' They all laughed as they left the inn with a spring in their step for the first time since the case had begun.

Not long after the old Saab disappeared down the road to Pateley, Oldroyd's prediction proved correct and a number of strangers' cars and SUVs started to arrive in Niddersgill. At about the same time, two very different characters met in the village. Wilf Bramley arrived in a dirty old van and parked it near to the shop. He walked over in his wellies, just as Tony Dexter arrived on foot wearing a Barbour jacket in the rain. Both men approached the shop, nodded to each other and suddenly halted when they saw the incident tape and the door closed.

'What's goin' on?' Wilf asked the PC outside.

She looked at him sceptically. 'Surely you know there's been another shooting?'

'No.' Tony Dexter joined the conversation. 'Who's been killed this time?'

The PC outlined what had happened. 'So you can understand that the shop is closed.'

'Bloody hell!' exclaimed Bramley. 'Peter Gorton! I've heard nowt abaht it, but ah haven't been into t'village for a few days and ah don't listen to t'news – it's just a lot o' gloomy stuff.'

'Me too,' said Dexter. 'We live up on the hills, don't we, Wilf?'

'Aye we do. Anyroad, let's pop in to t'Dog and find out more abaht what's goin' on.'

'All right, you're on. I haven't been in there for a while. It'll be nice to see people.'

'Ah thought ah hadn't seen thi for a bit. But ah don't think there'll be many in 'cos it's dinner time and folk'll be at work,' said Bramley.

'Never mind.'

The two men crossed the green and saw a number of unfamiliar vehicles in the inn car park.

'Ah'll bet that's them newspaper buggers again,' observed Bramley. 'They were all over t'village last week. Now there's been another murder they're back.' They entered the bar, in which, as Bramley had predicted, there were no locals. However, a number of brash-looking types, mostly men with shaved heads, beards and earrings, were clustered around one end of the bar, drinking gin and tonics and talking in loud voices.

Rob Owen looked pleased when Bramley and Dexter walked in. 'Well, I haven't seen you two for a while.'

'No, ah've been busy lookin' after a couple o' ewes that've been taken badly. They're OK now,' said Bramley.

'And I've been out making the best of the weather, but it looks like it's broken now,' said Dexter. 'I just came down to get a few provisions, and found the shop closed and the police on guard.' He explained to Owen that neither he nor Bramley had heard about the second murder. Owen pulled them a couple of pints.

'You haven't missed anything. It must be nice sometimes to be so out of things. I can't believe it,' he said. 'We were just starting to get on our feet again. God knows what will happen now. Who's going to want to come and stay in this village?'

'It'll blow over again, once this lot have had their fill,' said Dexter, nodding at the reporters. 'Have they been pumping you for information?'

Owen looked over at them. 'Yes, just like last time. They're not content with accounts of what happened, they want you to name who you think did it and then tell them some lurid details. I'm not playing their game. That chief inspector saw them off last week, but he's gone now – probably wanted to get out of their way.'

At that moment, two of the reporters detached themselves from the group and came over to Bramley and Dexter. 'I take it you live round here,' said one. He had stubble on his face and was wearing jeans and Dr Martens.

'Yes,' replied Dexter, while Bramley scowled at the man. 'So?'

'Did you see what happened last night? Did you know this bloke who was bumped off?'

'No we didn't see anything, but we knew the victim.'

'Of course, I forgot. Everyone knows everyone in a place like this, don't they?' said the reporter.

'That's right, so you must have an idea who did it,' said a fat man in a denim jacket; he had tattoos on the backs of his hands.

'Two murders in a place like this,' said a third, dressed in purple trousers and a yellow waistcoat. 'What's going on? Are you all getting so bored you've started killing each other for fun?'

'What the 'ell do yer mean by that?' exploded Bramley.

'Steady on, pops. Just a joke. We just want to know if you have any information for us.'

'Well, wi bloody don't, and if wi knew owt wi wunt be telling t'likes o' thee. So why don't ye all just tae thi 'ook and bugger off.'

The reporters reacted to this with consternation, as if not sure whether Bramley was speaking English. Dexter laughed. 'Well, you wanted to speak to a local person and now you have.'

The reporters left Bramley, who drank his beer and glared at them, and turned to Dexter. 'This is a small place, isn't it?' one of them asked. 'Some of you must have noticed someone behaving a bit bonkers. You know, the "village idiot goes berserk" kind of thing.'

Dexter winced. These people dealt in the crudest stereotypes. 'There's no one in this village you could describe as an idiot,' he replied. 'I think the police have their suspects. You should be talking to them.'

'We would, but they're not here. I think DCI Oldroyd's avoiding us.'

I don't blame him, thought Dexter.

'Aren't you all frightened that you're going to be next?' asked the reporter with the stubble. 'It's normally all cosy and safe up here, right? But now it's become dangerous and people can't sleep easily in their beds at night.'

They've written in clichés for so long, they speak in them as well, thought Dexter. 'I don't think people are cowering behind the doors of their houses,' he said.

'What about this bloke who was killed – Gorton, Peter Gorton?'

'What about him?'

'What was he like? Could he have had criminal connections? Two murders now; we might be talking about a criminal gang operating from here, and there's been a big argument. It's a nice cover, isn't it? Come and live among the yokels and no one suspects you.'

Dexter had to laugh at the outlandishness of this idea. 'Peter was just an ordinary, friendly bloke who did a good job of running the shop. The idea of him being in some underworld set-up is ridiculous. Look, can we just drink our beer in peace now?'

The reporters, realising they weren't going to get anything else, slunk back to their side of the bar, presumably waiting until another unsuspecting local person came in.

'Bloody nuisance,' muttered Bramley.

Behind the bar, Owen laughed. 'Yes, but they're spending plenty in here so I'm not complaining. They'll stay for a while until they realise that nobody has anything interesting to tell them.'

'You're right,' said Dexter.

Owen came closer and whispered, 'Actually I do know something about Peter's past, but I'm not telling them. I'm sure the police will have found out by now.'

'What?'

'Once, when he'd had a few drinks, he told me he'd been a prison officer.'

Dexter looked up sharply. 'Did he? Where?'

'He didn't say. Not that it has anything to do with his murder.'

'No,' replied Dexter, looking thoughtfully into his beer.

~

Back in the office in Harrogate with Andy and Steph, Oldroyd was approaching the case with renewed energy.

'So, we need the profile of Wilson from the Met, and check that it includes a photograph.'

'OK, sir.'

'Steph, contact Saunders and get him back up here for questioning.'

'Right, sir.'

They both left the room. Oldroyd was hoping to have a moment of reflection, but the hectic pace continued as his phone rang.

'Bloody hell, Jim, what's going on up there? Two murders now! In a dales village! What's the world coming to?' Tom Walker's gruff tones were unmistakable.

'It's a shock, Tom, I certainly wasn't expecting it. It's forced us to rethink everything. We have to assume the two are connected – the circumstances are so similar.' He outlined what they'd found out about Fraser's hoard of money and also Patrick Wilson and the Drover Road robbery.

'Well, at least you've got a couple of leads, then. Blackmail's always a good motive to look for if you've got a murder. And you really think this Wilson could have survived and be involved in it?'

'His body was never found, Tom, and he's the only person who had a motive to kill both victims.'

Walker grunted. 'It sounds a bit far-fetched to me, but you know best. It's certainly a weird case, so maybe it'll have a weird conclusion. Let me know if you need more help. I don't think Watkins will be bothered about this, he only starts getting agitated when somebody he thinks is important gets bumped off.'

Oldroyd laughed and spoke quickly to prevent a rant by Walker. 'OK, Tom, we're on it. Don't worry,' he said, and then he politely took his leave.

While he'd been talking to Walker, his phone had vibrated. Looking at the screen, he saw that he had a text from Deborah:

> *Booked us in for 'As You Like it' in York tomorrow evening. It's a little touring company and they all play a lot of different parts. They've got good reviews. Alice saw them in Ripon, said they were great fun.*

Oldroyd was pleased about this. He loved his Shakespeare, and he liked to see the plays performed in informal settings. And then something in his mind shifted – something which, as yet, he couldn't pin down.

～

It was late afternoon. The rain had subsided to a drizzle and part of the fells was visible again, although the tops were still covered in a thick mist. Ian Davis, wet and tired, had dropped his team off and then parked the Land Rover in the estate's garage, which was down a track behind the village. Although he knew that his long-term future was unclear, he was finding his work much easier without Fraser constantly on his back, even though the wet weather made things difficult. He walked back along the track, his boots splashing through puddles and his wet hair plastered to his head. As he turned a corner around a high hedge, he bumped into the one person he always tried to avoid: Liz Smith. She was dressed in a battered, mud-stained outdoor jacket.

'Oh, bloody hell!' he said as he moved aside.

Liz gave him a grim smile. 'Don't worry, Davis, I won't hurt you.'

He looked at her warily. 'I'm not sure about that. You're bloody fanatics, you lot. I don't know what you might do. Maybe it was you who got rid of my boss.'

'Oh, well maybe it was. It could be you next. Maybe we killed Peter Gorton too. Perhaps we're all mad.' She stared at him, wide-eyed in mock horror, and waved her arms. 'Anyway, I think you were glad to see the back of Fraser. I'll bet he was a sod to work for.'

Davis couldn't deny the truth of this and looked down. He noticed that her ankle was strapped up. He pointed to her leg.

'Did you get that on Evershaw Moor t'other day? I heard you were up there causing trouble.'

She glared at him. 'Yes, and I'm not ashamed of it. I got it for a good cause. The people who should be ashamed are those thugs, probably friends of yours, who beat up a young man who ended up in hospital. At least he'll survive. Not like Sam Cooper.'

Davis ignored this reference to the death on the moor. 'It's our jobs you're threatening, that's what you people don't understand.'

'Jobs which involve cruelty to animals. Shooting birds for sport! How can you do it?'

'What choice do yer think we have? Most of us have families to support.'

'You could leave here and find something better to do.'

'Oh sure, as if it was as easy as that. It's pointless talking to you.'

Davis looked away, waved at her in contempt and walked off without another word. Liz Smith shook her head, turned and made her way slowly, limping a little, in the other direction. Both remained as entrenched as ever in their attitudes to grouse shooting.

∼

'What do you fancy for tea tonight, then? And we might as well get things for a few days while we're here.'

Oldroyd and Deborah were doing a quick mid-week tour of the supermarket. Oldroyd was pushing the trolley and Deborah was consulting a list. As they both worked full-time, neither were particularly good at planning meals ahead. Any arrangement for dinner was further complicated by Deborah's aversion to meat. Oldroyd was quite happy to join her and reduce his meat consumption, but many of his ideas for meals turned out to be unsuitable. He enjoyed food but knew very little about cooking and ingredients.

He'd once suggested moussaka.

'But the original version has minced lamb in it, Jim.'

'Does it? I thought it was just aubergines and potatoes. What about lasagne?'

'Minced beef!'

'Yes, but not much. You could just leave it out.'

'You can do vegetarian versions of lasagne but they taste different,' said Deborah. 'I'm not sure you'd like them.'

'Well, I like a good curry: balti or bhuna.'

'Yes, but I bet you always have the chicken version.'

'Or lamb.'

'Jim! You're not taking this seriously.'

He'd laughed. 'Well, I'm happy to leave it to you. Your culinary knowledge is far superior to mine.'

'Hmm. You sound like a man trying to escape from domestic responsibilities to me. I don't like this meal-planning and shopping any more than you do.'

He smiled at the memory. Anyway, here they were again.

This time Oldroyd had some better suggestions. Stung by Deborah's criticism, he'd spent a little time consulting cookery books. 'How about roasted vegetables with feta cheese? I love that, and tomorrow I could do my macaroni with cheese and tomato sauce.'

'And ham?'

'I don't put much ham in – just a little to . . . flavour it.'

'OK then,' said Deborah with a sigh, as she picked items from the shelves and put them in the trolley. 'We'll have an omelette on Thursday, then we're going to your sister's on Friday. Good! That's the week taken care of. I'm just going down to get some bread. I'll meet you at the checkout.'

She disappeared into the next aisle, and Oldroyd pushed the trolley down past the magazines and newspapers section. He paused to have a quick browse through the headlines and Yorkshire-themed magazines, and his eye was caught by a headline in the children's comics section. It was a bold title in garish red: 'The Scarlet Claw!' The title referred to an evil monster which a hero would have to defeat, pictured in its blood-dripping horror on the cover. It reminded Oldroyd of something else he'd read or seen with that title.

Deborah found him reading the comic.

'Jim, what are you doing? I couldn't see you at the checkout. What on earth . . . ? The man's deranged: he's reading a children's comic. If you want it, put it in the trolley, but let's go.'

'Sorry,' replied Oldroyd, replacing the comic on the shelf. 'You know how ideas come to me at odd times. Have you heard of a novel or a film called *The Scarlet Claw*? I've seen or read something with that title but I can't remember what.'

'No, never heard of it. You'll have to google it, but not now please. I'm desperate to get back for a cup of tea.'

When they arrived home, Oldroyd made some tea while Deborah unpacked. Then he went to his computer and looked up *The Scarlet Claw*. It turned out to be an old Sherlock Holmes film from 1944 with good old Basil Rathbone and Nigel Bruce. In a contemporary poster there was Holmes smoking his pipe with Watson at his side, and in the background were vague shapes in a chilling mist. Oldroyd had a memory of watching it years ago, when he was a boy.

As in the comic, the 'scarlet claw' was thought to belong to a monster until Holmes proved otherwise. But what happened in the story that had struck a chord with him? When he had the time he would have to try to find it on YouTube and see if the story would relinquish its secret.

Six

White Beacon Hags
Dickens Dike
Great Shunner Fell
Rom Shaw Dike

It was really good to see you on Thursday. Could we meet
up sometime soon? There are one or two things I'd like us
to discuss. J. x

This text message came to Oldroyd's phone the next morning while he and Deborah were having breakfast. The text stirred up all the confused feelings he'd felt in Oxford. He looked at Deborah. He wasn't going to conceal this from her. That would only lead to trouble.

'Remember I told you Julia was there, down in Oxford?'

'Yes. Well, she would be for her daughter's degree ceremony, wouldn't she?'

'True, but what do you think about this?' He showed her the text. She read it and gave an arch smile.

'Oooh! It sounds to me like she might be interested in you again. Have you told me about everything that happened down there? Now be honest!'

Oldroyd laughed, knowing that she was joking, but he still found it difficult. 'No, seriously, I want to know what you think is going on in her mind.'

Deborah sniffed and read the text again. 'Well, from what you've told me, she hasn't been in the habit of sending friendly texts in the past, right?'

'Correct. In fact, ever since we separated, she's been fairly cold and distant.'

'So, to say it was "really good to see you" is obviously giving you a different and very positive signal about how she feels about you. Then she wants to meet up but doesn't specify what she wants to discuss with you. Is that a little tease? I wonder if there actually is anything, or does she just want to see you?' She gave him another meaningful smile. 'All in all, I think your wife might want you back, Jim. Oh dear!' She pretended to dab at a tear in her eye. 'Is this the end for me? Shall I pack my bags?'

Oldroyd was half amused and half alarmed. 'No, of course not.' He put his hand on hers. 'I'm with you now, and that's all there is to it.'

'I know,' she replied, grasping his hand. 'Don't worry, I'm not jealous and insecure. Just don't have anything to do with the bitch.' She burst out laughing. 'No, I shouldn't have said that!'

Oldroyd was laughing with relief. He loved her sense of humour. 'I'll have to reply and see if it's anything to do with Louise or Robert or the house or anything else. I'll let you know and I'll only meet her in a public place.'

'A cafe, and I'll sneak in and watch from a distance.'

'OK, you're welcome.' He looked at her. 'I'd never do anything to jeopardise our relationship. You know that.'

She smiled in a more serious way. 'I do,' she said.

~

Later that morning there was a knock on the door of the Fraser manor house. Henrietta opened it to discover a short, balding man dressed in a cheap-looking suit.

'Yes?'

'Good morning. Gideon Rawnsley, Elite Cars, Ripon. I'm sorry to say I've come to collect Mr Fraser's Jaguar XF.'

'What? Why is that?'

'He never paid for it I'm afraid. We only received the deposit and one payment. We won't be able to refund any of that because he's used the car. When that happens, it becomes a second-hand car and there's a large depreciation in its value.'

Henrietta shook her head at this latest blow. 'You'd better come in.'

'OK. I'll just tell my assistant. She's the one who drove me up here.' Rawnsley popped over to a nearby car in the lane and then returned to the narrow entrance hall.

'Just wait a moment,' said Henrietta. 'I'll have to ask my mother where the keys are.' She went back down the hall, opened a door and disappeared into a room.

Rawnsley looked around at the oak panelling and paintings in the hall. His encounters with the rich had left him cynical about people with money. The richer they appeared, the harder it was to get money out of them. Here was Fraser driving expensive cars, living in a seventeenth-century manor house and throwing out invitations to join shooting parties, while he was clearly in serious debt. There was a phrase Rawnsley had heard somewhere: 'Fine manners and unpaid bills'. It summed up Fraser exactly.

Henrietta returned with the keys. 'I must say, I think it's a bit heartless coming at this time when my father's not even buried yet, but here you are.' She handed the keys over. 'Luckily my mother won't miss it. It's far too big for her.'

'Many thanks,' said Rawnsley, and he immediately left the house. He wasn't going to get into an argument about morality after the way he'd been strung along by Fraser.

He got into the Jaguar, and passed straight out of the village followed by his assistant.

As he drove along the wet roads, he looked across the grey expanse of Gouthwaite Reservoir, its surface choppy and cold in the autumn wind. His relationship with Fraser had been an education. He realised now that the invitation to the shoot had been a way of controlling him: Fraser had thought that if Rawnsley shot some grouse and had a good dinner, he wouldn't press him so hard for payment on the car.

The truth about what Fraser really thought of him had emerged on the night of the murder: he saw him as an irritating little salesman who dealt in that inconvenient thing called money.

Well, Rawnsley had learned some good lessons in how to handle people of that class: keep your distance and don't socialise with them. And even more important: see the colour of their money before a big sale, and don't cut them any slack even though they think they deserve it.

As he arrived back in Ripon, the rain stopped and the sun broke through. He returned the car to the showroom, albeit now as a used car. He would still get a good price for it, and why not? He had a business to run and he would drive a harder bargain in future. There would be no more deference.

~

Oldroyd's second press conference on the Niddersgill murders took place at Harrogate. The press pack, disappointed with their pickings in the village, had descended on HQ hungry for some red meat from the DCI. Oldroyd didn't need to be told by DCS Walker that he had to face them again.

There was a room for press conferences and briefings in which Oldroyd, on his home territory, normally felt in control. If the atmosphere was tense he would first of all imagine walking up to the summit of Ingleborough from Clapham, one of his favourite walks. This always had a calming effect. But he felt much more on the defensive in this conference. There had still been no arrests and now there was a second death. The police were beginning to look defeated.

He'd thought long and hard about whether or not to mention the Drover Road robbery and Patrick Wilson, as they had no proof. On the one hand, he'd be releasing a hare and the dogs would go mad after it – it was such a juicy, dramatic story, 'Criminal Back from the Dead' and so on. And if it came to nothing, they would look very foolish. On the other hand, the press were always useful in broadcasting the message that the police were looking for someone, and sometimes this flushed a suspect out. He decided to take the risk and start the session with it. This would give him the initiative.

The press briefing room was packed. Oldroyd sat looking sombre, flanked by Steph and Andy.

'I want to begin with an important announcement in relation to the murders in the village of Niddersgill. We are working on the assumption that the murders are linked, as there are many similarities between them. We have identified a possible suspect who had a motive to kill both of the victims. This person is Patrick Wilson, who some of you may remember was a member of the gang who committed the Drover Road robbery in London.' There were expressions of surprise all around the room.

'Surely he's dead, Chief Inspector?' called out one reporter.

'So we thought. He fell into a river in Manchester trying to escape from prison. But no body was ever found and we now think that Wilson may have survived and be involved in these murders.' There were gasps of astonishment at this.

'Really? That sounds incredible. What evidence do you have?' This was a tricky question, which had to be handled carefully.

'We do not have conclusive evidence at this stage, but we believe the likelihood of his involvement is high, sufficiently high for us to ask for anybody with any information about the whereabouts of Patrick Wilson to come forward.'

The rapid murmurings of urgent conversations were heard about the room. As Oldroyd had predicted, they loved this.

'Is there any point in that, Chief Inspector? If he is alive and active as you suggest, surely the only people who know where he is are those who are hiding him. And they're unlikely to come forward.'

'Well, that may be true, but in the past crooks have been known to betray each other, so it's worth a try.'

'Where do you think he is?'

'My best guess is that he's disappeared back among the criminal fraternity of London, from where he's planned these murders.'

'So the two murderers were hitmen?'

'You could put it that way. It's significant that they've both disappeared without trace. They were relative newcomers to the village and I imagine they've returned to the capital too.'

'Is this your main line of enquiry?' There was scepticism in the voice.

'Yes, but not the only one. We're still following other leads.'

'Do you think there could be another murder in the village?' This was always a difficult question. A positive answer created alarm, but a negative one came back to bite you if there was another victim.

'We have no reason to think that anyone else is at risk, but until the perpetrators are caught, it is necessary for everyone to remain vigilant.'

At the end of the conference, Oldroyd was happy with the way he'd dealt with it, but when the detectives returned to the office he seemed morose. He sat in his chair and said nothing while Andy made coffee.

'Cheer up, sir,' said Steph, who had known Oldroyd a long time and recognised his moods. 'You handled that well.'

Oldroyd put his head in his hands. 'Yes, yes, it was OK, but something's not right. I could see the doubt on their faces when I was telling them about Patrick Wilson. I know he's the one with the motives, but these hitmen . . . Green and Moore.' He shook his head. 'I don't know. We'll have to wait until we get the full file on Wilson and see if that reveals anything. Saunders will be here shortly, so that might be interesting. I just don't have that feeling I normally get when we're closing in on the killer.' He sighed, then smiled at his two sergeants, slapped his legs and got up. 'We'll just have to press on like we always do.'

∼

Back in Nidderdale the weather was overcast but dry, and the wind had dropped. Tony Dexter, in corduroys and waxed jacket, was out with his binoculars moving carefully around the wet areas at the top end of Gouthwaite Reservoir. Bird migration would be starting soon and winter visitors to the UK would arrive. He watched a group of oystercatchers, and then found a place in the reeds from which he could see a small pool of water. After waiting for a while, his patience was rewarded when a shy water rail, crouching with its head forward, stepped cautiously out from the reeds. He focused the lenses and zoomed in on the red bill and red eye, the rich brown back and grey chest.

'They're beautiful birds, aren't they?' a voice whispered behind him.

He turned to see Liz Smith. 'Oh, it's you. Be quiet,' he whispered back.

Luckily the water rail was undisturbed. It stood for a while in the pool of water, then turned and walked slowly back into the reeds. Dexter turned to Liz. She was wearing brown dungarees and a woolly hat. Her ankle was still strapped up but she was walking more easily.

'What are you doing here?'

'Just out walking. I caught sight of you in the reeds and thought you might have found something interesting. I don't spend all my time sabotaging the activities of people who want to kill wildlife – I also enjoy being in the natural world.'

'Good. Does it calm you?' he said.

Liz laughed. 'You mean does it make me less angry? It does when I see a wonderful bird like that, but then I start to think about people who want to kill lovely creatures and I'm back to my sense of outrage. There are men with guns who'd shoot that water rail if they got the chance. It's all about bagging stuff for them.'

'Yes, it's terrible.'

'Why not join us, then?'

Dexter laughed a little nervously. Perhaps he was intimidated by forceful people.

'We've had this discussion before. I'd be pretty useless in a protest: too soft. I prefer to concentrate on my campaigns about the effects of the management of grouse moors on the environment.'

'So you don't have to get your hands dirty?'

'I've come up against a lot of opposition. I confronted Fraser once in his house about the environmental effect of his activities.'

They walked on through the boggy areas surrounding the reed beds. Dexter kept an eye out for birdlife.

'Did you get anywhere with him?'

'No. He didn't really listen to my arguments and I think that's the problem. I don't think you can ever change or defeat them. They're too determined and powerful. The only thing which is going to improve matters is legislation. Look at what happened with fox hunting.'

'A messy law, not properly enforced, which people get round or ignore. That's the problem with going through the politicians; you think they're committed but then if they see the wind is blowing in another direction, they'll water down what they've promised or desert you.'

'Your way is dangerous though, isn't it? You break the law and people get hurt.'

She shrugged. 'I don't care about the law of trespass; it's utterly ridiculous that people can't walk over open countryside, never mind who owns it. Most of those who get hurt are on our side, sabs who get beaten up by thugs. It happened the other day. A young man with me got punched in the face. And you remember what happened with Sam Cooper?'

They reached the water and saw flocks of Canada and greylag geese on the calm surface.

Dexter paused to focus his binoculars again. 'I know you hold Fraser responsible for Cooper's death. So did you retaliate? Was Fraser another casualty of this war?'

'You sound like the police. If you're implying that we murdered someone, even if they were one of our fiercest opponents and caused the death of one of our supporters, you're wrong. I keep saying to people: we preserve life, we don't destroy it.'

Dexter smiled. 'It's OK. I was only joking.'

'The police were all over us of course, once they knew we'd been in conflict with Fraser. I had that detective sergeant who works with the chief inspector round asking questions, and others in my group got visited by police from Pateley. Bloody typical! They weren't around when we were getting beaten up and kidnapped by the beaters the other day.'

'Kidnapped?'

'They frogmarched us into the jeep and drove us down to Pateley Bridge police station. Luckily Inspector Gibbs was there. I think he's quite sympathetic to us, really. He just warned me about our behaviour but he knows we'll take no notice.'

'You should listen to him and be more careful, especially when there are dangerous people about,' said Dexter.

'What do you mean?'

'What do you make of this second murder? Apparently Vic Moore is the main suspect . . . and he's disappeared, just like Alan Green.'

'I didn't really know him. Anyway, it should put the police off our trail, because poor Peter Gorton had nothing to do with grouse shooting,' said Liz.

'Off my trail too. I had the police asking me about Fraser. I think they thought I could have killed him because he was a danger to the environment. But nevertheless, two people have been killed. Doesn't it make you wonder who might be next?'

Liz shook her head as an oystercatcher flew past, emitting its characteristic *kleep*. 'I'm sure lots of people are terrified, but it doesn't worry me. I wouldn't like to be running the Dog and Gun at the moment. I'll bet there've been some cancellations. Jeanette, who works there, comes round to see me. She's interested in our cause. She says the atmosphere's a bit grim though the Owens are putting on a brave face. I'd go there to support them if they didn't serve so much meat and the food wasn't so expensive. Oh, by the way, she said that apparently Peter Gorton was a prison officer before he came here. He kept quiet about that.'

Dexter turned to her abruptly. 'Rob Owen mentioned that in the bar. Did Jeanette say where?'

'What do you mean?'

'Where was he a prison officer?'

'Oh, Manchester, I think she said. Strangeways.'

'How does she know?' He seemed serious and intense.

'No idea. Things leak out, don't they? It was probably one of those reporters who were all over the village, who'd been doing a bit of research and blabbed about it in the bar.'

'Right. Well, that is odd. He didn't seem like a prison officer, did he?' said Dexter, returning to a more light-hearted tone.

'No, but you can see why he wanted to come out here for a change. It must be grim working in a prison.'

They'd been walking across the marshy area and now reached a track.

'OK,' said Dexter. 'I'm going up this path back over to the barn, so I'll see you around. Be good.' He waved to her and walked off.

'There's no chance of that,' called back Liz with a laugh, but as she walked back along the track to the village she was puzzled.

Why had Dexter reacted so strangely to her information about Peter Gorton? It had seemed not only to surprise but also to worry him.

She shook her head. This was turning into one crazy village. And people had *her* down as the fanatical madwoman.

~

Henry Saunders sat in the interview room trying to retain his dignified manner, despite feeling distinctly rattled by his summons to

Harrogate Police HQ. He was facing a stern Oldroyd, with Andy in attendance.

'So,' began Oldroyd, 'you made the mistake of not being frank with us in our first conversation. It rarely pays off, and all you've succeeded in doing is bringing suspicion on yourself. Tell us about the payments you made to Sandy Fraser.'

Saunders looked extremely uncomfortable and sighed. 'Well, if I must. I don't suppose it'll do me any good to conceal it for any longer.' He looked at Oldroyd, whose expression was stony. 'Sandy was blackmailing me.'

'But he was a very old friend of yours.'

'He was, but he did it in such a discreet way that it hardly affected our relationship.'

'I find that hard to believe,' said Oldroyd.

Saunders laughed sardonically. 'Well, it's how our class behave, isn't it? Don't talk about unpleasant things directly, especially concerning money; preserve the surface chumminess.'

'What was he blackmailing you about?'

'He saw me in a restaurant in London with a woman with whom I was having an affair at the time. We both knew this had handed him some power and leverage in our relationship, if he chose to use it. Actually, I don't think he ever would have done if he hadn't become desperate.'

'In what way?'

'Sandy was a good judge, but he was no businessman. He completely overreached himself buying that grouse moor. He must have paid an enormous price for it. It wasn't long before he was struggling. I'm sure he never told Miriam anything about their financial difficulties.'

'Maybe not, but she was beginning to work it out.'

'I see. It must have been worse than I thought. Anyway, he began to ask me regularly for money, ostensibly loans, but we both knew the money would not be paid back. I didn't want my marriage to be damaged; I'm devoted to my wife, but we all like to play away a little at times, don't we?' He looked at Oldroyd, maybe expecting a smile of understanding, even complicity.

'Do we?' replied Oldroyd, in a tone that expressed his intense distaste.

Saunders cleared his throat, somewhat embarrassed. 'So I paid up. I could afford what he was asking. He never overstepped the mark and asked for too much; he would have thought it very ungentlemanly to be greedy and place me in difficulties.'

Andy shook his head in disbelief at the strange moral code of a 'gentlemanly' blackmailer.

'Even if the demands were not excessive, you must have wearied of handing over money to him,' Oldroyd said.

'I did, Chief Inspector, but I didn't kill him. I assume that's why I'm here, because you now think I had a motive to kill Sandy.'

'Correct. The victims of blackmailers often snap at some point and lash out at their blackmailer.'

'I didn't. It was a nuisance, but I could afford it. In a way I blamed myself. I shouldn't really have been there with Harriet, so in a way I was being punished. Also, you probably won't believe this but I still thought of Sandy as my friend, a friend who'd got himself into a mess. He must have been suffering a lot but he was too proud to admit it. I recognise that attitude and I didn't wish him any harm.'

There was a hardness in Saunders's expression when he talked about Fraser, and a faint curling of the lip that confirmed Oldroyd's scepticism about much of this. But he changed the line of questioning. 'Have you ever had anything to do with a man named Patrick Wilson?'

'Never heard of him.'

'He's one of our chief suspects in the murder of Sandy Fraser. When he was a judge, Fraser sent Wilson to prison for a long time, but we think Wilson escaped alive and planned his revenge. You would have made a nice accomplice for him. You both had a grievance against Fraser.'

Saunders laughed. 'I've absolutely no idea what you're talking about.'

'Have you heard of two men called Matthew Hart and Philip Traynor? They were involved in a robbery with Wilson.'

'No.'

Oldroyd looked at him, long and hard. 'OK. We'll leave it there. We have no hard evidence against you so you're free to go, but stay where we can contact you.'

'He certainly had a motive, sir,' said Andy after Saunders had left the room. 'But somehow I don't think he's involved. I can't see him as someone who would get in with the criminal underworld. And then, conveniently, in that underworld there's someone who also had a motive for killing Fraser. It doesn't stack up.'

'No, for the most part I agree,' replied Oldroyd. 'But I think he underplayed the anguish and anger of a person who is handing over money to a blackmailer. It's not impossible that he might have arranged for a hitman to relieve him of his tormentor. And remember, coincidences do occur. He may have met Wilson.'

'But what about the second murder, sir?'

'I don't think he was a part of that, but if Wilson was involved in Fraser's murder he may have discovered that Gorton was here in the same village, and then continued with his revenge killing alone.' Oldroyd yawned and rubbed his forehead. The stress was taking its toll on his energy levels and he didn't find his own theories very convincing. He could do with another escape into his new poetic creativity. 'Has the information on Wilson arrived from the Met yet?'

'I'm expecting the file soon. I've heard from Inspector Gibbs. He says that the Manchester police and prison authorities had nothing new, but they did confirm that Gorton had been accused of assault and that he'd taken early retirement under a cloud.'

'OK, well, let's see if anything's arrived.' He slouched over to his computer, desperate for a breakthrough.

~

The bar at the Dog and Gun had a very sombre atmosphere. The reporters had left and the group of locals who gathered there regularly had now lost three of its members – one dead and two disappeared; they had no idea what to make of it. Ian Davis, grabbing a quick pint or two at lunchtime, was at the bar with Wilf Bramley. There was no one else there. The two hardly managed a conversation and instead stood sighing, tutting and murmuring phrases such as 'I dunno' and 'What the bloody hell's goin' on?' in between taking swigs of beer.

Kirsty was behind the bar. She was feeling better but still worried that Alan Green or even Vic Moore might come back to get her, and she had insisted on a male member of staff being close by during her shifts.

'How's Jeanette?' asked Davis.

'Not brilliant, as you can imagine. She's gone home to her parents in Northallerton for a while, to get away from here.'

'Ah don't blame her, poor lass,' said Bramley. He sat on a bar stool, rubbed his unshaven chin, and shook his head as if trying but failing to make sense of it all. 'It's a bloody funny do that both you and 'er witnessed them murders, in't it?'

'That's what everybody's saying,' replied Kirsty as she dried some beer glasses. 'I don't know what to make of it. It could just be coincidence, but the really creepy thing is that both me and Jeanette felt that Alan and Vic wanted us to see them. To see their faces. They looked at us before they ran off.'

Davis drained his glass. 'Just time for another, Kirsty.' She pulled him a fresh pint. 'That's bloody crazy, but what's worse is that we knew Alan and Vic. They drank in here with us. They were good blokes and then they go committing murder and . . . Peter . . .' His speech trailed away and he shrugged.

'If it really was them,' said Kirsty.

'Eh? What do yer mean? Ah thought you said you both had a good look at 'em?' said Bramley.

'We did, but Harry's got a theory.'

'Oh yeah,' said Davis, sounding sceptical.

'Yes. He says we saw them, but only at a distance. It could have been someone impersonating them.'

'But you saw their faces.'

'Yes, but not really close up. They could, you know, have been made up to look like Alan and Vic.'

'What!? So what's happened to the real Alan and Vic?'

'Harry says they could have been kidnapped, and then this person – or there could have been two of them – disguised himself, or themselves, as Alan and Vic to put suspicion on them. And that's why they wanted us to get a good look at them – that's the murderers – but not too close, so that we would say it was Alan and Vic. Oh shit, I've not explained that very well!'

Davis laughed. 'I think I followed it. Is Harry going to tell the police about this big theory?'

'He might. You have to admit, it makes sense. Do you really think Alan and Vic would murder people for no reason?'

'Where did these . . . mystery folk come from, then?' asked an also-doubtful Bramley.

'That's for the police to find out.'

Davis laughed again. 'What a load of tosh! He's got an imagination, I'll give him that, and too much time on his hands by the sounds of it. I don't think you're keeping him entertained at night.'

Kirsty hit him with the tea towel. 'Hey! You cheeky bugger! Shut your face! Everybody seems to know about Harry and me.'

'You haven't exactly kept it a secret. We're always spotting you two making out by the back door.' Grinning, Davis nodded towards the other end of the inn. 'One night, me and some of the lads I work with were here late and we crept round to the back where you can see the window of Harry's room, and guess what? No light was on, because he wasn't there, was he?'

Kirsty was outraged but she took it humorously. 'You rotten sods, there's no privacy with people like you around, is there?! It's a wonder you didn't try to look into my room as well!'

'We would have done if it hadn't been at the front.' Davis's eyes twinkled with mischief.

'No!' cried Kirsty. 'You disgusting voyeurs!'

'Never mind, lass,' said Bramley with a chuckle. 'It's only because they wish they could have been there themselves.'

Kirsty laughed uproariously at this, and Davis went bright red. 'Oh! Look at him. Blushing! And him a married man. Does Jenny know you like to stalk couples?' she taunted.

'No . . . Don't say anything . . . I . . .' stammered Davis, on the defensive. 'Bloody hell!' he laughed. 'I should have kept quiet. Anyway, to get back to Harry's theory. What's going to happen to the real Alan and Vic now? Are the murderers going to release them? Then they'll both say they were being held captive, won't they?'

Kirsty frowned. 'I'm not sure. Harry hasn't said anything about that.'

'And why did these people want to murder Fraser and Peter Gorton anyway?' continued Davis. 'And why bother dressing up as someone else in the village? Why didn't they just kill them?'

'Maybe to lull their victims into a false sense of security or . . . Oh! I don't know! You'll have to ask Harry.'

'I will, don't worry. I'm glad he's not in charge of the investigation.' Davis had enjoyed pulling Newton's theory to pieces, but Bramley was not so sure that it lacked credibility.

'Aye, well,' he began with a lugubrious sigh. 'What if Harry's reight? Who maht be kidnapped next? And waar still: who maht be shot next?'

This silenced them all.

The humour and laughter had been a welcome relief from the shock and horror of recent events, but Bramley's comment brought them back to the reality: two people had been shot, the reasons were unclear and there was no guarantee that there would not be another victim.

'Anyway, I'm off back to work,' said Davis, who staggered a bit as he left the bar. Kirsty looked after him and frowned.

It was time she made a call.

~

At Harrogate HQ, Oldroyd was poring through all the information that had finally arrived from the Met about Patrick Wilson. His form was impressive. Although it seemed that he'd come to crime late, in his early thirties, he'd built up a large portfolio of criminal acts, beginning with fraud and then progressing to burglaries and armed robbery. He was clearly a hardened and dangerous career criminal who despised law enforcement and was capable of violence. He'd attacked police and prison officers several times. Oldroyd could imagine the provocation that had led to Peter Gorton confronting him in some way in Strangeways jail. The planning of his robberies showed that Wilson had a sharp and cunning brain.

This led Oldroyd to muse, as he often did, on the cliché that if these intelligent criminal minds actually used their intelligence in a legal way, they would probably make more money and not end up incarcerated in prison.

The file contained a police photograph of Wilson: an ordinary-looking man with thinning hair, grey eyes and a moustache. Oldroyd searched the face for clues. Was there anything familiar in the features?

Oldroyd felt some vague sense of recognition, but it was easy to imagine that you'd seen someone before; people were more similar to each other than was commonly thought, and every face had many like it in the population as a whole.

Where was Wilson now? A man like him would have many links in the underworld, so the likelihood was that he was holed up somewhere plotting his revenge on the people who, in his view, had treated him badly. Maybe they should try offering a reward for his capture. That might tempt one of his cronies to betray him. Personal gain was always paramount to these people, but there was a rough code of behaviour among them: the penalties for betrayal, especially to the police, were severe.

This made Oldroyd think of Matthew Hart, the man who had turned against Wilson's gang. Presumably the Met knew where he was and had warned him that Wilson could be alive and free. If the police had done their work properly there should be little chance of Wilson tracking him down.

Oldroyd looked up from the screen and rubbed his eyes. Where did they go next? It was really up to the Met to try to find Wilson. All the other theories seemed to have led nowhere. Wilson was the only suspect who had a motive to kill both Fraser and Gorton – that is, if he really was still alive. It was all so insubstantial and there seemed to be no immediate prospect of bringing things to a conclusion. It left Oldroyd feeling powerless.

Soon, he knew, Watkins would be on to Superintendent Walker complaining about the lack of results, and then Oldroyd would be called in and would have to listen to one of Walker's tirades about Watkins, while trying to explain why no further progress had been made. He grimaced at the thought.

At least he was going to York that evening to see *As You Like It* with Deborah. It would be a welcome break from this frustrating case.

～

'Look, you're not going there tonight, right?'

'Oh come on, love. I work hard – everybody goes for a pint when they've finished work.'

Ian and Jenny Davis were having a row in the kitchen of their cottage. It was early evening and the kids were upstairs playing. Jenny was by the door with her arms folded and Ian was on the sofa looking away from her.

'You never have one pint though, do you? It's always a few and then you come home tipsy or drunk. Kirsty rang and she told me you're going there at dinner time in the middle of the day as well.'

'What? Wait till I see her. I don't go every day. It's just for the odd pint. She should mind her own business.' He looked sheepish.

'She's worried about you, like I am. You're drinking too much, Ian. It's not doing you any good and we can't afford it.'

Davis looked very uncomfortable. 'OK, it's been a bit over t'top recently, I admit, but it was all because of that bloody Fraser. He was making my life a misery. It cheers me up to be in that bar with the others. We always have a laugh.'

'I'm sure you do, while her indoors does the ironing and puts the kids to bed.'

'I put the kids to bed a lot!'

'Sometimes. Anyway, it's got to stop, Ian. Do you want to be a father who drinks the family money away?'

'No, but it's under control – I know how far to go.'

'That's what they all say until they end up alcoholics.'

'Alcoholic!'

'You heard what I said. What makes you think you're different to everybody else? As if we haven't got enough problems in this village without you drinking our money away. And that's another reason I prefer you at home at the moment. Two people have been killed and I worry when you're out.' Unexpectedly, she burst into tears. Davis was shocked.

'Oh love, don't. Look, I'll stay in tonight, and why don't you come with me to the Dog more often? Then you can watch how much I drink.'

'I'd like to, but what about the kids? We haven't got a babysitter.'

'Well, there's a bloke I work with. He has a teenage daughter and she'd like to earn a bit o' money. So I could ask him if she's available. We wouldn't have to give her much and it would be a change for you.'

She dried her eyes and looked at him. 'Yes. Why not? I want to get back to playing darts again. I used to be good, remember?'

'I do. It's time you got out more. And I promise I'll cut down on the boozing.'

She stopped crying and gave him a hug.

∼

Out in the Vale of York, the evening weather was calm and the sky clear. The lines of trees and small copses in the flat fields were starting to go yellow, with hints of orange and brown. Huge machines were moving up and down, doing some harvesting of wheat and barley in the last hours of daylight.

Deborah was driving the Saab as she and Oldroyd entered the old part of the city. As they crossed Lendal Bridge, Oldroyd looked over to see that the river was very high after the recent rains up in the dales, from where the Ure, Swale and Nidd flowed down and joined to form the Ouse near York. Flooding was a notorious problem in Yorkshire's ancient capital.

They parked in the big car park down Gillygate and walked back past the Theatre Royal, down Davygate, Parliament Street and Piccadilly to the magnificence of the fourteenth-century Merchant Adventurers' Hall. The stunning timber-framed Great Hall was being used by the small touring theatre company, and what an amazing setting it was for Shakespeare! Oldroyd and Deborah took their seats, and he looked up into the high ceiling. The indoor performances by Elizabethan troupes of actors in some of the great houses of the day and London's Inns of Court must have been very much like this: a small but attentive audience, polished wood reflecting candlelight, voices echoing up among the high roof beams of the steeply pitched wooden frame.

The performance was a great success. The energetic group of four young actors managed to present the play with minimal scenery, props and costumes, and by each one playing numerous parts. Deborah and Oldroyd enjoyed glasses of wine in the interval in a magical atmosphere of conviviality inspired by Shakespearian comedy.

After the show, it was dark as they walked back through the narrow streets.

'Well, that was wonderful!' said Deborah, who was full of enthusiasm. 'I've been taken to a different world and I don't want to come down to earth.'

'I know what you mean,' replied Oldroyd. 'Bottom in *A Midsummer Night's Dream* is described as having been "transported" into a new place and self. Shakespeare always gets the right word.'

'Yes,' said Deborah, very laconically for her. She was still absorbed by the play and its atmosphere. Oldroyd was content to walk on quietly for a while too, because, yet again, Shakespeare had given him an idea to work with.

'Do you know,' he said when they arrived back at the Gillygate car park, 'we need to keep coming to see Shakespeare. This is the second time a play has given me an idea about a case.'

When he and Deborah had watched a promenade production of *A Midsummer Night's Dream* at Ripley Castle early in their relationship, that too had kick-started his brain into solving a seemingly impossible crime.

'Well, that's fine with me,' replied a tired Deborah.

~

When they got back to Harrogate it was quite late, but Oldroyd said he was staying up to watch something.

Deborah looked at him suspiciously. 'This is work, isn't it?'

'I'm afraid so, but it does involve watching a film, so it should be quite entertaining.'

Deborah yawned. 'OK, but don't stay up too late, and don't wake me up when you come to bed.'

'I won't. It's been a great evening.' They kissed and Oldroyd went to his computer. What he'd heard tonight in the play had reminded him that he'd been so preoccupied with the case in the last few days that he'd forgotten to look up the Sherlock Holmes film. He soon found it on YouTube.

For the next hour and a quarter he was plunged into the black-and-white world of the film with its sinister music and melodramatic dialogue. It transported him back to his childhood, when these films with Basil Rathbone and Nigel Bruce had thrilled and scared him. Despite the dated corniness there was still a power about the film, especially in Rathbone's steely and commanding presence as Holmes. Oldroyd could see how, in 1944, the film would have been terrifying. By the end, he had not only been entertained, but enlightened.

He crept to bed in the dark, making sure that he didn't disturb Deborah, and then lay awake for quite some time feeling the excitement of the possible breakthrough.

~

John Gray was up early the next morning, even though the weather was very wet again and a thick mist had returned. He liked to listen to the news bulletins or read the latest stories on his laptop. Niddersgill had featured prominently in yesterday's news, including Chief Inspector Oldroyd's press conference. In today's early bulletin, there hadn't been anything new.

Things felt odd in the house now that Vic had gone. He missed him, but of course he knew that he would never come back, not after a crime like that. After recent events, the village didn't feel the same either. Even though he spent most of his time in the studio, he could sense a change in the atmosphere. It was no longer relaxing and he felt once more that his stay in Niddersgill was limited. In fact, it seemed the right time to move on. He was tiring of the small-village atmosphere. Now that the shop was closed, you couldn't get even basic things like milk and bread without going into Pateley Bridge. Actually, he'd found a way round this. He had an arrangement with the Dog and Gun to provide him with milk and a loaf of bread every other day until the shop reopened. It was time to collect these.

He put on a waterproof coat, and walked across the green. He encountered no one in the frightened and shut-up village except David Eastwood, who was wearing a light, waterproof coat over his red T-shirt. The two men exchanged nods. At the back of the inn, the door was answered by Harry Newton.

'Morning, Mr Gray, have you come for your bread and milk?'

'That's right.'

Harry went back inside and returned with a sourdough loaf and a carton of milk. 'Weather's broken,' he said, as Gray handed over the money.

'Yes, but we can't complain, we've had a good run of fine days. Bye.'

After this routine exchange, Gray walked back across the green. The weather didn't concern him. He had a busy day ahead.

∼

When he'd seen John Gray on the wet village green, a thought had struck David Eastwood and he'd stopped to watch Gray walk over to the inn. Yes, it was curious. He would have to contact Inspector Gibbs.

∼

When Steph and Andy arrived at Harrogate HQ, Oldroyd was already there. This was unusual and a sign that he had fresh ideas about the case which he wanted to pursue.

'Andy,' he said abruptly before Andy had got properly into Oldroyd's office. 'Get on to the Met again. I want more information about Patrick Wilson. That stuff they sent us was all well and good, but it was just his criminal record. I want to know more about him as a person and I'm particularly interested in what he did before he embarked on his criminal career.'

'OK, sir,' replied Andy, somewhat puzzled, and went immediately to the general office where he had his desk.

'Are you on to something then, sir?' asked Steph, who'd known her boss a long time and had learned to read his moods. This morning he looked upbeat and animated.

'Maybe, Steph. I'm hoping to confirm my theory when Andy gets the information. If I'm right, we'll need to get back to Niddersgill fairly sharply, although I don't think anyone else is at risk. Can you get on the phone to Inspector Gibbs and warn him that we may need his help?'

'OK, sir.' Steph left the office with some eagerness to perform the task. She was also pleased that at last it looked as if some progress would be made.

The phone rang and Oldroyd answered it, expecting Tom Walker, but it was Andy.

'Sir, I've got DCI Riley from the Met on the phone and he wants to speak to you urgently.'

'Right, put him on.'

'DCI Oldroyd?'

'Yes.'

'It's DCI Riley here. I'm in charge of undercover operations at the Met. I'm sending you the information you asked for about Patrick Wilson's early life.'

'Good, but why are you ringing?'

'Because there are things going on in that village in Nidderdale that it's time you knew about, and you'll have to move quickly if you want to take advantage of them.'

∽

Andy and Steph heard the sound of Oldroyd's voice on the phone and he seemed to be getting more and more excited. They edged into the office, sensing that things were about to kick off. As soon as he came off the phone, Oldroyd scanned through the file on Patrick Wilson that DCI Riley had sent.

'Good Lord! That's it. That confirms what I thought. My God, those idiots at the Met! Why didn't they tell me earlier?' He turned around, both anxious and exhilarated, and saw Andy and Steph looking tense in anticipation of what might be about to happen. 'Right, you two. This is it – it's all falling into place. Get a fast squad car, we need to get up to Niddersgill as quick as we can. There is someone else at risk. I'll tell you about it on the way. And we're going to need armed support. I'll clear it with DCS Walker.'

~

Tony Dexter was reading a book on the geology of the dales while he waited for the rain to ease off. Then he was going to walk further up the dale towards Angram Reservoir and see what the bird life was doing. It was very quiet in the barn, apart from the drumming of the rain on the roof.

There was a knock on the door. He had few visitors and wasn't expecting anybody. He looked through the window and tried to see who it was, but he could only see a huddled figure in an outdoor jacket with the hood pulled up. As soon as he unlocked the door, it was forced wide open and Dexter saw the muzzle of a shotgun. The man holding the gun came in out of the rain and threw back his hood.

'Matt,' he said. 'How nice to see you again.'

'You!' said Dexter.

'You don't sound surprised. You knew I'd turn up at some point, didn't you? You have to answer for what you did, but first you're going to show me where you've hidden the loot.'

~

Bill Gibbs took the call from Andy and was about to leave the Pateley Bridge station when his phone went again. It was David Eastwood.

'Yes, David, make it quick, I've got to get up to Niddersgill pretty sharpish.'

'OK. It's just that, remember you asked me the other day if I'd ever delivered any mail to Vic Moore at that cottage in the village and I said I hadn't?'

'Yes.'

'Well, I don't know whether it's important, but in fact I don't think I've ever delivered anything to John Gray either, except junk mail with just the address on, you know. As far as I can remember, nothing's ever gone to that cottage with their names on. It's as if they don't exist.'

~

Andy drove the police car swiftly up the narrow roads through the pelting rain. By the time they arrived in Niddersgill, the rain was less heavy. They were followed by another car containing two armed officers. Gibbs was waiting for them by the village green with DC Potts.

'There's no answer at the door of Gray's house,' he said.

'We'll have to break in. He could still be in there and, by the way, we need to start using his real name: Patrick Wilson,' said Oldroyd. They walked over towards the cottage.

'The bank robber who was supposed to be dead?' said an amazed Gibbs. 'He's the artist?'

'Yes, he's very much alive, ruthless in exacting his revenge, and, it seems, a master of disguise. He's managed to live in this village for quite a while, posing as a painter, without anyone recognising him.'

'But why should anyone here recognise him? He's a criminal from London.'

'Correct. But the man who gave him a long jail sentence was Fraser, and the man who he thinks mistreated him in Strangeways was Gorton. There's more, but I'll come to that later.'

They had arrived at John Gray's cottage. Oldroyd rapped on the door. 'Wilson, open up. We know what's been going on. We've got armed police officers with us.' There was no response. Oldroyd stood back. 'OK, break in.'

The door soon gave way under a heavy assault from the hefty officers, who went in first and moved quickly through every room in the cottage, reporting back that there was no sign of anyone.

'Blast it! But I think I know where he is. He must have decided to make his final move. He knew we were on to him after that press conference yesterday.' Oldroyd turned to Gibbs. 'Bill, take these officers and go up to Tony Dexter's barn. And we need to call him by his real name too: Matthew Hart.'

'Who's he?'

'The bank robber who turned Queen's evidence. I'll tell you more later – just get up there. He's in terrible danger. I just hope you're not too late.'

Gibbs, Potts and the armed officers left.

'Sir,' said Steph. 'You haven't said what's happened to Alan Green and Vic Moore. Were they hitmen after all?'

'Yes, but I don't think they've disappeared back to London or anything. I think we'll find them here.'

'Here, sir? In this cottage? Do you mean Wilson's locked them up?'

'Bloody hell, sir,' said Andy. 'But where?'

'We need to look for another room that's concealed. It was probably a cellar at one time. It shouldn't be too difficult to locate. Let's get these rugs up.'

The three detectives searched through the ground floor. It was Andy who found it, under a piece of carpet in a small utility room.

'Here, sir. There's a trapdoor with a metal ring flush with the wood.'

Steph and Oldroyd rushed over.

'Excellent,' said Oldroyd. 'Now let's take care. I have a feeling we may only find what's left of them.'

At this, Andy and Steph steeled themselves to find some gruesome remains, and Andy pulled up the trapdoor to reveal a stone staircase leading down into darkness. There was a switch near the top. Oldroyd clicked on the light and led the way down. What they found at the bottom shocked the two sergeants.

~

Gibbs managed to get the police car slowly up the track to the converted barn. All the officers piled out and surrounded the building. The door was already open. Gibbs went inside cautiously with one of the armed officers, but the barn was empty. The open door and the fact that a laptop had been left on suggested a hasty departure. Gibbs was still reeling from Oldroyd's revelations about the real identities of two people in the village. So Tony Dexter was really Matthew Hart, one of the Drover Road robbers. Why was he here in Niddersgill? Whatever the answer to that was, he was clearly in danger now. If DCI Oldroyd was right, Patrick Wilson would want revenge on the man who'd betrayed him.

It seemed likely that Wilson had abducted Hart. *Blast it!* They'd clearly been several steps behind this character throughout the case.

Gibbs looked round. There must be a reason why Hart had not been shot immediately, the most likely being that he had some information that Wilson needed. Could there be any clue as to where they might have gone? It seemed unlikely, but they were desperate to find something before it was too late. Just inside the door, Gibbs saw a small piece of folded paper on the floor.

Was it possible that Hart had dropped this to leave a clue?

Gibbs looked at the paper: on it was a picture of a spider.

Steph, Andy and Oldroyd gazed in wonder at the contents of the cellar room in Wilson's cottage. It was set up like an actor's dressing room, with mirrors, lighting, make-up, props and costumes on racks. There were some wigs on a model head. The eyes in the head stared at them. There was no sign of Alan Green or Vic Moore.

'This is spooky, sir,' said Steph, who shivered at the ghoulish atmosphere of the secret underground lair. 'But there's no one here.'

Oldroyd was sorting through an old wardrobe. 'Yes, here they are!' He pulled out two hangers containing clothing: a dark suit with a padded jacket, and a green jumper with corduroy trousers. 'I'm judging this on the descriptions of the two men, but I present to you: Alan Green and Vic Moore.'

'What, sir? You mean the clothes they wore?'

'No, Andy. This is all they were, because they never actually existed. They were parts played by Patrick Wilson. He put on these costumes and he murdered Fraser and Gorton. His third identity was John Gray, the artist.'

'What?' said Andy, still not following.

'Sir, on the way up you said Wilson was in disguise in the village but you never said he had three identities,' said an astonished Steph.

'No, because I wasn't completely sure about it until we got here, and now I've found all this. It took me a long time to realise that Wilson had sent us on a wild goose chase looking for people who weren't real. It was supremely audacious; he even talked to us about Vic Moore and showed us his bedroom. He also told us that Moore had had instructions to do something he didn't want to do, which lent weight to the idea that he was being controlled by someone. I was completely taken in for a while.'

'So that's why "Alan Green" and "Vic Moore" made sure that those two women recognised them as the killers – so we would be confused. God! Poor Inspector Gibbs; he spent all that time trying to trace Alan Green in Pateley Bridge and the other villages,' said Steph.

'I know. He's not going to be pleased. Except that we've finally cracked it.'

'Hold on though, sir,' said Andy, who was flabbergasted by this outlandish discovery. 'How could he be three people at once in a village like this? Surely someone would realise?'

'That's what I thought for a long time. I suspected that something might be going on with disguises but I never contemplated the extent of Wilson's deception. It was an exquisite piece of acting. We found out from the Met file that he was an actor before he turned to crime, and earned quite a reputation as being the kind of performer who could utterly transform himself into different characters using make-up, prosthetics, wigs, accents and so on.'

'Even so, sir, surely someone would notice. I mean, they could never be together at the same time, could they?'

'That's right, and that's where another piece of consummate skill came in: timing. He arrived here as John Gray after he'd discovered that Gorton and Fraser were in this village, and found the ideal cottage with a cellar to rent. It was a very convenient coincidence for him that two of his targets were in the same place. So remember, no one here had ever seen him in his real identity as Patrick Wilson, and "John Gray" kept himself to himself in the role of the semi-reclusive artist. It gave him a reason not to mix much with other people.

'So then he waited, and suddenly Alan Green appears in the village: Geordie accent, brown wig and false moustache. No one would ever think: that's John Gray dressed up. He makes sure that "Green" becomes well known in the village, but no one asks too many questions about where he lives. He can invent a back story if he has to. He drinks in the inn and does odd jobs for people, even Fraser and probably Gorton; it's a good way of monitoring them.

'After a while he introduced his third identity. This was trickier, but he pulled it off. "Vic Moore" was taller than Green – that would be due to inserts in his shoes – and fatter; that's why he wore this padded jacket. He wore more formal clothes, spoke in a Birmingham accent and always wore dark glasses. There was probably some kind of prosthetic to fatten his face. All of this was very subtle, nothing crude like stage make-up. It was so good that no one recognised "Green" in this new identity. The difficulty is that he needed Vic to be a part of village life too, and for that he also had to be a regular at the Dog and Gun.'

'So how come no one realised that they were never there together?' persisted Andy.

'It's the illusionist's trick of suggestibility. Unless you're actually thinking about it and looking for it, why would you notice that they never appeared together? As Green he would talk about Moore and vice versa. They would ask where the other one was and maybe call each other on mobile phones, pretending to have a conversation. It was all so skilfully done that I'll bet if you sat down now with Bramley, Davis, the people behind the bar and any other regulars, they'd all probably say that they were sure that Green and Moore were often in the bar together and they got on well with each other. The idea of them being separate people had been presented to them so many times that they actually believed it. And why not? You wouldn't even consider the idea that there's a man in the village disguising himself as different people. Even if you were sure you'd never seen them together, you'd think that it was probably just you who hadn't seen them and others had.'

'Why did he need to have three identities, sir?' asked Steph.

'Green and Moore were like the shotgun cartridges Wilson used to kill Gorton and Fraser. Once they were spent they were discarded. They disappeared after the murders when the witnesses had seen them fire the shots, or thought they had. Those two young women, who were so insistent that they'd seen Green and Moore, unwittingly did a great job of putting us off the scent. Using a shotgun, of course, got us also thinking about the possible involvement of Fraser's enemies in the shooting world. We started to look all over the place, but all the answers were here.'

'What put you on to what was actually happening, sir?' asked Steph.

'It just dawned on me slowly. I went to see *As You Like It* with my partner.' Oldroyd wandered around the room as he spoke, examining everything. He'd always fancied being an actor. 'She'd already told me that in the small touring company we saw, the actors played lots of different parts, and then there is a famous speech by a character called Jaques. He says, "All the world's a stage" and "one man in his time plays many parts". That really implanted the idea in my mind, and I realised what could have happened. None of the three men were native villagers and they'd all arrived relatively recently. So, unlike the local people who had no reason to question what they saw, I was looking for a pattern, and I could see one. Three men who arrived in the village one after the other, not too far apart but not too close for it to seem odd. They were all very different from each other in voice, dress, stature, facial appearance, and I realised that a skilled actor specialising in disguise could play all three.

'Then, believe it or not, I got further confirmation for my theory from an old Sherlock Holmes film, a black-and-white thing from the 1940s. It's amazing where you get help from if you keep your mind open.'

'What happens in that, then, sir?' asked Steph. 'It sounds a bit obscure.'

'It is, and I'm sure Patrick Wilson never saw it, but what happens is uncannily similar to what happened in Niddersgill, just made a bit more melodramatic. Holmes and Watson go to this village in Canada where people are being murdered, apparently by a strange beast with a huge claw. Holmes works out that there is a link between the victims, and that the murderer is disguised as a villager but they don't know which one. His weapon is a five-pronged garden fork which keeps the myth of the beast alive. Holmes traps him by taking on a disguise himself. At least I didn't have to do that. It's great stuff. I'd seen it years ago and something about this case jogged my memory.'

'Bloody hell!' said Andy, shaking his head. 'Well, this is really one for the records, isn't it? Two murders committed by people who didn't exist. Sometimes I wonder what on earth's going to happen next when I'm working for you, sir.'

Oldroyd started to laugh, but then they heard Gibbs shouting for them in the room above and they went quickly back up the stairs.

'I see you've found another room, sir,' observed Gibbs. 'Anything down there?'

'Yes, and it confirms everything. We need to get a forensics team up here to go through it all. Did you find Matthew Hart?'

'No, sir,' said Gibbs, clearly disappointed to bring bad news. 'The door was open but there was no one in the barn. No dead body either, you'll be pleased to know, but there were some signs of a hasty exit. I found this on the floor and wondered whether it could be a clue.' He handed the picture to Oldroyd. 'Maybe Hart dropped it deliberately. I know it's a long shot but—'

Oldroyd could not contain his excitement and turned to Gibbs. 'Stop there, Bill. You've done brilliantly: tremendous attention to detail.' He brandished the paper. 'I know what this picture means and where Hart has taken Wilson. I'm not sure why he's taken him there, but I have an idea. Let's go – we may still be able to save him.'

Seven

Amerdale Dub
Scosthorp Moor
Huntershaw Ridge
Sourmire Moor

The two former partners in crime were trudging across the wet fields. Hart was in front, closely followed by Wilson with the shotgun. A fine drizzle still fell and the mist was now very low, obscuring the view in every direction. Wilson stayed on the alert for anyone else who might be on the path.

'You were right, Pat. I have been expecting you,' said Hart, grim-faced but calm.

'Well, here I am, you piece of shit,' snarled Wilson. He spoke in a cockney accent. His face, stripped of all make-up and hair, looked hard. His voice was harsh and his manner slouching and aggressive. He was totally unlike any of his three identities in the village.

'Oh yes,' said Hart. 'I heard the news yesterday morning too. The police are on to you so you had to make a move. I have to congratulate you on your disguises. You had me fooled.'

'Good try at changing your appearance, but not good enough. I recognised you straight away when I saw you in the village,' said

Wilson. 'When you're good at disguises yourself, you can also see through them. Did the cops plant you here?'

They'd stopped. Hart kept the conversation going, playing for time. 'Yes. They thought you might show up, as Fraser and Gorton were here.'

Wilson laughed. 'You weren't clever enough, were you? I'd come up here to get Fraser, who I'd tracked down to his nice little retirement house. I couldn't believe it when I found Gorton here too. And then . . . when I saw you!' He grinned and shook his head. 'It was almost enough to make me believe that God, or in my case the Devil, was on my side. I had to take more time and make my scheme more elaborate.'

'You're a great actor, Pat. Why didn't you stay in the theatre?' Hart hoped a compliment might distract his enemy.

'You can't make any money unless you're a big name. I had to work hard at a poncey drama school, where people made fun of my accent, to train to be an actor. I always wanted to do it, but then I soon got sick of all those posh glamour types getting all the best parts, just because they'd got the looks. None of them were better actors than me.'

'I'll bet they weren't.'

'The bloody directors got on my nerves too. Half of them didn't know what they were talking about. I lost a lot of parts through saying what I thought, and the work dried up.'

'So what happened?'

'I watched a lot of crime films, robberies and stuff, and I thought: Patrick, you're wasted, you could use your talents to make a lot of money. I had a few old friends from my schooldays who'd been in trouble. I put feelers out and got in with the right – or some would say wrong – people.' There was a nasty grin on Wilson's face. 'I was a great asset to any team planning a robbery, as you know. I could impersonate a security guard or the manager of a bank. I only had to observe for a while without them knowing. I got into all kinds of places and when they realised it was a hoax, it was too late.' He smiled again with fond remembrance. 'Anyway.' He raised the gun again. 'We haven't got time for this. Move on.'

Hart said nothing. They were gradually making their way to the wooded area recently visited by Oldroyd and Dexter. He hoped that the message he'd left had got to the chief inspector, although it was very unlikely. He wasn't unduly worried. It would be good to have their support, but he could deal with the situation himself.

'Phil was a good mate of mine. He bloody topped himself inside because of you, and I knew why,' said Wilson.

'Yes, he made the mistake of showing me an old lock-up garage he had in the back streets near where he used to live in Balham. He must have realised once he was inside that I would work out where his share of the money was. And I did.'

'You bastard.' Wilson dug the gun hard into Hart's back. 'You not only double-crossed us but you took his money as well. No wonder he couldn't stand the idea of you having it. Poor sod.'

Hart turned round and looked at Wilson with blazing anger.

'Double-crossing!' rasped Hart. 'Well, you and Traynor should know all about that. Do you remember Tony Anderson?'

Wilson lowered the gun and looked at Hart. 'Anderson?' he said.

'Yes. Tony Anderson. He was only a young lad. He was awe-struck by your glamour, and then you and Traynor took him out on his first robbery, swearing him to silence. You left him on guard outside that jeweller's shop, and when the cops arrived you both disappeared out of the back leaving him to take the rap. Without realising it, his role was to slow the police down and give you time to escape.'

'That's how you learn in our world: the hard way.'

'It was bloody hard for him, wasn't it? He wouldn't say who else was involved as he'd been brainwashed and threatened into loyalty by you and that set of bastards you worked with. He was sent down for four years at the age of eighteen. He rotted in prison for some of his best years, thanks to you.'

'What the hell do you care about all that?' Wilson raised the gun again.

'Because he was my sister's boy. My nephew.' Wilson lowered the gun and looked at Hart in surprise. 'Janice tried hard to keep him out of trouble – she didn't want him to go the same way as me and Dad. She was heartbroken when he went to prison.'

'Shit!' exclaimed Wilson, realising where this was going. 'So that's what it was all about! You ratted on me and Phil to get revenge.'

'I did.' Hart spat this out with contempt. 'I planned out exactly what I was going to do. There was no other way I could get back at you other than by getting involved with you on a job, and then betraying you just as you did to Tony. You never suspected a thing. And I took Phil's money from the garage. I've given some to Janice to help her with the family and to get Tony some training and a job. I'd have got hold of yours too if I could. Neither of you two bastards deserved anything.'

Wilson laughed. 'Well, well,' he said. 'That explains a lot. But it's all fallen apart now, hasn't it? You're going to show me where you've hidden Phil's money and then I might let you go. Just for old times' sake.'

Hart knew that was nonsense. Wilson would shoot him immediately when he knew where the money was hidden. They continued to walk through the fields on the edge of the bank of mist.

∾

The two squad cars sped along the sodden lanes until they could get no nearer to their destination by road. Then they abandoned the cars and continued on foot along muddy paths.

'Wilson is a ruthless criminal and he's already killed two people. Bill, I want you to deploy and control the armed officers. Get near to the target and circle it. We'll try to talk him round. I just hope we're not too late.'

'Where exactly are we going, sir?' asked Steph.

'To an ice house.'

'A what?' said Andy, so surprised he forgot to add 'sir'.

'An ice house. One with spiders in it.'

Andy gave Steph a glance of incredulity. She smiled and shrugged her shoulders. Sometimes, with DCI Oldroyd, you just had to play along, however bizarre things seemed.

～

Wilson and Hart were walking up the path from the pond towards the ice house, which had appeared out of the mist.

'What the bloody hell is this?' said Wilson.

'It's an ice house, a deep pit where they used to store ice for use in the summer.'

'OK, quit the history lesson, I'm not stupid. And you've hidden the stuff in there?'

'Yes. We go in here.' Hart showed Wilson the iron entrance gate to the short tunnel which led to the brick-lined pit. 'This gate is usually left open, but I've brought a padlock. We don't want anyone coming in while we're here getting the money and diamonds, do we?'

Wilson stepped just inside the gate. He looked around suspiciously for a few moments, then said, 'OK, but don't try anything stupid.'

While Hart locked the gate with the padlock, Wilson trained the gun on him.

'Right, so where is it?' he asked.

Hart walked down the tunnel.

'Just over here, but I thought you'd like to see these first.' Hart suddenly produced a flashlight from his pocket and shone it on the roof of the tunnel, which was only inches above their heads. The flashlight illuminated the large cave spiders, their long legs gripping the cold damp stone and the numerous strange, round white egg sacs hanging from the roof between them.

Wilson uttered a piercing scream and ran back to the gate. He shook it. 'Open it! Open it now,' he yelled. 'You know I can't stand spiders! Open it or I'll shoot you!'

Hart was standing by the entrance to the pit. He had the key in his hand and was holding it over the deep drop into the circular chamber.

'Come over here and put the gun down by me. If you don't, I'll drop this key and you'll not get out of here until someone else arrives and they break the padlock. That could be a long time.'

'No!' screamed Wilson. 'I have to get out now,' he gasped. 'I can't breathe.' He stumbled across to Hart and dropped the gun. Hart picked it up and handed Wilson the key. Frantically, Wilson ran back to the gate and fumbled with the padlock, his hands shaking. He managed to open it and lunged out of the tunnel. Figures loomed up ahead of him, coming out of the woods, and he heard a voice shouting.

'Stop! There are armed police officers surrounding this area. If you have a weapon, put it down and raise your hands.'

Wilson recognised Oldroyd on the path. As soon as he had got out of the tunnel, the terrifying grip of his arachnophobia relaxed and he regained control. He ran diagonally up the hill and disappeared into the mist.

'Damn!' shouted Oldroyd. 'Bill, stand the armed officers down. I don't think he has a weapon. We can't use them to pursue him in this mist, they'll never get a clear view and they'll end up shooting us.' Inspector Gibbs gave the order and the other officers gathered round Oldroyd.

'OK. Steph, you and I are going to pursue him. You know the terrain around here.'

'Sir,' replied Steph.

'Bill, Andy, go in and see what's happened to Hart. I haven't heard any shots so I hope he's OK. Arrest him. He's got a lot of questions to answer. You should also be able to start the process of recovering some of the loot from the Drover Road robbery.'

'Right, sir.'

'I'm OK, Chief Inspector.' At that moment, Hart appeared from the tunnel with the shotgun. One of the armed officers trained a gun on him, but Hart placed Wilson's weapon on the ground and raised his hands. 'Don't worry, I'm not trying to escape or anything. I'm finished with all that.'

'Fine,' said Oldroyd. He nodded to Steph. 'Let's go.'

~

Patrick Wilson blundered over a stile and up through the woods towards Yorke's Folly. His only hope was that the mist would hide him and he would be able to somehow get back to the village. He had hidden a motorbike near the cottage so that he could make a quick getaway. Unfortunately, the mist made it impossible for him to see where he was. It would have been difficult even if he'd had a better knowledge of the area. He paused for breath and listened. Sounds were muffled in the mist, but in the distance he could just about hear rustling and the cracking of twigs. He was being followed. Damn that Hart and the bloody spiders! Then he heard voices. One was that chief inspector, who called out.

'Wilson!' The sound came eerily through the mist. They were not far away. 'You can't escape. There are too many of us. Give yourself up.'

Wilson plunged on, trying to put some distance between himself and his pursuers. The swirling mist had soaked him through. A large branch loomed up and he ran into it. He uttered a curse, which was heard by Oldroyd and Steph.

'He's over there, sir. He'll be at the folly soon. We might have a chance to corner him there. I'll go down this way and try to get ahead of him and you chase from behind.'

'OK,' replied Oldroyd, who was glad that his running with Deborah had increased his fitness. He carried on after Wilson, calling out at regular intervals, partly to distract him from noticing that Steph was moving in front of him.

Suddenly the trees thinned out ahead of Wilson and the stone edifices of the folly appeared out of the mist, looking dark and sinister. He hid behind one of the stone pillars, breathing heavily and looking from side to side. He thought he must be at that stone thing on the hillside which he'd seen many times from the road, so if he went down through the woods from here and kept in a straight line he was bound to hit the road. Then, hopefully, he could creep his way back to the village, get the motorbike and escape. He moved off quickly before Oldroyd could catch up with him, but suddenly found his way barred by a female officer.

'Stop there!' shouted Steph firmly, but Wilson ran on. Steph tried to stop him but he hurled himself past her. He was on the top of the ridge now and the mist was at its thickest. He heard Steph shout behind him.

'Watch out! You're on the edge of the cliff, it's dangerous and—'

Those were the last words that Wilson heard. Suddenly there was nothing under his feet as he stepped over the cliff edge and, with a cry, fell forty feet on to a huge boulder of millstone grit.

～

Inside the tunnel entrance to the ice house, Hart was calm as he showed Bill Gibbs and Andy where he'd hidden the money and diamonds. Andy prised a loose stone from the wall to reveal a cavity filled with canvas bags. He pulled them out and opened them. Some were stuffed with rolls of banknotes; some were filled with diamonds which glimmered weakly in the dim tunnel.

'There's a fortune here,' said Gibbs.

'There is,' agreed Hart. 'The Drover Road robbery was very lucrative. This is only a third of what we took. But I'm not proud of it. I've used some of the money for a good cause but I haven't touched the diamonds.'

Andy looked at the money and the jewels. It suddenly struck him how weird the whole thing was: all this effort and struggle and violence over some bits of paper and sparkly rocks in some grubby bags. He looked up and saw the spiders on the roof. Sometimes the world of basic creatures like those was easier to understand than that of your fellow humans.

～

At the top of Guisecliff, Oldroyd appeared through the mist. Steph strode out to stop him.

'What was that cry?' he asked.

'We're right at the edge here, sir, be careful. I'm afraid Wilson's gone over. I doubt he's survived. I tried to stop him but he pushed past me.'

Oldroyd crouched down to regain his breath. 'Oh God! Well, that's that, then. We did our best. You'd better alert the others. At least no one else has been hurt and now it's all over.'

Steph contacted Andy and explained what had happened. Leaving Hart with an officer in the police car, Andy, Gibbs and the remaining officers hurried up the path to join Steph and Oldroyd, who were sitting silently on the trunk of a fallen tree in the mist waiting for them. Steph showed them where Wilson had gone over. Two officers went back and followed a path that led to the base of the cliff. Here they found Wilson's body. His neck was broken, and his head had been smashed in at the back. One of the officers immediately phoned HQ to get an ambulance, and then waited by the body. The other returned to inform the detectives.

Oldroyd stood up. He was damp, stiff and increasingly cold in the persistent mist and drizzle. 'Right, we can't do any more. Let's get out of here.'

The troop of police made their way slowly back to the police cars and then to Niddersgill. All the tension had drained away. Outside the Dog and Gun, for the last time in the case, Oldroyd thanked Gibbs and his officers for all their hard work.

'Thank you, sir. I must say it's been a puzzler and not something we encounter very much up here,' said Gibbs. 'I'd like to read your full report on what was behind it all. You say both murders were committed by that artist who had a lot of disguises?'

'That's the essence of it. We'll know the full story when we've interviewed Hart and I'll let you know all about it.'

'Bloody hell! So the postman was right: those two suspects didn't exist.' He explained to Oldroyd what Eastwood had told him about the mail.

'Well, there we are then: one of our early suspects had the answer all along,' mused Oldroyd.

On his way back to Pateley Bridge, Gibbs reflected on the weird events of the past two weeks. The whole case had been well out of his comfort zone. He was a rural copper who preferred the country pace of life, and a community he knew, to the glamour of city-style investigations into robberies and murder. He was returning now to his steady world of occasional shop break-ins, minor drugs offences and a stolen car or two. However, he thought as he smiled to himself, he'd enjoyed the excitement of working with DCI Oldroyd again. There was nothing like it to shake you up a bit and remind you how thrilling police work could be.

'So it wasn't a coincidence that you were living near Niddersgill?'

Matthew Hart was in the interview room back at Harrogate HQ with Oldroyd and Steph. He was very calm and seemed relieved that things were over. He was still dressed in his outdoor clothes and looked like a rambler and birdwatcher rather than a bank robber.

'No. I'm sure people at the Met have told you what happened. I was given a new identity after I turned Queen's evidence because my life would have been in danger if people knew I was a rat. I returned my share of what we stole, but I told the police I didn't know anything about where the others had hidden theirs. I don't think they ever believed me and their instincts were right. I did know where Traynor's money was. I used it carefully and sparingly to help my nephew and sister.'

'So did you think that was the end of it?'

'Yes. I'd had enough of crime. I'd seen what it does to people. That last job was part of my plan to get revenge. You have to remember I was brought up in a tough family in a rough place. My father was part of a gang – my brother is inside for robbery.'

'So what changed you?'

Hart went quiet for a moment before he replied. 'It was when I saw my nephew going the same way. I never had any kids and I was close to him. He was such a nice little boy, so innocent and loving. I used to take him to the park to play football. My sister tried hard to bring him up well even though her husband had walked out and she had no money. I understood what she was trying to do: get a different future for him, but it was hard in that neighbourhood. When he was a teenager he started to get into the gangs just like we all had. And you know the rest.'

'So tell me what happened next.'

'I moved right out of London and I rented a room in a house right out in the country, in my new identity as Tony Dexter. That's when I got in touch with something in myself which must have always been there, but never developed because I'd lived all my life in raw and ugly parts of the city. I found I loved the countryside, everything about it but particularly the birds and wildlife. I got myself some binoculars and began to read about environmental issues. My eyes were opened and I saw what a futile life I'd been leading: all that violence and lawbreaking in pursuit of money. I was overwhelmed by the beauty of it all and I started to write poems. Imagine me, a hardened criminal from London's under-world, writing verse about the landscape.' He shook his head as if he still couldn't believe it.

'Then you heard that Wilson was supposedly dead, and the police came back.'

Hart sighed. 'Yes. Things were fine and then I read that he'd fallen in the river trying to escape and was presumed dead. I was suspicious about that, and so were the police. Pat was a tough and wily character. He would have had no trouble finding places to hide in London, and he would have retrieved his money from the robbery from wherever he'd hidden it.'

'So the police made you help them?'

'Yes. They checked on me from time to time and they still had a grudge against me because of the money. They were suspicious about some of the expensive things I had like the binoculars, and the fact that I didn't seem to do much work. So they came and said they needed my help. They implied it wouldn't do me any good to refuse, but when they explained what I had to do I was happy to do it, though they didn't know the reason why.

'They told me there was a good chance that Pat was alive and that there was this village in Yorkshire where the judge who'd sentenced him and the prison officer who'd mistreated him were now living. They knew what a vindictive sod he was and they were concerned that he would come after them. I asked why they couldn't watch over them but they said they didn't have the resources to have someone permanently in the village and they didn't want to frighten Pat off. The idea was to trap him there and recapture him.'

'I presume they told you about his abilities as an actor and disguise specialist?'

'They did. I knew he'd used disguises on some of his jobs but I'd no idea how good he was or that he'd trained as an actor. None of us in the gangs ever talked much about our private lives or what we'd done in the past. We were too busy planning robberies and break-ins. Anyway, the police said he would be disguised but I'd known him for a long time so I should recognise him. My appearance was different and he wasn't expecting me to be there so he wouldn't recognise me. They were bloody wrong about all that! His disguises and acting were brilliant and he did recognise me.'

'Don't worry, he took in everybody, including us.'

'The undercover police set me up in the barn near the village. What a fabulous place with the fells and the beautiful reservoir! It was a paradise for me. My job was to keep watch over the village, particularly Gorton and Fraser, and report immediately if I saw anything suspicious. The main problem was that Pat was ahead of us. He'd already arrived in the village as John Gray the artist. When his other personas arrived, it was so carefully and subtly done that I didn't suspect anything.'

'Neither did anyone else. It's only afterwards when you're looking for the pattern that you see it.'

'I suspected that one of these newcomers to the village could be him, but I'd no idea which one – and anyway, it was only a possibility that he would come to the village at all. I'd no idea that he was all three.'

'So what happened when things started to kick off?'

Hart shook his head. 'It was a shock when Fraser was killed. I knew then that Pat was here and that he'd tricked us. There was talk about other people who had a motive to kill Fraser, but I was sure that it was him.'

'What did your minders in the police say?'

'They weren't pleased. I'd told them about my suspicions but they said they had to be sure which person he was before they could move. If they got the wrong person that would cause trouble and frighten Pat away.'

'And now everyone was pursuing Alan Green, even though they didn't know it was really Patrick Wilson.'

'Yes, and so he outwitted us again. I didn't know what to do, and while I was thinking about it Gorton was killed and the suspect was Vic Moore who disappeared: same pattern, but there was a difference. This time the suspect lived in the village, supposedly with John Gray the artist. I wasn't convinced that that was the end.'

'Why not?'

'Vic Moore was supposedly lodging with John Gray but there was something that I didn't find convincing. If Moore was one of

Pat's disguises it surely meant that Gray must be an accomplice, unless . . . And I began to wonder if John Gray was also one of Pat's personas.'

'But you didn't tell the police?'

Hart looked at Oldroyd. 'No. The police didn't know I had my own agenda with Pat. I wanted to bring him down myself. I began to think that maybe he had recognised me and would try to make me his third victim. I also knew that he would want to get his hands on Phil's money.'

'And you were right?'

'Yes. I planned how I was going to trap him and then hand him over to the police. I hid the money and diamonds in that tunnel entrance to the ice house. I knew Pat had severe arachnophobia; I'd seen him freak out before when he saw a spider, however small. I was confident I could overpower him in there due to that fear, which immobilised him.'

'But you had a backup plan involving me?'

Hart smiled. 'Yes, Chief Inspector. I gave you a broad hint about the ice house and hoped that if things weren't working out, you might come to help me. I knew you would be on to things when Liz Smith told me it had come out that Peter Gorton worked at Strangeways. I knew you'd realise that was the connection between Fraser and Gorton and you'd be back. That was confirmed by that press conference which was on the news. I thought Pat would hear it too so I was ready for him to make a move.'

Oldroyd felt some satisfaction that his risky strategy of announcing to the press that they thought Patrick Wilson was still alive had succeeded in flushing him out.

'I dropped that picture on the floor of the barn,' continued Hart. 'And it seems the message got to you.'

'Yes.'

Hart took a deep breath. 'OK. It was a long shot but it worked. As it happened I was in control by the end, but it was nice to get some assistance.' He looked at Oldroyd and then at Steph. 'I wasn't intending to kill him, you know. I've finished with violence, but I think he got what he deserved in the end. Fraser and Gorton didn't deserve such a terrible revenge.'

'We'll have to hold on to you for a while until we've reported everything that's happened to the Met. They won't be pleased with the fact that you went it alone and that you knew where Traynor's money was,' said Oldroyd.

Hart looked very sanguine about the prospect and shrugged. 'I don't care, Chief Inspector. They can send me down for a while if they want. I'm a changed man and I'll survive. Then I'll be back to the countryside, in this area I think. I love these wild fells. The call of that curlew gets into your soul. You're a Yorkshireman, aren't you, Chief Inspector?'

'I am,' said Oldroyd. 'And you won't find any countryside anywhere else that's better.'

'True. I'm glad I inspired you to write poetry. It's a better legacy than terrifying people and stealing money.' Hart smiled as he was taken out of the interview room. Oldroyd and Steph returned to the office to join Andy, who was completing some admin concerning the case. They told him what Hart had revealed.

'What do you think will happen to him, sir? Do you think the Met will press charges?' asked Andy.

'No. In the end he got them what they wanted, didn't he? Although they may have preferred to capture Wilson alive. Also, I think they'll want to keep their involvement quiet. What they were doing was risky, especially not telling us about it, and particularly after the first murder. We might have worked out what was going on more quickly. Not that we could necessarily have stopped Wilson. He was a cunning and malicious character, but

I gave that DCI Riley a piece of my mind, I can tell you. He's in deep trouble now. His plan risked the lives of two men and it failed spectacularly. If he really believed that Wilson was alive and a threat to Fraser and Gorton, he should have warned them, not used them as bait to trap Wilson.'

'I remember Riley, sir. He had a reputation for being flashy and taking risks, going for glory, you know what I mean?'

'I do, and it's not my style. Policing's not about our personal egos, it's about upholding the law and protecting the public.'

'Hear, hear, sir!' said Andy with a touch of mockery.

'I'll tell you what, though, sir,' said Steph mischievously. 'You remember that press conference when that bloke from one of the tabloids talked about the criminal underworld and hitmen. You made fun of him, but actually he wasn't far wrong, was he?'

'Hmm, I suppose not,' said Oldroyd, realising they were both teasing him. 'Maybe I should ring him up and apologise,' he laughed. 'But I don't think I'll bother.'

'Absolutely, sir.'

Andy and Steph liked to pull Oldroyd's beard occasionally, as the saying went, but at the end of another perplexing case in which their boss had triumphed, their admiration of him, and their loyalty, went deep.

∾

In Niddersgill, the relief was almost palpable. The drama was over, the tension subsided and there was a gradual return to the area's age-long identity as a sleepy village, famous only for its inn and the quality food and drink served there.

Reporters were no longer interested and no one feared for his or her safety. A group of local people had temporarily taken over the running of the shop, so milk, bread, newspapers and locally produced honey were once again on sale.

In the Dog and Gun, Wilf Bramley and Ian Davis were propping up the bar and holding their usual pints of bitter. Jenny was there, too, after the potential babysitter proved to be very keen to start.

Kirsty was behind the bar, smiling and looking relaxed. She was very relieved that the crime had been solved and that she had done the right thing in telling the police she'd seen Alan Green.

'Ah still can't bloody believe it,' said Bramley, shaking his head. 'A village like this wi' a mad bloke shootin' other folk for revenge. Who the bloody 'ell would believe that?'

Davis laughed.

'And Alan Green and Vic Moore didn't exist.' Kirsty shuddered. 'That's the really spooky bit. Those blokes who came in here and we got pally with were just that bank robber in disguise. It makes you think about what's real and what isn't.'

'Yeah,' said Davis mischievously. 'I'm really an American serial killer in disguise and one night I'm going to creep up and get you all.'

'How would you disguise your accent?' said his wife, laughing at the prospect.

'And you'll have to be quick. Harry and I will be moving soon.'
'Oh?'

Everyone looked sad. Kirsty was a popular character in the village.

'Yes. He's going for an interview next week for a job in a restaurant in Leeds. If he gets it we'll move there. I'll get a job there too – there'll be plenty of bar work. To be honest, we've had enough of being here, miles away from anywhere, and this carry-on hasn't helped. I'm not relaxed at night now after what happened; I keep imagining I'm going to wake up to the sound of a gun going off.'

'Aye, I can imagine,' said Bramley. 'How's that other lass gettin' on?'

'Jeanette? She's still at her parents' in Northallerton. I don't think she'll come back.'

'I don't blame her,' said Davis.

'Looks like changes in the village,' said Bramley. 'Lot of people leavin'.'

'Yeah, but more will come in. That's the way these days, Wilf. Most people don't live in a place like this all their lives like you have,' said Davis.

'Aye, you're right,' said Bramley, then he laughed. 'Let's hope that t'next folk that come are real and none of them are bloody robbers and murderers!'

'I'll drink to that,' said Davis. 'Kirsty, two pints o' bitter please.' He looked at Jenny, who frowned. 'Or maybe not. I think I've had enough.'

~

Andy and Steph were relaxing in their riverside apartment in Leeds. Andy was scrolling through his texts and grinned when he got to a particular one.

'Jason wants to come up and stay for a weekend. He's between jobs apparently.'

Jason was an old friend of Andy's. He lived in London and worked in the City 'moving figures around on screens', as Andy cynically described it, but he made a lot of money.

Steph was reading a novel and looked up. 'Is he between girlfriends, or does he want to bring one with him?'

'He doesn't say, but I think it's over with that Alice.'

'Good. God she was awful!'

Andy laughed. 'Yeah, the classic empty-headed rah.'

'Do you remember, they came up in August and she brought that thick coat because she thought it would be cold up north?'

'Yes, well, she was right – it is.'

'Get lost.'

'She was good-looking though.'

'Oh yeah, well that's all that matters in a woman, isn't it? Never mind the brain, look at the breasts.'

'Yes, but I'm all right because you've got both.'

'Andy!' She threw a cushion at him.

'You know, he says he's between jobs but he doesn't say why, but I bet he's been given the push again. One of these times he'll go too far.'

Jason had developed a habit of breaking the trading rules in the stock market and had come very close to breaking the law on occasion. His behaviour had lost him a number of jobs, but he always bounced back because he was so good at what he did. Andy dreaded the moment when his friend would get arrested for being involved in some scam involving millions. He'd known Jason from his schooldays.

He turned to Steph in a more serious manner. 'What do you think turns gifted people into criminals?'

'Whoa! Deep stuff! You've been working with the boss so long now, you're turning into a thinker. Have you got the brains for it?'

'Cheeky! You're right, actually. He makes you think about all kinds of stuff. When I first came up here, I was just interested in locking bad people up. I never thought about them as individuals and that things had happened to make them like that.'

'It's an important thing you learn from him: to think about the psychology of the people involved in a case.'

'Yes. I can see how poor people with no education and skills might turn to crime, but why someone like Jason, or Patrick

Wilson? Jason was a whizz at maths and stuff at school, he could have done all sorts of jobs, but here he is spending his time in a glorified casino – and, this is what worries me, getting more criminal. Wilson was a brilliant actor and an artist. He could have done all sorts of stuff and he ends up robbing banks and shooting people.'

Steph put down her book and paused before answering. 'I think people like that have big egos.'

'Too right, in Jason's case!'

'And they don't like being told what to do. Nor do they like people getting ahead of them who they don't think are as good as they are. Jason hates his managers who are paid more than him, and I'll bet Wilson got frustrated not being able to make the big time as an actor. Breaking the rules is a way of putting two fingers up to the system – even better if they can get away with it. That makes the others look like fools.'

'Wow, that's amazing! You haven't been working with the boss for all these years for nothing.'

'And some are at their most dangerous when they're thwarted or betrayed by someone. Their egos can't take it. That's why Wilson got so violent against people who'd mistreated him.'

'Do you think Jason's going to end up like that? I don't mean robbing banks and killing people, but, you know, in trouble and in prison?'

'Naw, he's too much of a softie. There's nothing malicious in him, it's all bravado with Jason. Anyway, he likes the good life too much – he'd never risk going to prison.'

'Yeah, I suppose. When I was working in the Met, I used to think that some evening I'd have to arrest him for drink-driving or something. I've worried about him a lot.'

'Well, don't, and tell him of course he can come up here, with or without a partner.'

'That's what he needs: a partner – someone who will clip his wings and make him live a steady, dull life like me.'

She threw another cushion at him.

～

'So it's another success for you, Jim? How on earth are you going to cope with his gigantic ego, Deborah?'

Alison was entertaining Oldroyd and Deborah at the vicarage in Kirkby Underside where she was the vicar of the local church. The three of them were seated at the table. She'd cooked an excellent vegetarian dish with aubergines and tamarind. Oldroyd reflected on how this would have been enhanced with tender cubes of lamb, but kept such thoughts to himself. He stood up from his seat and performed an elaborate bow.

'It was another complicated affair,' said Deborah.

'He specialises in them,' said Alison.

'I know, but this one was beyond the pale: two murderers who didn't exist and a disguised bank robber taking his revenge on people in a small dales village.'

'All in a day's work,' said Oldroyd, laughing and taking a sip of red wine.

'Wasn't it a weird coincidence that all those people were in the same village?'

'Good question. It was only the two murder victims who were in Niddersgill by chance. Hart was there to keep watch on what was happening in a secret operation that was a disastrous failure. There will be some repercussions from that, so don't say anything.'

'OK, but still, the two people Wilson was after just happened to end up in the same small place?' said Deborah sceptically.

'I know, people struggle with things like this and start thinking there's some weird fatalistic or supernatural force at work that's organising events from behind the scenes. In fact, if you think about how many events are taking place continuously in time and space, statistically, unusual things are going to happen. Apparently if only twenty-three people get together, there's a fifty per cent chance that two of them will share the same birthday.'

'Wow, that's a low number of people! So what you're saying is that coincidences are far more likely to happen than we think.'

'Yes. And also when you look at many coincidences, there are often at least partial explanations for them; they're not as random as they might seem. In this case, Niddersgill is very picturesque and an ideal retirement village, with houses available because there are fewer local people living there and working in farming nowadays. Alexander Fraser bought a grouse moor and a manor house, which he was likely to do as he'd grown fond of shooting and probably fancied moving to the country. If a local shop becomes vacant it's going to attract another person from outside: Peter Gorton in this case, who wanted to make a similar move. So yes it's a coincidence, but not quite so far-fetched as it might sound. It's probably the kind of coincidence that happens fairly regularly.' Oldroyd finished his drink. 'It was also a coincidence that the two young women who worked behind the bar at the inn were the witnesses to the murders. I wondered about that for a while: were they involved in some way, but then what's the big deal? They were both around the village and happened to be in the right place – or wrong, depending how you look at it – at the crucial time. What do you think, sis, with your theologian's cap on?'

'I agree with you, Jim. I think the whole notion of some kind of supernatural agency or fate which is determining what happens is untenable. Nor do I like the idea of a God who intervenes to do things if we pray to him. Events in this life appear to be random and there's no obvious indication of any organising force behind it all. Having said that, Christians believe that God cares about us and is somehow involved in human history and our lives, so I keep a corner in my mind for the idea of Him, or Her of course, just nudging us in certain directions. It can't be any more than that, otherwise we would lose our freedom to make choices.'

'There have been people like Thomas Hardy,' observed Oldroyd, 'who believed that if there is an active force in the universe it is malignant, thus all the terrible twists of fate in his novels. What do you think, Deborah?'

'Well, this is all heavy stuff,' said Deborah, laughing. 'I feel I'm in a university seminar. OK, well my perspective would be that, yes, events are random, but it's difficult for us to accept this as it makes us feel insecure and out of control. So we try to look for patterns which might suggest that there is some purpose in things, even if we can't discern what it is. It's more reassuring to think that way.'

A vigorous debate ensued as the trio retired to the comfortable armchairs in the huge rectory lounge and drank coffee. All three enjoyed a discussion of the deep existential questions of life and came at them from different perspectives. It was very late when Oldroyd and Deborah left.

Deborah had stayed off alcohol and drove them back to Harrogate.

'I like Alison, she's such an interesting person. I'm not religious, but when you meet someone like her it makes you think,' she said as she drove through the dark country lanes.

'About what?' muttered Oldroyd, who was dozing in the passenger seat.

'I suppose about whether there is anything in it or not – you know, religion. Someone like her obviously derives a great deal of wisdom from her faith.'

'She does, that's why I like talking to her about these issues. I used to try to be like her, but I couldn't be. I just don't believe all the supernatural stuff, and you have to be yourself. You can't pretend.'

He put his hand on Deborah's shoulder. He found her a wise and interesting person too, and he valued their relationship very much. It confirmed his decision to avoid any sort of involvement with Julia beyond the purely practical.

Deborah yawned as they entered the flat on the Stray. 'Oh, look at the time, I'm going straight off to bed.'

'I'll be along in a minute.'

'Don't stay up late, remember it's parkrun tomorrow morning.'

'No.' Oldroyd grimaced at the prospect, then went to his computer and brought up a photograph. It was Basil Rathbone playing the part of Sherlock Holmes in *The Scarlet Claw*. How amazing that he'd been helped to solve the mystery by the great fictional detective! What a part to play, and how well Basil Rathbone had played it!

He saluted both the actor and the character before he went off to bed.

~

The weekend went well and Oldroyd even improved his personal-best time at parkrun, but by Monday morning he was feeling his usual sense of anti-climax at the end of a difficult and tense case. Once the adrenalin stopped flowing he tended to flop. He arrived at the office fairly late and went to see Tom Walker. For once, the old boy was in a good mood.

'Well done, Jim. Excellent work! You're a crack team, you and those two sergeants. I've spoken to Bill Gibbs at Pateley too. I hear he put in some sterling work. He's a damn good copper but not flashy: just the type that Watkins doesn't appreciate.' Oldroyd was expecting the usual growling diatribe at this point, but Walker was smiling. 'Did you see him on telly last night? He was on that Yorkshire news programme being interviewed about management costs in the force. Someone got hold of some figures showing that he and his cronies are paid huge salaries while police numbers are going down. You should have seen the bugger squirm! He had no bloody answers of course.' Walker's relish of the chief constable's discomfort was keen. Oldroyd kept quiet as usual, so as not to encourage him further.

'So it was an escaped robber who had multiple identities? How did he get away with that in a dales village?'

'Very skilful, Tom: a master of disguise and a brilliant actor. He took us all in.'

'Well done,' said Walker, then he sighed. 'Anyway, I'd better get on. I've got to write a bloody report for Watkins on "Optimising Resources and Improving Performance in Negative-Revenue Circumstances". He can never speak or write in plain English. What he means is how can we do more with less after the bloody cuts? I'll bloody well tell him what I think and no mistake. Don't forget to tell Johnson and Carter they did a good job. They're the people who matter, not twerps like him.'

With that, Oldroyd made his escape.

Back in his office, he felt lethargic and dull. Why not go out for a while? Nobody questioned his movements, especially as he always got results and put in so many hours on difficult cases. Soon he was in the old Saab and driving out of Harrogate.

The weather had cleared and it was sunny again in Nidderdale. The crisp temperatures and developing colours on the trees showed that autumn was progressing. Oldroyd drove slowly up the dale, enjoying the scenery now that the pressure was off.

Passing through Pateley Bridge he saw that preparations were underway in Bewerley Park for the famous Nidderdale Show, one of the biggest, and traditionally the last, of the season of the north of England's agricultural shows. It was good to see rural life continuing after the recent burst of unexpected violence. He thought he caught sight of Bill Gibbs talking to a farmer as he turned up the road to Niddersgill.

He was able to drive at a leisurely pace, in marked contrast with that of the previous week, when they'd driven urgently through the rain at top speed trying to prevent further violence. He parked in a lay-by just outside Niddersgill and grabbed his rucksack. Inside was his notebook; he'd decided to have another session in solitude contemplating the landscape and working on his poem. He walked quickly up a steep path on to the wooded slopes of the fell, and settled in a place from where he could see across Gouthwaite Reservoir to the fells beyond. There was a breeze which ruffled the surface of the water, making it sparkle in the sun. High fleecy clouds drifted across the sky and created moving shadows on the fellside, which was covered with a pattern of stone walls and barns. The distant peaks between Nidderdale and Wharfedale loomed higher – wild, remote and mysterious. It was the country of his heart, as D. H. Lawrence once said about Nottinghamshire.

A voice disturbed the quiet.

'Ah, Chief Inspector, I thought that was you.'

Blast, thought Oldroyd, not again! He never seemed to be able to escape attention for very long. He looked round to see Liz Smith in red boots, moleskin trousers and a multicoloured home-knitted jumper.

'Good morning,' he said tersely, hoping she wouldn't stay long.

'Don't worry, I won't disturb you,' she replied, echoing his thought. 'But as I've run into you, I thought I'd stop to say thank you. I've said some pretty negative things about the police in the past, but you and your team were amazing.'

'Thank you. That's what we're here for,' replied Oldroyd.

'Yes, I agree: catching the dangerous criminals and not harassing honest campaigners.' She couldn't resist making a political point.

'Laws apply to the honest campaigners – as you call them – too.'

She ignored this comment. 'I was shocked about Tony Dexter . . . or the man who turned out not to be Tony Dexter. I met him out by the reservoir only the other day. I thought he was an OK guy. He seemed to have the right attitudes to the environment and stuff. I can't believe he was a bank robber.'

'I think we can say he was a reformed bank robber. His attachment to the countryside was genuine and he helped us to bring down the murderer. I think he'll be back.'

'It makes you think about people. They're not always who they seem to be.'

'No, and it's not a good idea to divide them up in a black-and-white way into heroes and villains.'

'Maybe.'

'Anyway, don't you have some shoots to disrupt?'

Liz laughed. 'Not at the moment. We're taking a break after what happened at the last one, but we'll be back. The fight goes on. I could never stop while birds are being shot for fun – it's who I am.'

Oldroyd smiled at her. There was something about her that he liked and respected. She reminded him of his daughter in her feisty refusal to accept things she thought were wrong.

She looked at his notebook. 'Are you writing poems?' Her tone was sceptical.

'Yes, why not?'

'Just a stereotype, I suppose. I don't expect policemen to write poetry.'

Oldroyd liked her frankness. He handed her the notebook opened at the poem he'd been writing since the day he'd interviewed Hart in his barn. He'd started it the day he'd met Hart in the woods, but had had no time to work on it since. She read it aloud.

'That's really good. So you've taken place names and fashioned them into a poem?'

'Yes. All from Ordnance Survey maps.'

'That's such a simple idea but it works really well. Those old words and names convey the atmosphere. You've made a lovely rhythm out of it.' She looked out over the landscape. 'People think that activists like me are only interested in the politics of the countryside: kicking up a fuss and causing trouble. It's not true; I told Tony or whoever he was the other day when I met him out here. I love the peace and beauty of places like this just as much as anyone else. What I do is not just about protecting the birds. All that shooting and blood and keeping people off the moors really disrupts the beauty and spirituality that people need. These places are sacred.'

Oldroyd looked again across the wide expanse of Nidderdale, which had recently been desecrated by human violence of a different kind. As he contemplated the beauty and stillness of the landscape, Oldroyd reflected that the disruption of the last two weeks had left no sign. The place was as serene and majestic as ever.

'I agree,' he said.

Dales Incantation

Crutching Close Laithe,
Yarnthwaite Barn,
Hawkswick Clowder,
Pikesdaw Barn.

Stony Nick Crag,
Low Dowk Cave,
Dumpit Hill Moss,
Swinsto Cave.

Bracken Pot Wood,
Outgang Hill,
Darnbrook Cowside,
Greenhaw Hill.

Numberstones End,
Lumb Gill Wham,
Seavey Crook Bank,
Lower Wham.

Tatham Wife Moss,
Quaking Pot,
Black Edge Shake Hole,
Jingling Pot.

Amerdale Dub,
Scosthorp Moor,
Huntershaw Ridge,
Sourmire Moor.

Gollinglith Fleet,
Crookrise Crag,
Oughtershaw Side,
Healaugh Crag.

Smearsett Copys,
Gaping Gill,
Warrendale Knotts,
Sourmilk Gill.

Attermire Scar,
Fountains Fell,
Lee Gate High Mark,
Wether Fell.

Dodderham Moss,
Agill Well,
Cumma Know Gate,
Cotgills Well.

White Beacon Hags,
Dickens Dike,
Great Shunner Fell,
Rom Shaw Dike.

Grey Mare Yethersgill,
River Dibb,
Jenny Twigg and her daughter Tib.

J. Oldroyd

Acknowledgments

I would like to thank my family, friends and members of the Otley Writers' Group for their help and support over the years.

The fictional village of Niddersgill is based on a number of settlements in Nidderdale. Other places are real, including Brimham Rocks, Yorke's Folly, Guisecliff, Gouthwaite Reservoir and How Stean Gorge. The ice house containing the cave spiders also exists, but I have decided not to reveal its precise location so that the spiders may remain there undisturbed!

All the place names in 'Dales Incantation' can be found on Ordnance Survey Explorer maps of the Yorkshire Dales area.

West Riding Police is a fictional force based on the old riding boundary. Harrogate was part of the old West Riding, although it is in today's North Yorkshire.

About the Author

John R. Ellis has lived in Yorkshire for most of his life and has spent many years exploring Yorkshire's diverse landscapes, history, language and communities. He recently retired after a career in teaching, mostly in further education in the Leeds area. In addition to the Yorkshire Murder Mystery series, he writes poetry, ghost stories and biography. He has completed a screenplay about the last years of the poet Edward Thomas and a work of faction about the extraordinary life of his Irish mother-in-law. He is currently working on his memoirs of growing up in a working-class area of Huddersfield in the 1950s and 1960s.